David

ALSO BY RAY ROBERTSON

David

RAY ROBERTSON

BIBLIOASIS

Library and Archives Canada Cataloguing in Publication

Robertson, Ray, 1966–
    David / Ray Robertson.

ISBN 978-1-926845-86-9

    I. Title.

PS8585.O3219D3   2013   C813'.54   C2012-901705-1

Canada Council   Conseil des Arts   ONTARIO ARTS COUNCIL
for the Arts   du Canada   CONSEIL DES ARTS DE L'ONTARIO

            Canadian   Patrimoine
            Heritage   canadien

Biblioasis acknowledges the ongoing financial support of the Government of Canada through The Canada Council for the Arts, Canadian Heritage, the Canada Book Fund; and the Government of Ontario through the Ontario Arts Council.

PRINTED AND BOUND IN CANADA

MIX
Paper from
responsible sources
FSC® C107923

Mara Anita Korkola

Roll on Babe

If the fool would persist in his folly he would become wise.

— WILLIAM BLAKE,
The Marriage of Heaven and Hell

1

God and whiskey have got me where I am. Too little of the one, too much of the other.

Aristotle said that the virtuous man is a man of moderation, the kind of man who avoids excess and scarcity in both action and feeling. But then, Aristotle wasn't born a slave. And Athens, Greece, is a long, long way from Jackson, Louisiana.

The man who owned my mother and whoever grew in her womb didn't need to read Aristotle to know that *Some men are by nature free, and others slaves, and that for these slavery is both expedient and right*. Wouldn't have disagreed, of course, and probably would have been pleased to be reminded of just one more virtue of procuring a classical education for one's male offspring. To care for one's children materially but to neglect their intellectual and spiritual needs would be simply uncivilized.

Fate or luck—take your pick, both have their backers— meant that the teacher my mother's master hired to instruct his sons in the wisdom of Western literature was William King, the same man who taught me to read Greek, to recite Virgil, to know the best that has been thought and said.

Knowledge is power. Thomas Hobbes. *Leviathan*, 1668.

I learned that one on my own.

*

"One more, David, if you please."

I walk the bottle to the other end of the bar; pour out the shot, take the twenty-five cents. No one carries credit at Sophia's. Even after-hours saloons need rules, even criminals need laws.

A chill, and everyone looks up, waits to see who's going to push through the heavy green velvet curtains hanging over the doorless doorway. In the wintertime the cold always calls ahead, whenever Tom at the door upstairs lets someone inside, the freezing air rushing ahead and down the stairs to mingle among the living. Sometimes someone will complain that Sophia's is like a cave—the low ceiling, the absence of any windows, the fact that we are in the basement of an under-taker's—especially when, no matter how well the fire is kept, it's winter and unavoidably damp. But no one ever complains when all the other saloons in town are locked tight for the night and mine is the only one with liquor for sale.

It's just Franklin—Franklin who runs the mortuary upstairs—so everyone looks back down. I nod, pour him a whiskey. I've known him long enough for my nose to know he's been working on a body. An undertaker's hours are never his own.

"Thank you, David."

Franklin drinks his whiskey standing up and sets the shot glass back down on the bar, pulls a wad of bills—this month's rent—out of his pants pocket. It's already the sixth, but Franklin's been my tenant for nearly seven years now and has never missed the rent yet. Besides, we've got a side busi-ness together and I wouldn't be partners with any man who didn't honour his debts.

I take the money and count it. I know it's all there, but I count it anyway. Why not? It's my money to do with what I want. I put the bills in my pocket and rap the bar and pour

Franklin another whiskey. I always feel generous on rent day.

Franklin holds up his hand. "I'm just resting, I'm not done upstairs." The shot glass is almost half full by the time I stop pouring, but I splash it into the basin behind the bar. I hate to waste good whiskey—or even the stuff I sell at Sophia's—but even if it was the jug of Wild Turkey I keep locked away in the back, I only drink among friends. Work is for working.

"I've got a rush job, but it ain't no rush job, if you know what I mean," Franklin says.

"A real mess, is it?" Meyers says from the other end of the bar, snorting up some snuff from the back of his hand. Meyers runs the chemist shop over on King Street and fancies himself a man of medicine, a doctor lacking only a degree. What Meyers really is is a glorified dry goods merchant who believes that if he gets a new suit made for himself every year from Savile Row, then he qualifies as an honorary English gentleman. But he's a regular. And people don't come to Sophia's to be what they are. They can get that at home.

"Nah, just old age, I guess. All things considered, looks as fit as you or me or David."

Some people believe that formaldehyde is a miracle cure, can erase the torture of six months of TB or straighten out a broken neck. Formaldehyde just buys time. Some undertakers have started to offer grooming and cleaning services for the deceased, but I advised Franklin to forget it—who would pay a stranger to be the last person on earth to care for their loved one? Besides, Franklin can barely groom himself, and the same goes but double for his personal hygiene.

"His people want him preserved because there's lots of folks out there who want to pay their respects, I guess," he says. "But them coloured boys that brought him in, they let it be known in no uncertain terms that he was to be returned to

4

Ray Robertson

them looking in the exact same condition as when he arrived. Didn't even go back to Buxton to wait, said they was gonna wait right out front until I was finished."

I set down the glass I'm drying. "Who is it?" I say.

"Who is what?"

I force myself to take a deep breath before I answer. One tends to do that a lot when talking to Franklin. "Who is it that the coloured men are waiting on?"

"The Reverend King," Franklin says. "The Reverend King, he died tonight."

I pick the same glass back up. It's already clean, but I wipe it again anyway.

"Well, I better get back at it, not unless I want them coloured boys upset with me." Although he's only going to be outside long enough to walk around to the front of the building, Franklin pulls his cap back on. Elbow on the bar, leaning my way, "A little too high-profile to be a candidate for us," he whispers, winks.

I watch Franklin disappear back through the curtain. I pick Meyers' shot glass up off the bar and toss out what's left into the basin. Everyone can feel the creeping chill of the door opening upstairs.

"I'm sorry, I wasn't quite done with that, Old Boy," Meyers says, pushing his glasses up his nose. Whenever Meyers attempts to make a point, he pushes his glasses up his nose.

"Yes, you were," I say. "And so is everyone else." It's early for an after-hours saloon, I've only got four other patrons—three men in one corner playing cards and, in the other, Thompson sitting by himself as usual, with his opened notebook on the table in front of him for company—but I raise my voice anyway. "That's it, I'm closing."

"But it's"—Meyers pulls his watch out of his vest pocket—"it's not quite even eleven."

"I don't need you or anyone else to tell me what time it is, Meyers. And what time it is is time for you to go home—all of you." I stare Meyers into his hat and coat. The men in the corner finish their drinks standing up, slip into their coats and hats. Even Thompson, whose company I usually have time for and whom I sometimes let nurse a final whiskey while I tally up the till, knows it's time to leave.

As soon as the men and Meyers and Thompson have left, I hear Tom limping down the stairs. Tom's worked the door for me almost from the beginning, since I opened Sophia's back in the summer of '87, during prohibition, but he still parts the curtains when he comes inside like he might be in the wrong place, isn't sure he isn't somewhere he's not supposed to be. I was only born a slave; Tom *was* a slave, came to the Elgin Settlement in '52 after Congress passed the Fugitive Slave Act, when it became not only allowable but legally compulsory to assist in the return to his Southern master of any escaped slave living in the free states. Some people continued calling them the *free states* even after that. Some other people didn't.

"Early night tonight, Boss," Tom says.

"Early night," I say.

I peel a five-dollar bill from the roll in my pocket and slide it across the bar. Tom looks at it, then at me, like a smart bear at a trap.

"Take it," I say.

This time Tom looks just at me. "Everything all right, Boss?"

"Everything is just fine."

Tom keeps looking at me. If he was a white man, I would ask him what he thought he was staring at.

"You know the Reverend King died today," I say.

"I do."

"Who told you?"

"Don't recall, Boss. Everybody knows. Is all anybody talkin' about."

I nod. "You'll be going to Buxton tomorrow to pay your respects," I say.

"I will."

I pick up the bill and hold it out to him. "Then get yourself cleaned up at the baths."

"Don't cost five dollars to get cleaned up at no baths in this town."

"Take it anyway," I say, shaking the bill like autumn's last, barely hanging leaf. "And it wouldn't kill you to buy a new shirt."

This time Tom accepts the money, more for my sake than for his. "If you say so, Boss."

I walk Tom upstairs, want to lock the door behind him. I won't be going home tonight.

Tom takes his coat down from the nail over the stool he sits on every night, turns down his lantern until it flickers the stairwell black. We both step outside. The stars in the sky a thousand August suns. I shut my eyes and see an explosion of silver, listen to Tom start down the frozen walkway. Before he gets too far:

"An important man died today, Tom."

Tom limps to a stop but doesn't turn around. He's waiting for me to say something else.

"Good night, Tom," I say.

"Good night, Boss."

*

You could never plan it out the way it happens. Too complicated, too many twists and turns to culminate simply in the circumstances of one human life. But no one's life is ever simple. Only seems that way when it's your own.

An Irish-born, Glasgow-educated, American-immigrated man marries the daughter of a Louisianan plantation owner while teaching at a private school for the sons of wealthy planters. Unable to live with himself for being the owner of the four slaves his wife brought into their marriage, he soon emigrates again, this time with his wife and two infant children, and enrolls as a theology student at the University of Edinburgh. The son dies on the journey there, the daughter and wife two years later, the same year the man is ordained a minister of the Presbyterian Church of Scotland and selected to do missionary work in Canada West. While working among the Black refugees in the area, the man formulates his idea of founding a self-sustaining Black settlement where former slaves will be free not just in form but in function—education, religious instruction, and economic self-determination the practical prescription for both spiritual and material self-elevation and lasting emancipation, a City of God on earth. But before the man can put his plan into action, his father-in-law dies, leaving him fourteen slaves as his personal property. The man returns to Jackson, Louisiana, with the intention of travelling with his human inheritance to his parents' and brothers' farm in Ohio, where he will legally set them free but also offer them the opportunity to spend the winter on the farm, going to school and learning about northern farming, before joining him in Canada to live as truly free men and women on the proposed settlement.

Before the fourteen soon-to-be ex-slaves and the man can board the steamboat he'd booked north, however, one of the fourteen pleads with the man to buy back her only child—recently sold to a neighbouring plantation—so that mother and son can be reunited and the boy can accompany them to freedom. This the man does, for the sum of $150.

The woman is so thankful—not only that her only off-spring is to be free but that they are to live together again as mother and child—she gives her son the man's last name as his own, a tribute to the white man's remarkable beneficence.

The boy born a slave had been known as simply *David*. The boy reborn a free man became *David King*.

*

After I've counted and recorded and put away the evening's take into the safe, I decide to go home after all. Sometimes owning your own bar isn't a good thing. All the liquor you can drink and no human voice or face to say you shouldn't try. In my case, Loretta's voice and face.

"Henry, let's go," I say, slapping my thigh twice to let him know I mean it, and Henry pushes open the door to the back-room with his nose and trots beside me up the stairs, overtaking me as usual by the time we get to the top. Ordinarily, the spin of the safe's lock after I've deposited the money inside and shut its door is his cue to come out of the back, where he sleeps during business hours, and sit and wait by the bottom of the stairs—the spin, a walk, home, then bed—but tonight he's thrown off by the early hour. Me, too.

Especially if it's winter, the only sounds we're likely to hear on the walk home are ourselves: the crunch of freshly fallen snow under my shoes; the sniffing of Henry's snout; the hot hiss of urine whenever he lifts his leg. I know I've made a mistake in taking our usual route home along King Street as soon as we pass the Rankin Hotel. The Rankin advertises itself as one of the finest hotels in Canada, with fifty-five different dishes on its menu, including lamb chops and buffalo tongue, but the people laughing and shouting and climbing into their carriages out front aren't after anything different than the people who come into Sophia's every night. Oblivion is oblivion. The only difference is the hours of operation and the overpriced food I don't serve.

Pascal said that the sole cause of man's unhappiness is that he doesn't know how to stay quietly in his room. The last time I saw the Reverend King, I had a copy of Pascal's *Pensées* underneath my arm and the smell of whiskey on my breath. Mrs. King had been ill—not with the illness that had cost her her mind, but the illness that would eventually kill her, an illness of the lungs that made it almost impossible for her to breathe, like she was drowning in her own body—and I'd been coming back to the Settlement every couple days for the first time since I'd left for good twenty-two years earlier, after the War Between the States was over, the year I turned eighteen.

Of course he knew I'd been visiting Mrs. King, sitting beside her bed, reading to her for hours even if she couldn't hear me. Nothing happened at the Settlement that the Reverend King didn't know about. When I was a boy, I believed that not only did he know everything that I'd done and was doing, but everything that I was going to do, even if I didn't. But that was when I believed that God's eyes were everywhere. Back then I would have believed that Mrs. King's moans were somehow all a part of His divine plan. Back then I did believe that the man who raped my mother, her master, wasn't my real father, that my real father was waiting for me in heaven.

The Reverend King looked as surprised as I felt as I exited Mrs. King's bedroom. Someone must have told him I'd left already. Someone had been wrong.

"David," he said, nodding but not stopping.

"Reverend King," I said, doing the same.

It wasn't until I was outside and getting on my horse and went to put on my hat that I realized I'd taken it off when I'd passed him in the doorway. I had sworn to myself that I would never do that again. Halfway back to Chatham, I'd almost convinced myself that the tears I was crying were all for Mrs. King.

*

As soon as Henry sets paw inside the house, he tears upstairs; before I've had time to light the lamp in the library, he's scouring the main floor, including the pantry, the door of which he pries open with his nose. Nothing. Not much chance that Loretta would have been in there waiting for us to come home anyway, but dogs don't like secrets, not even closed doors.

I leave the fire alone. If Loretta was here, I'd have to add another log—Loretta can never be warm enough—but when it's just Henry and me I keep the house cool, the temperature outside one's head an honest thermometer of what's going on inside. Imagine Socrates on a clear Athens morning in the fresh open air of the agora, busily corrupting the city's youth in the art of being virtuous. Then think of the thousands of slithering gods and goddesses of India hatched from the steaming brains of overheated believing millions. People or places, weather is soul.

Satisfied, or at least resigned, that it's just the two of us, Henry circles the rug in front of the fireplace three complete times before collapsing in a heavy heap to the floor. I watch him watch the fire from my chair, head resting on his front paws, eyes slowly, slowly closing until finally fluttering shut, an extinguished candle on a drafty windowsill. Not forever, though. Not yet, anyway. Not like the Reverend King. Nearly eighty-three years of morning after morning of waking up— the world's most ordinary miracle—and tomorrow morning he won't. The truest truth that makes absolutely no sense.

Times like this, only Mr. Blake or whiskey will do. A time exactly like this, I need both. Henry's eyelids slide open as I stand up, but he stays lying where he is. Although it's *Songs of Innocence and Experience* that's behind glass and under lock and key, it's the whiskey I should probably be concerned with protecting. Not much chance that anyone in Chatham would ever want my 1831 first edition—the only edition preceding it the illuminated, engraved copies produced by Mr. Blake himself—as much as they'd want a bottle of whiskey. But sometimes philistines make good neighbours. I'm going to own one of those copies made by Mr. Blake's own hands one day, and when I do, I won't even have to lock my front door at night.

Favourite books are like old friends: beginnings and endings don't matter, you take what you need when you need it. I swallow, savour the familiar burn of the first sip of whiskey, and set the glass on the table beside my chair, open up the Blake on my lap. The fuzzy black type reminds me that I've left my spectacles upstairs in the bedroom. If I bring the book nearer, I know I won't need them, won't have to get up again, but whenever Loretta catches me attempting to read without them, she warns me that my eyes will only get worse. But Loretta doesn't really warn me, not about anything; warning isn't Loretta's way. Loretta explains the situation, points out the potential advantages and disadvantages, advocates the most reasonable course of action. I wonder if all Germans act the way that all Germans are supposed to act or just the only one I've ever known. If Loretta gets her way, I'll find out for myself, and sooner rather than later. Only last week:

"You have the money, yes?" she said.

"I could afford to go, if that's what you mean."

"Do not be modest, David. You could afford to go one hundred times over. The only question that remains is whether or not your affairs here prohibit you from being away for an extended period."

Loretta didn't speak English until she arrived in Canada a little more than ten years ago, a sixteen-year-old girl knowing no one and not knowing where she was going to go, but in spite of a thick German accent, speaks with a clarity and exactitude unequalled by anyone I've ever known except one. And now, after today, the only one I still know.

"There are a lot of things that would need to be taken care of first, arrangements that would need to be made."

"But these arrangements, they *can* be made. These affairs, they do *not* prohibit you."

"They don't *prohibit* me, no, but—"

"No, they do not prohibit you. And you would like to see the birthplace of Goethe, of Schopenhauer, of Beethoven, would you not? To learn their language, perhaps?"

"I don't need a holiday, if that's what you mean."

"You say this word like it is a curse word."

"What word?"

"*Holiday*, obviously."

"I think you're hearing things. I only meant that I'm not complaining about my life. You've never heard me say I'm unhappy. You've never once heard me complain about my life."

Once I've retrieved my glasses, I decide that while I'm in the bedroom I might as well relieve myself. I was the fourth man in Chatham to have indoor plumbing, but I decide to use the chamber pot instead. Out of habit I aim for the left-hand side of the pot, let the urine silently run down the side and slowly gather and rise at the bottom of the bubbling bowl. It's my mother's pot—*was* my mother's pot—and I can still remember how pleased she was when she was finally able to own a store-bought, Detroit-manufactured chamber pot decorated with blue horizontal stripes. When her rheumatism got so bad she rarely left the house except to attend church—the highlight of her day the dragging of her gnarled limbs out of bed to sit in her chair by the window—she still made a point of every day dusting that chamber pot. By then she'd bought another, cheaper pot to use for what it was intended for, but the blue-striped chamber pot sat pride of place on top of the bureau in her bedroom, right between her bible and a copy of the legal document declaring her and her son free Negroes.

In the five minutes it takes me to return to the library, Loretta has let herself in, is squatting on her heels and scratching Henry's stomach, a long canine grin carved into his face, all four black legs pointed straight up in the air like he's unconditionally surrendered. "This is a most unimpressive watchdog," Loretta says, still scratching.

Sitting back down in my chair, "I'm afraid you've ruined him forever for that line of work." We both know that's a lie, that it's only her familiar footsteps or mine on the front porch that elicit whimpers of expectation rather than howls of aggression. One of Loretta's tenants is a butcher from Dresden who always gives her a cow bone along with his rent for what she tells him is her dog. Loretta's business contacts, past and present, know as much about her as mine do about me.

She gives Henry an all-done slap on his belly that makes a hollow sound like a single tap on a drum and stands up. Henry flips over onto his side and we both watch her rise to her full height of six feet. Henry wags his tail; I smile. What man doesn't want more—more whiskey, more money, more years? And yet, when it comes to women, it's tiny feet they desire, a pinched waist, a doll's dimensions. *Enough! or Too much*, Mr. Blake wrote. A world in a grain of sand wasn't the only blessed vision he knew about.

"You are home early tonight," Loretta says, settling into the other chair on the other side of the fire. She's the only one who uses it—it's covered in the blanket she knit while sitting in it—but like the key to the front door she carries in her bag, it's never referred to as *hers*. It's as if we've discovered a way to not be what we don't want to be and yet still have what we want.

"I decided to close early," I say, picking up my drink, reminded of why I poured it in the first place.

"Yes, of course, that is obvious. But why? This is not like you to not want to make money."

I finish the rest of my drink in one long swallow and almost gag. Whiskey is not water, is made to do other things.

"Is that who you really think I am?" I say. "Just another greedy shopkeeper?"

I take my empty glass with me into the kitchen without asking Loretta if she'd like a drink too. It doesn't matter. By the time I've finished refilling my glass, Loretta is beside me at the kitchen counter, taking another glass down from the cupboard as well as her bottle of schnapps. We walk back into the library with our respective drinks without exchanging a word.

Loretta will not argue—she'll discuss, deliberate, even debate, but she will not argue—and the way she picks up her needles and yarn from underneath her chair and straightaway begins knitting without acknowledging either me or my sour mood has its intended effect, makes me madder than if she'd confronted me with the bile of my words and shown me I'd been wrong to use them. I reopen the Blake and bring the book close enough that I don't need my glasses to make the type stop smearing. That'll show her.

Except that in five minutes I've got a headache from reading without my glasses and a cloudy brain from drinking the whiskey too fast and a strong desire not to feel distant from one of the two human beings I know in this world whom I don't ordinarily feel distant from. Good liquor and immortal literature are necessary but not sufficient.

"I'm sorry," I say.

Loretta stops knitting, looks up. "You are forgiven," she says. Needles immediately working again, "So. You closed early this evening. This is not like you."

I want her to know what happened tonight—who died, what it means—but I'm not sure that I know yet myself.

"Can we just pick up where we left off last night?" I say. I say it like a child asking for a sweet, but that's how I feel, so, so be it.

Eyes still on her work, "Are you sure that is what you need for yourself right now?"

I nod. She doesn't look up, makes me say it. "It's what I need," I say.

She finishes a last row and then slides the yarn and needles back into the box underneath her chair; stands up and wipes away an imaginary mess from the front of her dress. She offers me her hand. I take it and we walk side by side up the stairs, the click of Henry's nails on the steps behind us serenading us all the way to the bedroom.

By the time I've undressed and am already underneath the covers, Loretta is only just down to her undergarments. The light from the bedroom fireplace is less than what I'd like—watching Loretta bathe by the natural light of bright morning is my favourite way of beginning the day—but the gentle glow it creates all around her suits where we are and what we're going to do.

She meets my eyes and doesn't release them while unfastening her corset and then pulling off the white chemise underneath. Next, foot up on the metal end of the bed, the unhooking of the garters, always the left then the right, followed by the slow roll of stocking down thigh, calf, ankle, toes. Finally, the removal of the belt itself, tugged around to the front and unclasped and set on top of the heap of clothes on the fireside chair. I pull back the blankets from her side of the bed, let Loretta slide in.

What happens next, I don't have to ask her to do. Loretta reaches across me, raises herself up on one arm above me, two identical pallid moons rising over me, perfumed warmth all around me. Getting what she's after from the table on my side of the bed, she lies back down on her side. Begins.

"'Warum nun aber erblickt man im Alter das Leben, welches man hinter sich hat, so hurz?'"

I close my eyes, let the heavy words smoke the air, mix and merge with Loretta's scent that couldn't be anyone else's but Loretta's.

"'Weil man es fur so kurz halt wie die Erinnerung desselben ist.'"

I feel myself already drifting off, Schopenhauer's words no longer words but music without worldly referents, a perfect, impenetrable language saying everything and nothing and all at once.

"'Aus diesser namlich ist alles Unbedeutende und viel Unangenehmes herausgefallen,'" Loretta reads, "'daher wenig ubrig geblieben,' and sleep now, my David, sleep now, little boy of mine."

And soon, very soon, I do.

2

I was seven or eight years old the first time I heard someone say, "If a job is worth doing, it's worth doing right." As I was shovelling horse shit at the time, the wisdom of these words failed to leave a lasting impression.

Luckily for me, I was only one year old when the first fifteen settlers, my mother and myself included, along with the Reverend King, arrived at the Elgin Settlement in 1849, so the earliest, most difficult of those pioneering years I spent either cozied in my cradle or wandering around the Settlement barefoot and blithe, making life miserable for the chickens and any other farm animal I decided needed chasing. Unlike alcohol, which was forbidden in writing by the Reverend King as one of several non-negotiable conditions for purchasing Settlement land, dogs weren't illegal in Buxton, but they might as well have been for the number of times you saw one, which, in my case, was exactly once.

The land that the Reverend King and the Presbyterian Church chose for the Settlement was six miles long and three miles wide, bounded on the north by the Thames River and on the south by Lake Erie. The swampy land was thick with oak, hickory, elm, and walnut trees—valuable timber in years to come, but also the first exhausting order of business upon the settlers' arrival. I sucked my thumb and cried whenever I was hungry or needed changing, while everyone else cut and burned trees and cleared brush and opened roads and dug drainage and built housing and planted vegetable gardens; and by the time I was old enough to write my own name, what had once been silent miles of empty forest had become home to 130 families with their very own Negro-run post office, school, church, sawmill, gristmill, and potash factory. What was left of the surrounding woods was put to use, too, deer and wild turkey and rabbit in abundance to supplement the cattle and hogs and chickens raised right on the Settlement.

The dog I saw was when I was ten, hunting with my best friend, George, and his father, Mr. Freeman. Most of the men of Elgin were happy to include a fatherless boy in whatever it was that fathers and sons did together, but when the Reverend King would speak on Sunday about how self-reliance bred self-respect, about how a fulfilled, contented man before God and society was a man who didn't ask another man to undertake his appointed tasks or shoulder his worldly burdens, I knew he wasn't just talking about not buying with credit what you knew you'd never be able to afford with cash. In my case, it meant that an encouraging word and a shiny apple from a friend's father wasn't the same thing as a bond born of blood. It meant that if I really wanted a father of my own, it was up to me to find him.

Mr. Freeman was even kinder to me than any of the other fathers because George had been my best friend almost from the day he and his father arrived in Buxton in '55; plus, he knew what it was like for a boy to grow up with only one parent, George's mother having died giving birth to George. Mr. Freeman had been born a slave in Mississippi and had fled for the North Star three separate times, on each occasion that he failed and was recaptured, was beaten, lashed, starved, and sold off to a new master, the belief being that "You can't let a peach get too ripe." If it was hot when we'd go hunting, sometimes we'd detour to Deer Pond for a swim. The marks on Mr. Freeman's back like long, fat red worms that wouldn't leave him alone.

It was the season's first snowfall, yesterday's brown and green gone missing overnight underneath a frozen dusting of fine white baking flour. Sometimes, when we'd be walking in the woods, Mr. Freeman would suddenly stop on the path to bend down on one knee and finger the leaves of a plant or to rub the back of his hand over the bark of a tree, occasionally slicing off a bunch of leaves to take home with him or uprooting an entire plant with the long, shiny knife that always hung from his belt. He wasn't a doctor, but for a long time was the closest thing Elgin had to one unless you were willing to ride all the way into Chatham.

When he'd lived in Mississippi, he said, another slave, an old man everyone called Tuttle, had taught him all about roots and herbs and how to use them to stop a toothache or to make a burn feel better or to cure sleeplessness. Mr. Freeman farmed like almost everyone else in Elgin—tobacco mostly, but corn and oats, too—but if it was cold and damp and the rheumatism in my mother's knees would flare up, she'd send me over to George's house with a nickel to ask for some of the powder that his father would grind up for her to mix in with her tea. She'd always make a face when she drank it—you were supposed to prepare the water as hot as you could stand it and to swallow the whole thing down as quickly as you could—but within a couple of hours the pain in her legs would have subsided and she'd be ready to get back on her knees to scrub the floors of the Reverend King's house and to sweep underneath his and Mrs. King's beds. My mother was the Kings' housekeeper.

"Ah, Pa," George said.

Mr. Freeman didn't pay any attention, brought the winter-wilting limb of the plant he'd stopped to inspect closer to his nose; breathed in hard, like he was smelling an apple pie cooling on a kitchen table.

"We're never going to get there," George said, shutting an eye and following with his rifle end the flight of a bird taking off from a tree branch. Mr. Freeman had taught us never to shoot a gun except for food or protection. Higher up the same tree I watched a squirrel jump from branch to branch and then from that tree to the next, billows of powdery snow avalanching down with every expert leap. Directly below this last, a dog sat determinedly scratching one of his ears, looking at me looking at him with no more concern than if I were just another elm or oak. Finished, he rose to all fours and shook his head from side to side several times, like he was trying to wake up. He stayed where he was, unsure, it seemed, whether to approach us.

"A dog," I said, lifting a single finger, as if to do more would mean scaring him away.

"Where did he come from, do you think?" I heard George say, but didn't turn around, didn't want to break the connection the dog and I shared, didn't want to startle him away.

"Lost, I guess," I said.

"Somebody's from Chatham who was hunting out here, maybe," he said.

"Maybe."

Like he knew we were talking about him, the dog wagged his tail; didn't make a move toward us, but slowly wagged his black tail back and forth, back and forth. He was black all over, but with a white stripe running from just below his neck down his chest. I wanted to pet him like I'd seen white people do with their dogs in Chatham, but I didn't know what to do next. Mr. Freeman would know what to do next.

Before I could ask him, though: a shotgun blast from behind me and a single, sharp-pitched yelp from the dog, and the crows in the treetops caw-cawing their angry escape. The dog tipped over onto its side like he'd all of a sudden frozen in place and been pushed by invisible hands, his eyes wide open but unseeing, his mouth opening and closing as he lay there on the snow-covered ground like a fish in a bucket of stale water running out of fresh air. For some reason, only his two back legs, and not all four, twitched and trembled and spasmed. Mr. Freeman walked between us and past us and carefully aimed the rifle just above the dog's eye and pulled the trigger. He wiped down the barrel of his gun on the dog's long back, four dirty red streaks for each cleaned side.

Seeing George and I still standing there, looking at the thing that two minutes before had been the dog, "Don't you worry, boys, that's one hound won't be tormenting no poor Negro no time soon," he said. Placing one of his big, warm hands on my shoulder, "No hellhounds on no poor slave's heels in this free land of ours if we can help it."

*

Closing time isn't for another couple of hours, but I've already scrubbed the bar and basin gleaming clean and washed every empty glass as soon as it's been dirtied and hauled in enough fresh kindling from outside to get us through tomorrow night and probably the night after that. Bringing in the wood is Tom's job ordinarily, but even if I hadn't given him the time off for the wake tonight, I probably would have found a way to do it myself anyway, busy hands cooling medicine for a burning brain. I'm also extra diligent about keeping every glass filled, am toting the bottle of whiskey over to Thompson's table before he's had time to nod to me for a refill.

At the clink of my bottle to his glass, Thompson looks up and slides his notepad across the table his way, an experienced card player careful to keep everyone else in the game in the dark. I'm the only one in Sophia's who knows what's supposed to be written there, even if I don't have any inkling what actually is, but I wouldn't peek if I could. Prayers and suicide notes are privileged information.

"And how is Song of His Self this evening?" I say, sitting down in the empty chair opposite him.

Slipping the notebook into the inside pocket of his jacket, "Loafing and inviting my soul," he says.

"As usual."

"As usual."

Together we silently observe the men all around us drinking and smoking and playing cards and laughing and looking at their watches and considering how much longer they can put off the inevitable: having to go home. Meyers' voice, of course, is the loudest. It has to be—no one is listening.

"From Hitching's, Hitching's Baby Store. It's where Queen Victoria bought *her* prams when *she* was a young mother. Now, the thing to remember when you're buying a pram is that what you want is the wickerwork or bassinet model. This allows the child to be laid flat on its back with plenty of room to move about, but not so much that the little terror can get himself in any trouble. And you want the Silver Cross Bassinette. Believe it or not, some of these American versions are actually made of cane or some other beastly vegetable product. No, no, it's always best to buy the best, that's what I always tell Mrs. Meyers, so get the Silver Cross, it's quite simply the finest there is. You can order them directly from Hitching's Baby Store, you know. It's where Queen Victoria bought *her* prams when *she* was a young mother."

There are men standing on either side of Meyers at the bar, but both appear to be more interested in studying the row of whiskey bottles displayed along the wall behind it than in acknowledging Meyers' words or even his simple physical presence. No matter—Meyers pulls his silver snuff box out of his vest pocket and snorts a fat line from the back of his fatter hand before continuing. "As I was saying to Mrs. Meyers just the other evening . . ."

It's unfortunate Darwin wasn't born twenty-five years later, or he wouldn't have had to sail all the way to the Galapagos Islands to discover that only the most adaptable animals endure; all he would have to have done was spend some time at Sophia's observing Meyers. Any lesser man would have decided years before to do his drinking somewhere where he wasn't so steadfastly ignored. The survival of the oblivious.

Thompson is the only customer I've got whose conversation I'll occasionally seek out for its own sake. Thompson is Scottish and a bachelor and an ex-lawyer, but most of all he's an ardent admirer of Walt Whitman—evidenced by the cheap copy of *Leaves of Grass* that always shares the tabletop with his glass—for reasons not entirely aesthetic. And he's a drunk. Which only somewhat explains the ex-lawyer part.

"Missed Tom on the way in this evening," he says. Thompson always tips Tom a quarter at the end of the night.

"He's in Elgin."

"Everything's all right, I hope." Thompson's long, Scot-taught rolling vowels echo the same way as the Reverend King's did. It used to sound as if the whole of history was in that voice.

"Someone died."

"Oh?"

"Not anyone he was close to. He'll be back tomorrow night. Everything will be back to normal by tomorrow night."

I stand, wipe the table everywhere that Thompson's drink isn't. I didn't sit down just so I could talk about what I'm trying not to think about. I lift his drink, finish wiping, set it back down.

"The minister, the white one who started the Negro settlement, I can't recall his name—it's his wake, I'm sure. There was something about it in the *Planet*."

Thompson's been in Chatham not even ten years, never knew Elgin when it was two thousand people thriving, when reporters from as far away as New York and Boston and even Britain would come to see and write about the Reverend William King and his exciting new experiment in free Negro living, amazed at how the children of former slaves would stand at the front of their log-cabin classroom reciting long passages of Virgil and Homer in their respective native tongues as part of the school's everyday curriculum.

"No doubt," I say.

"Well, here's to Tom, then," he says, lifting his glass.

I take my place back behind the bar, can sense my body readying my mouth to snarl at the next person impudent enough to ask me for something outrageous like another drink. Instead, I take a deep breath and interlock my fingers and rub my palms, hard, over and over again, like Loretta's taught me to do whenever I feel myself getting angry. I do it below the bar so that no one can see me, and it helps, I don't even snap at Meyers when he orders another round and there's a speck of brown snuff clinging to his flabby white cheek.

I give Meyers two dimes and his drink and the first line of Lucretius that lifts off my lips. "*Inque brevi spatio mutanteur saecla animantum et quasi cursores vitai lampada tradunt.*"

"Sorry, David, old boy," he says, pocketing the change and taking his whiskey. "I'm embarrassed to have to say that my French just isn't what it used to be."

*

Not just the newspapers wrote about the Reverend King. Harriet Beecher Stowe modelled a character by the name of

Clayton after him in one of her novels, *Dred, a Tale of the Dismal Swamp*. In honour of the famous author of *Uncle Tom's Cabin*, the Reverend and the second Mrs. King returned the favour by naming their home Clayton House. Of course, by then, adding Mrs. King's name to anything her husband did or said was considered merely being polite. By then, everyone—even me, the nine-year-old son of their housekeeper—knew something was wrong with Mrs. King. The only difference was, I didn't mind. More than that: I liked the way Mrs. King was.

Married to the Reverend King in 1853, the second Mrs. King gave birth a few years later to a stillborn son and almost immediately began, as my mother and everyone else around Buxton used to say, to turn "queer." For a while she gave free piano lessons to any child in the Settlement who wished to learn, but even these stopped when, one day, mid-lesson, she simply rose from the piano bench, went into the bedroom, shut the door, and refused to come out.

A cot was placed in the Reverend King's study, the piano was moved into the couple's old shared bedroom, and my mother would bring Mrs. King's meals to her in her room. The bedroom door would always be closed, and everyone—the Reverend King included—would go about their business around Clayton House as if there was nothing at all unusual about the muffled sound of a piano playing Beethoven and Schumann sonatas hour after hour, day after day. Until the day the music stopped forever and every time my mother would bring Mrs. King her food, she'd find her in the exact same place, sitting silently at her bedroom window.

I was the house pet Clayton House never had. After school, and before school after my chores at home were done, I'd help my mother in the kitchen or push around the furniture while she dusted and swept or emptied out back the buckets of dirty mopping water. The jobs I liked best were the ones I got to do all by myself, like beating the rugs on the back porch or carrying in the firewood that would be left at the end of the front walk by Mr. Johnson or one of his sons and their horse, Midnight.

"Good boy," my mother would say, kindling piled high to my eyes. "When the Reverend King sits down at his desk in front of his fire tonight, it'll be the wood you brought in that'll be keeping him so nice and warm." The Reverend King was almost never at home in the daytime, but would work in his study late every night, sometimes until midnight. "I don't know when that man sleeps," she'd marvel. "Lord, please look after our dear Reverend King." I felt proud I was helping him do his work, felt a little like it was my work too.

There was a special stick for beating the rugs. It was oak and heavy and nearly the length of my arm. With every smack, I'd pretend that each fresh explosion of flying dirt and lint was actually hundreds of hurtling meteors like the ones we'd learned about in school, every one of them racing against the others to see who could collide with the earth first, competing amongst themselves to destroy every Slave State and all of the helpless slave owners and their slave-owning families along with them. I never worked out how the abolitionists and the slaves themselves would escape being crushed to death at the same time, but I knew I didn't have to worry about it very much. God, I knew, would find a way.

*

"And this one?"

I pause before I say what we both know I'll say, a moment's hesitation meant to imply concentration, contemplation, consideration.

"Interesting," I say.

Loretta doesn't respond, probably doesn't even hear me, flips over the photograph onto the pile of already-viewed others laid out on her skirt. What was once my large kitchen pantry is now her small workroom, but freshly developed photos are always formally scrutinized fireside, Loretta's spread skirt the only desk she needs to do her job.

"And this one?"

I look up from the book I'm only staring at anyway, and Loretta holds up a new picture for me to see. Before I can automatic another "Interesting," though, something makes my eyes stay where they are, linger longer than they ordinarily do. Loretta notices this. Loretta notices everything.

"Ah, this one—it *is* interesting, yes? And why is this? Please be specific."

I stand up from my chair and take the photograph from her, step closer to the light of the fire. "I don't know," I say, lying, knowing that she knows I'm lying, knowing, too, that the lies we allow each other are one of the ways we know we're in love. The flame flickers the picture brighter but not any clearer—turns it softer, even, as if the man belonging to the face in the photo had fallen asleep in his Sunday best on a bursting autumn orange afternoon. He's not asleep, of course; Loretta doesn't make it her business to take pictures of dozing gentlemen. Loretta is a portraitist of the dead. The only sleep her subjects sleep is their last.

"I suppose he reminds me of someone," I finally say, handing her back the photo. I take the poker and push around the logs even though the fire is burning just fine on its own.

"That is all?"

"That's all."

"This is disappointing."

I keep poking around where I'm not needed, eventually succeed in reducing a hunk of previously blazing white ash to a furious red lump. "I'm sorry if I don't share your belief that pictures of the recently deceased are on par with lyric poetry," I say. I know Loretta is staring at the back of my head, so I squat down where I am, keep prodding and rearranging.

"Must art be made only of words?" Loretta says.

"Of course not."

"And can we agree that we would be wise not to decide what is and what is not art based solely on its subject matter, but to withhold our judgement until we have experienced for ourselves the essence of the piece of art in question?"

"I guess," I say, waving away a sudden swarm of sparks, nearly tipping over on my heels in the process.

"You guess?"

"No—yes, I mean. Yes."

"So perhaps the product of an art form in its infancy—photography, for instance—could be as valid as, say, lyric poetry? As practised by the right artist, I mean, obviously."

"Obviously."

I give up, abandon the fire for my chair. Never argue with a German woman with a dialectical mind.

"Good, then," Loretta says, rising, just as I've sat back down. "And now we go to bed, yes?"

"I think I'm going to read a little more."

"But you have not turned a page all evening."

"Of course I have," I say, holding up my book as if somehow this made it true.

"I see." Loretta slaps her thigh once, twice. "Come along, Heinrich, it is time for all of us non-readers to retire for the evening."

Henry is on his feet and stretching in place in front of the fireplace—nose to the carpet, ass-end in the air—as soon as he hears his name, or at least its Prussian translation. One more slap of Loretta's thigh later and I watch the two of them, and then their shadows, slide up the stairs.

I take up and then set back down my book, consider and then reject the idea of a drink. And, just like I knew I would, just like she knew I would, I pick up the stack of photos left behind on Loretta's still-warm seat. I begin at the bottom of the pile.

Even sightless, every one of them—every man, every woman, every child; the Whites, the Blacks, the single Chinese—wants you to know that they know something that no one alive can ever understand. I despise the smugness of the dead. The dead never look a man in the eye.

*

Eight years ago, I watched them lower a different dead person—Mrs. King—into the ground from the back of my horse, drunk but steady in the saddle. No one had told me I wasn't welcome at the funeral, but no one had to. A carrion knows he's not wanted.

I wanted more whiskey, not a woman—especially not a woman whose touch I had to pay for—but Dresden was closer to the Settlement than Chatham, and I remembered that there was a tavern there that would sell you a bottle and a room to drink it in if you paid for a girl to go along with them, so I rode right at Bear Creek where ordinarily I would have ridden left.

Every nearby Negro knew about Dresden—how it was the site of the real Uncle Tom's cabin; how Josiah Henson, a slave for forty-one years who escaped with his family using the Underground Railroad in 1830, purchased a two-hundred-acre tract of land as a refuge for fugitives from the United States; how he helped to establish the community in and around Dresden as well as the British American Institute, a school for the advancement of fugitive slaves; how he was the inspiration for the Uncle Tom character in Harriet Beecher

Stowe's famous novel—but all this particular Negro wanted to know this steadily sleeting night was alcoholic asylum with as little accompanying chit-chat as possible. When the man who ran the place told me he had just the girl for me, a nice Prussian girl who didn't speak English too well but who was a good girl who knew what to do, I handed him his money and took my whiskey and room key with me upstairs.

A full bottle, a clean glass, a door that locked from the inside—I had everything I needed until morning or unconsciousness, whichever came first. I was already on my second drink when I got up from the bed to answer the heavy knock on the door. I opened it and felt immediately disappointed with myself, not the ideal emotion you hope to inspire when deciding to spend the night at a brothel. The girl forced me to find her beautiful. Whorehouses are for a lot of things, but beauty isn't one of them.

"It is expected for you to let me in, yes?" the girl said.

I stepped aside, closed the door with my free hand. I lifted my glass. "Would you like a drink?" I said.

She walked to the side table and inspected the label on the bottle. "Not of this, thank you, no."

Face-flushing disappointment again, this time for swilling liquor that was, yes, the girl was right, fit only for someone who either didn't know any better or—worse—did know better but who'd convinced himself it didn't matter. I spilled out another two inches anyway and stretched out on the bed.

The girl stepped closer to the fire and began to slowly undress while facing me with all the enthusiasm of someone dutifully carrying out an employer's instructions, carefully placing each removed item on the small room's only chair. To prove to her and me both that I didn't particularly care, I stared at the end of the bed while sipping my whiskey. Draining my drink, reaching for the bottle on the floor, Damn it, I thought, this was not the way this evening was intended to turn out. I'd paid for oblivion, not titillation. And the customer is always right.

"You can stop," I said. "We're not . . ." I tried to think of some physical gesture to finish my sentence, but ended up just raising my glass to my lips. "You can leave your clothes on," I said.

But don't put back on what you've already taken off, I didn't say that. Not that more exposed flesh could have made her any more appealing, everything about her body harvest-time ripe and robust, her black lace bustier shouting out her cantaloupe breasts, her matching stockings and heels screaming her cornstalk-long, surprisingly muscular legs. Just a big, healthy farm girl, I thought. She couldn't have been more than eighteen.

"All right," she said, moving her discarded clothes to the fire's hearth so she could sit down, crossing one leg over the other, entwined hands resting on her knee. Her eyes never left mine, as if she was waiting for me to entertain her, like I was the one who was half naked and she was the one calling the tune.

"Where are you from in Prussia?" I said.

A raised eyebrow. "You are familiar with Prussia?"

"No."

"Then where I am from will not make any difference to you, yes?"

"No, I guess not."

"You guess?"

"No, it won't."

She nodded like I'd finally come up with the right arithmetic answer; idly scratched her kneecap through sheer black stocking. I'd never seen anyone do anything more erotic in my life.

"I am from Rocken," she said. "It is in the province of Saxony. Rocken, it is farming town, there is no reason for you to know it even if you did know Prussia. For anyone to know it."

A farming town, I was right. "And why did you come here?" I immediately regretted my words. "Here to Canada West, I mean." Canada had been its own country for nearly twenty years by then, but I still hadn't gotten used to calling it by its new name.

"Someone I knew from Rocken I come here with two years ago."

"Does she live in Dresden too?"

"*Him.* In America, perhaps, the last time I saw *him.* If he has not returned to Rocken by now. A very weak man this man was."

"But still your friend."

"Never my friend—the father of my baby."

"Oh." I tipped my drink, hid my eyes in my glass.

"And so you do not have to ask, the baby, he die coming here from Halifax, after we come from Rocken."

"I'm sorry," I said.

She recrossed her legs and tilted her head a little to one side, as if registering a previously undetected physical deformity on my face. "But this is surely not the thing to say?"

I shook my head. "I don't know what you mean."

"I mean, how can you be sorry for something you have nothing to do with, obviously."

"*Had* nothing to do with," I said before I knew I was saying it. Ten years of Latin grammar lasts a lifetime.

The girl sat silent for a moment. Eventually: "*Had* nothing to do with." The way she repeated it made you believe she would never use the wrong verb tense again.

"It's just an expression," I said. "A way to show someone sympathy."

"But it is not true."

"No, it's not true."

"No."

She got up from her chair and picked up the first item of clothing on top of the pile beside the fire; stepped into her dress and made her long legs disappear, a cruel magician, sad magic. Now I was back where we'd started, me disappointed at myself for being disappointed. I lifted my glass, but it was empty.

Hand on her hip, head tilted again: "You are disappointed my clothes are going back on," she said. And smiled, if only a little, more amused than actually pleased.

"No, I was just . . ." I raised my glass. "I didn't know I was out of whiskey."

"I see," she said, the corners of her mouth journeying a little higher this time, her chestnut brown eyes smiling along for the ride.

I swung my boots over the side of the bed, stood and stuck out my hand. "My name is David," I said.

"Hello, David. My name, it is Loretta."

*

"I think we have a candidate."

"Have a drink, Franklin."

Franklin's idea of discretion is to wink at you when he says something too loud in the company of people who shouldn't be hearing what he's saying.

"I'm not thirsty." A promising candidate can do what little else can, make Franklin decline an offer of free whiskey.

"Have one anyway," I say, making it clear—clear enough even for Franklin—by the way I look only at him when I pour his drink that magnanimity isn't the source of my suggestion.

Cluing in, "Well, I suppose I wouldn't mind wetting my whistle just a little bit," he says, taking up his glass, although not before letting me know he knows what's going on with a long, lazy wink.

I walk to the other end of the bar. "The devil's boots don't creak," the Reverend King used to say, but even proverbs can't be right all of the time.

I part the curtain at the bottom of the stairs, call out for Tom.

"Yes, Boss?"

"Watch the bar for me for a few minutes, will you, Tom?"

"Sure thing, Boss."

I wait for Tom to limp downstairs. It hadn't been enough for his last master to have him whipped when he was caught attempting to run away again, he'd personally broken both of his knees with a sledgehammer, the loss of an able-bodied slave easily worth the valuable lesson it would impart to all his other slaves about what happens to itchy-footed, uppity niggers.

"And tell Franklin to wait five minutes and then to meet me upstairs."

"Sure, Boss."

"And remember, no credit, I don't care who's asking."

"Never have yet, Boss."

I bow my head to the sideways-blowing snow and walk around to the side of the building, am letting myself in with my own key when Franklin is suddenly at my side with his.

"Here, I've got my key, David," he says, pushing his way past me.

I leave mine lodged in the lock. "Franklin, you can clearly see I've already got my key in the door. Why would I need to use your key?"

Franklin stares at the key in his hand like he's waiting for it to tell him the answer to my question. Putting it away, "Well, you've got yours out already, we might as well use it."

"And didn't Tom tell you to wait five minutes before you left?"

"Yes."

"And?"

"And what?"

"And it clearly hasn't been five minutes. There was a reason I wanted it to seem like you weren't following me out the door."

"Are you sure?"

I inhale, I exhale, I watch the freezing air transform my breath into what it wants. "Am I sure of what, Franklin?"

"Are you sure it wasn't five minutes? I'd swear I waited five minutes. Just like Tom told me you told him to tell me to do."

I give up and unlock the door. He probably did think he'd waited long enough, time as illusory to Franklin when there's money to be made on the quick turnaround of a fresh corpse as it is to a child suffering the torture of a neverending night before Christmas. Without saying a word, we both head for the arrivals room. We've done this before, we know why we're here.

A little over a year after it became law, prohibition was repealed, so I became overseer of an after-hours saloon, not nearly as lucrative a job as my previous vocation as all-hours illegal liquor supplier, but better, anyway, than being a mere law-abiding publican. By this time I'd met Loretta and was already having a house built on some land I'd purchased on Park Street and wondering what to do with Sophia's soon-to-be-vacated upstairs. Then Franklin—a weasel-faced little man with a plump cherry red wart in the middle of his right cheek—showed up at Sophia's one night asking for whiskey. By the time of his third free drink I asked him if he wanted a job. By the look of him, I knew he needed one.

"I'm thinking of opening a funeral parlour," I said. "I'm looking for a mortician."

Franklin scratched his head, not entirely because he was thinking.

"Undertaker," I said, refilling his glass.

"I don't know anything about being an undertaker."

"That's not important."

"I mean, all I know about corpses is that they're dead."

"Exactly," I said.

When I moved into my new house nine months later, Franklin moved in upstairs as undertaker and tenant, and it wasn't long before I was making more money than I had before liquor was legal again.

Franklin ignores the naked body lying on the table and picks up his ledger, flips through a couple of pages until he finds the one he's looking for.

"Gerald Dawson, labourer, fifty-two, only living family member a brother who lives up near Kingston—he's the one who's paying, already paid up in full, by post—heart attack, Doc thinks, organs and all the rest of him just fine and dandy." Franklin looks up from the accumulated facts of the life and, now, death of Gerald Dawson; looks at me like a dog waiting for permission to eat the treat balanced on the end of his nose.

"Pine, oak, or lead?" I say.

"Pine."

I nod. A pine coffin is the cheapest Franklin sells, which means that the family isn't overly concerned with their loved one's material afterlife, which is good news for us. Lead coffins are more expensive because they're most effective at holding off the worms. A guaranteed five hundred years of undisturbed sleep, Franklin tells them. No one ever asks what happens after that.

"No funeral?" I say.

"Nope."

"And the doctor's all done with him?"

Franklin flips again, holds up the form he's after. "Signed, sealed, and delivered."

The call is mine to make, we both know it, so I give Gerald Dawson, labourer, fifty-two, a silent, head-to-toe once-over to make the decision feel official. There's not much to see, to say.

Sad, yes, but not because he's dead—I've seen too many corpses in my time to be moved to melancholy by looking at one more—but because of how he probably lived. Although over fifty, and silver and thinning on top where he isn't balding, his biceps and forearms are still sinewy strong, none of that old-man flesh turkey-necking from the bone, the long, blue, healthy veins rivering up each forearm nature's sole reward for likely decades of day-after-day, soul-starving drudgery. And now, his heart exploded, his labour's still not done; he's going back to work one more time, no resting in peace for you quite yet, Gerald Dawson. The working class are history's niggers.

"Okay, let London know we've got a delivery for them."

"Right, good, right," Franklin says, already spending, I can tell, his cut of our usual twenty-five-dollar payment plus the cost of delivery. I wouldn't be surprised if he hasn't got the cable already written and ready to send.

"And don't skimp on the sandbags," I say. "I want that casket filled up pound for pound."

"Sure, David."

"Which means weighing him *and* the bags."

"Sure, sure, of course."

I let myself out, let Franklin get on with his work so that the medical students in London will be able to get on with theirs, so that we'll be able to get paid. Officially, indigents and condemned murderers satisfy the demand for bodies in university anatomy classes, but the dean of any medical school will tell you that, unfortunately, there just aren't enough poor people and convicted killers around these days. *Ergo*, Franklin and I, supply and demand, laissez-faire economics, study your Adam Smith.

When I was a young man, when finding bodies meant doing it the old-fashioned way—at night, by moonlight, with a shovel and a pick—it was easier to believe that Lucretius was right, that *The greatest wealth is to live content with little, for there is never want where the mind is satisfied.*

But a satisfied mind isn't easy to achieve when you're walking around with shackled feet. Later on, I found what I was looking for in Voltaire. Books, gods, people—if you're lucky, you find the right ones at the right time.

Liberty is power, Voltaire said.

But don't take his or my word for it. Just ask Gerald Dawson.

3

Sometimes it seemed as if I was the only person in Buxton who didn't embrace July and August's back-to-back blasts of broil as a long-lost, much-missed friend, the summer sun so hot, the still air so sticky thick, the flicker of a single fly's wings almost cooling relief. I may have been born in Louisiana, but the air I breathed from my second year onward blew a thousand miles north. For two entire months and parts of two others on either side, my mother, George, his father—everyone, one way or another, who followed the North Star to Canada—savoured the damp of their clothes and the sweat on their faces as some sort of seasonal blessing.

Of course, I wasn't the only person who suffered the heat and humidity, just the only dark-skinned one. Summertime found the Reverend King's brow as dotted with wet as mine, my mother dutifully struggling at the washbasin to supply him daily with a clean white collar. But the Reverend King was always too busy to be bothered by anything as trivial as the weather. The original settlers liked to tell the story of how, that difficult first winter, chopping down trees and burning their stumps and boiling the smelly black ash, the Reverend King worked as hard and as long as anyone, how he once called out during an outdoor supper break when they were one plate short, "Give me a wood chip. I can eat off a wood chip as well as off any plate of china."

It was the heat that made Mrs. King and me allies.

Mrs. King's bedroom wasn't officially off limits; to have forbidden entry to it would have meant admitting something inside was wrong. Instead, it was simply understood that Mrs. King needed her rest, was busy embroidering or practising the piano, wasn't feeling well and shouldn't be disturbed. But I wasn't anyone who had to be put off anything, I was just David, the housekeeper's little boy.

I was eight years old when Mrs. King gave birth to her stillborn child. Until then, she played the piano at services at St. Andrew's Church but was otherwise seldom seen around the Settlement, and when she was, she walked with lowered eyes and a thin-lipped, nervous smile and with her arm tightly entwined in the Reverend King's like she was afraid, if she let go, she'd lift off and disappear like a lost balloon. Everyone had high hopes when it was announced she was pregnant, no one more so than my mother.

"She have her baby, she be fine, you see. A woman without a child never be happy, never. All she need to do is have her baby to look after and she be fine, keep her mind off her own self."

And everyone was just as pleased for the Reverend King, who had already lost a wife and two infant children so early on in his own life.

"God is using the Reverend King to teach us all a lesson," my mother said. "Such a good man don't deserve all the family hardships he have to endure so far, and him being so young. But God gonna reward his patience now, gonna give him a new baby child, a son to grow up to be just like him, too, I bet, you see."

Actually, my mother did see, was one of the few people besides Mrs. Abbott, the midwife, to view the little lifeless body that passed through Mrs. King into the unwelcoming world. I overheard my mother tell Mr. Johnson, when he came to deliver the Kings' firewood the next day, "It want no sickly child, either, not like most that die before they's born. Was a good weight and had all its ten fingers and toes. It like the Good Lord, He *wanted* that child to be born just so as not to live. And I was right, too, it *was* a boy, just like I told everyone it would be."

After the baby was buried, Mrs. King didn't play the piano at church anymore, and when one did spot her on the street, which was rare, she'd always be wearing a black shawl, which she'd use to hide her eyes as she hurried by. And then one day you never saw her around the Settlement at all. Which didn't mean I didn't see her.

My last after-school job of the day, before I walked my mother home at the end of her long day's labour, was helping her serve Mrs. King her evening meal in her room. My mother would carry the tray of food and utensils and I would follow behind, carrying the water pitcher and a glass. Especially during the summer, when Mrs. King spent most of her time fanning herself by the window, my mother was always trying to get her to drink more water. My mother was an indefatigable believer that there existed no ill in this world that reading the Bible every day and keeping well hydrated couldn't overcome.

"Why, good evening, Mrs. King." My mother would knock twice and then immediately enter, something I was taught never to do. When I asked her why she did what I wasn't supposed to, "Because I be out in the hallway knocking all night otherwise, that's why," she said.

"Look what we've got for you for your supper tonight, Mrs. King—some nice green beans, a corn on the cob, some nice cold ham right off the bone, and look at this nice peach cobbler Mrs. Semple make up just for you and Reverend King 'specially." My mother would carefully place the tray on the table beside Mrs. King's chair by the window and proceed to lay out the silverware and unfold the linen napkin like a salesman presenting his most irresistible wares. Mrs. King would turn around just far enough in her seat to manage a nearly indecipherable little smile and an accompanying slight nod before returning her attention to the window and her fanning, no sale today, thank you, maybe next time.

That was my cue to pour from the pitcher and for my mother to say, "You drink up now, dear, a nice cool glass of water is just what a body needs in weather like this." Mrs. King would do as she was told, like a child who knows it's pointless to argue, and raise the glass to her lips. "That's a good dear," my mother would say. "Now you enjoy your nice dinner now and I'll see you bright and early tomorrow morning with your breakfast." And then my mother and I would close Mrs. King's bedroom door behind us and make sure there wasn't any final thing that the Reverend King needed if he was home, which he usually wasn't, and we'd walk home together, fireflies and crickets and hard bright silver stars splashed across the summer sky.

And then one day Mrs. King looked at me; looked at me, for the first time, as something more than the person who lugged in her pitcher of water and her glass. Hearing the Reverend King at the front door returning home from some-where, my mother had stepped out of the room, leaving me to wait for Mrs. King to take her obligatory swallow of water. It was August and I wanted to be finished and outdoors, where at least there was a breeze, if only a steamy warm one. A line of sweat ran from my forehead into my right eye, and it stung. I blinked, rubbed my eye, blinked again.

Mrs. King stood up from her chair. I didn't know what I'd done, but whatever it was, I knew I shouldn't have done it. I don't think, up to that moment, I'd heard her speak more than twenty words, let alone ever seen her rise from her window-side perch. I wished my mother was there to protect me. I thought of Mrs. King's nameless dead baby buried underneath the ground and how no one said it but everyone knew she was crazy.

"You poor child, take this," she said, handing me her fan.

I was too surprised, too scared, not to. Her words shared the same overseas lilt as the Reverend's, but whereas his were big and booming, hers were tiny and seemed almost apologetic.

Somehow, "No, ma'am, this is yours," I managed.

Mrs. King smiled—an honest smile, not like the ones she manufactured for strangers on the street or for my mother delivering the food she didn't want.

"Now, how can that possibly be? It's my gift to you. Didn't anyone ever teach you it is considered unkind to return a gift to a friend?"

"No, ma'am."

"Well, thankfully, now someone has."

*

I was a good boy. Of course I was a good boy. What other kind of boy could I have been? A stray dog no longer stray is a happy dog, an appreciative dog, an indebted dog. Understandably.

In the classroom, I never spoke until spoken to. I did not giggle, whisper, or squirm in my seat. I used proper language at all times whenever speaking. I always abided by the Golden Rule hand-lettered and framed and hanging at the front of the classroom, *Do unto others as you would have them do unto you.* I always assumed good posture and always faced forward, my feet flat on the schoolhouse floor and my hands folded on top of the desk. I raised my hand when I wished to speak and I stood beside my desk before speaking. Whenever Mr. Rapier, our teacher, asked me to, I would assist a fellow student in disentangling a point of incomprehension, never vain in my superior understanding, only pleased to be able to share my knowledge with another.

At home, I did all of my chores without ever having to be reminded to do them. I carried in old Mrs. Cross's firewood for her and shovelled her walkway and never accepted the nickel she never forgot to offer. I took my mother's arm when we walked to church and dropped my very own earned dime into the collection plate. When I was old enough, I helped the Reverend King and Mr. Rapier run the evening classes they organized to teach the older adults how to read. I wrote letters for the blind and the illiterate to their relatives and friends still in chains back in the South. I prayed every night for my mother's and my souls and the swift death of slavery and the Reverend King's continued good health. I breathed so that my mother and Jesus and the Reverend King would be proud of me.

Understandably.

*

The bottle and two glasses and the bowl of ice and the silver tongs laid out on the kitchen table; Henry with a fresh busy bone, oblivious for hours in front of the fire; the new gramophone waiting in the corner, wound and ready to go to work: everything is set, all that's missing is George. I get up and go to the front window and part the curtain, sit back down. I rearrange the contents on the table—this time the bowl of ice and the tongs on the left, the glasses side by side in the middle, the bottle flanking the right—then get up and go to the window again, the same result as before. I sit down and open the bottle. A watched door never darkens.

At nine p.m. on the first Saturday of every other month for the last eight years, George has shown up on my doorstep like he'd just dropped by on the off chance I just might be in. We didn't hear much of each other after the war, after we both turned eighteen—him staying behind in Buxton, intent on raising a family and working his way up to the top of the potash factory, me moving away to Chatham—until, eventually, from the ages of thirty to forty we didn't even share that uncomfortable silence that is owed to those who discover one day that their best friends have turned into strangers. We don't talk about what brought us back into each other's lives, but for eight straight years now we've passed the first Saturday night of every other month sitting together drinking whiskey at my kitchen table, haven't missed a single night yet.

George's tap at the door lifts Henry's head from his chewing, springs him to his feet and peels back his gums, bone time over now and ready to protect his family, or at least die trying. Dogs are never less than exactly what the moment calls for. This more than compensates for them never visiting the World's Fair or believing that they're going to heaven. Dogs are born Buddhists.

As soon as Henry sees George and me shake hands, he's wagging hard and moving in, waiting for his new friend to give him the rubs between the ears that common greeting courtesy demands, but I tell him, "Lie down, Henry, get your bone and lie down." Puzzled, he pauses, then does what he's told.

"He's a good dog," George says without looking at him, the same thing he says every time he arrives, and begins to unbutton his overcoat on the way to the kitchen. No former slave keeps a dog. None but me. I keep Henry away from George when he visits, and George acts like it's perfectly normal to allow a wild animal that's been known to hunt down our ancestors to live in one's home.

George settles his bulk around his chair while I pour out our first drink. I already opened the bottle to help pass the time, but my glass is as clean as his. The best part of drinking is getting drunk; or, if drinking with another, getting drunk together. Drunkenness itself is never as intoxicating as slowly sipping sobriety behind, everything not as it should be gradually dissolving into everything it should, body and soul both exulting with every additional swallow in the inevitable libation liberation.

"You look good," George says, watching me pour his drink. This is the second thing he always says.

"You don't look too bad yourself," I answer. "Considering what you've got to work with, I mean."

George laughs, rubs his fat stomach like Henry wished he'd rubbed his. "Two weeks ago Mary made me go see the doctor on account of how I was a little short of breath whenever I'd climb the stairs at home and how the joints in my knees were aching a little. I told her it was nothing to worry about, I felt just fine otherwise, but she made me go anyway, that's Mary." George laughs harder now, pats his stomach even more affectionately. "Five dollars later, the doctor said the only thing I was suffering from was too much good living. I said to Mary when I got home, 'He should have given *me* five dollars, I could have told *him* that.'"

George laughs so loud this time, Henry looks up from his bone, wags his worship at the joyful noise coming from the kitchen. I hand George his whiskey.

George wears every hard-earned badge of well-deserved worldly success there is: a hand-cut, three-piece suit; always-shining shoes, a different pair for every day of the week; a gold pocket watch he'll one day hand down to one of his two sons; and a bulging, nearly perfectly round stomach that serves not only as a convenient resting place for his folded hands but also as an emblem of everything that his life—and the lives of his wife and their five children—has come to exemplify: accomplishment, satiation, pride. Skinny folks are poor folks are slaves. George, and George's children, will never be poor again.

We sit, sip. The first glass of whiskey is always for tasting, especially when it's whiskey as good as this; after that, alcohol's sundry other pleasures tend to elbow appreciation to the back of the line. We listen to the trees outside creak in the cold; to the wood in the fireplace crackle its warm, dry heat. It's good to grow up poor together. To know that the wall that separates you from the freezing wind is as arbitrary as it is necessary. To know it and not have to say it.

"How's business?" George says.

Business is Sophia's, of course, but since Sophia's is an illegal business, whenever George and I talk, it's just called *business*.

"Good, good. Not bad. You?"

And, as usual, George proceeds to tell me all about all of the expansion they're considering at the factory and all of the new products they're hoping to develop and all of the new markets in Michigan and Ohio and as far away as Kentucky they're hoping to one day reach, and I let him tell me and tell me. Potash and its resultant commercial uses aren't, in and of themselves, enlivening conversation, but a Black-born, Black-owned, Black-run organization full of an every-year-increasing number of Black men building, expanding, *growing*—I could listen to that all night. A team player? Me? No, never, not even if I wanted to be. But I can still cheer, I can still root for the home side. Can't *but* cheer.

Besides, as good as we both are at not talking about things that talking about can never change anyway, there's one thing neither of us wants to acknowledge that we both know needs to be said before we can spend the rest of the evening sitting in this house that I own mortgage-free, drinking expensive whiskey that I can easily afford, and feeling pleased with ourselves for how pleasantly our past has turned into our present. Any topic, then, just as long as it's off-topic.

"So they're calling Mr. Brown a Father of Confederation now," I say.

George leans back in his seat. "Mr. Brown from the board?" George is a Buxton man, usually only comes into Chatham to visit me. George pays his taxes to the Dominion of Canada, but his real country is Elgin.

"One and the same."

George Brown was not only the publisher of the *Globe* and an editorializing abolitionist and an early, outspoken supporter of the Elgin Settlement, but he, along with two Black businessmen from Toronto and Buffalo—who sent their children to the Buxton school because it was so superior to any coloured schools near where they lived—formed the Canada Mill and Mercantile Company to promote businesses in Elgin. The potash company, for one, was launched with seed money borrowed from them interest-free.

"The only white man on the board of directors," I say, tending to George's empty glass. I'm behind the bar every night at Sophia's—why would I pay someone else to do what I can do better and for free?—but the first Saturday of every other month, I'm George's personal bartender.

George takes his freshly poured glass of whiskey; looks at it, doesn't drink it. "The only white man except for the Reverend King."

I finish fixing my drink but don't waste any time staring at the glass. When I set it back down empty, George has turned his attention from his glass to me.

"I didn't ask you why you weren't at the funeral," he says.

"You didn't have to."

He holds up his hand like I imagine he does at business meetings when an idea is proffered that he wants to stop in its tracks before it can waste any more valuable time. "That's all . . . your business," he says.

"That's right, it is."

"And you know I've never made it mine."

I watch Henry lying in front of the fireplace getting serious with his bone, a paw slung over one of its gnawed ends to better keep it in place while he chews and chews his way to nothing. I don't have any choice but to nod.

"And I don't see any reason to make it mine now."

"Good," I say, picking up my glass.

"But I'll tell you this, too—I don't think we should let this night go by without at least toasting him, David. I don't think that would be right."

I look back at Henry.

"We don't even have to say anything, not out loud, anyway. Just raise our glasses and each of us can think whatever he wants to think and that'll be that." George lifts his drink, holds it in the air experimentally, like a man sticking his wet finger in the breeze to determine which way the wind is blowing.

I clink my glass to his, hear the telltale ping of a genuine crystal-to-crystal kiss, and that's that, it's just George and me again.

"Good," he says, massaging his stomach clockwise then counterclockwise, already laughing at what he's going to say next, as if it's so damn funny he just can't wait until it's out of his mouth to start snickering. "Now how about some of that music you were talking about last time I was here, music that comes out of a *machine*?"

I get up and go to the other room and can't help almost laughing myself, although I don't have a clue why, which only serves to make me laugh for real, which naturally sets George really roaring. Placing the arm of the gramophone on the record already in place, I realize why I'm laughing: I'm laughing because whenever I'm with George, we laugh.

The needle digs out the sounds buried deep in the grooves of the thick black shellac, a minor musical miracle that even Mrs. King, the person who taught me how to listen, never would have believed possible. Mrs. Reverend William King.

Some dead men simply refuse to stay dead.

4

Once, while Mrs. King was playing the piano, I was watching when I should have been listening.

It wasn't as if ordinarily she had to persuade me to pay attention. From the first time I'd been present when she played—leaning up against the ledge of her bedroom window while the music passed from her fingers to the piano to the air to my ears—I was compelled to listen. We always sang in church, and sometimes either George or I would start up a song when we'd be roaming alone in the woods, usually something we'd picked up from one of the older settlers, an old plantation song that didn't, mercifully, make much sense to us word-wise but which still felt good on our tongues and, somehow, even in our souls.

> *I'm going away to the Great House Farm! O, yeah! O, yeah!*
> *I'm going away to the Great House Farm! O, yeah!*

All those punctuating *O, yeah!*s were particularly stirring to sing, especially when you had someone else to shout them out with.

The music Mrs. King made was different, yet wasn't. Vocal-less, yes, and no tick-tocky rhythms to root you to the beat, but beneath the ostensibly tumultuous surface, bubbling up just underneath the ever-eddying notes, the same sounds of anguish and longing and even occasional jagged stabs of anger that characterized the slave songs. It was as if one rang out with the raw call for liberation while the other sang the sound of freedom finally achieved and Oh my God, now what?

Like that very first time, Mrs. King had simply sat down at the piano and begun playing. I'd been her only audience for long enough now to know it was her favourite, Schumann's Symphony no. 4 in D Minor, op. 120. She never tired of it, and neither did I. It was like Heraclitus's river: every time you stepped into it, you heard something different.

I liked to listen to Mrs. King play the piano while looking out the window, the view of the garden—whether tucked away under cold winter white or, as it was that day, bursting green throughout the hot, humid summer—a convenient place to set aside your eyes awhile so as to allow your ears temporary dominion over the rest of your senses. I must have been listening for fifteen minutes when it occurred to me that the bird I'd been watching hadn't moved, not once, the entire time. How she knew I was paying more attention to the bird than the Schumann, I don't know, but suddenly the room was quiet. I felt embarrassed that I was the one who'd made the music stop.

"What is it?" Mrs. King said, hurrying, for her, to the window. "What's out there?" She squatted down beside me, less, it seemed, better to see what I was seeing than to keep whatever it was that was out there from seeing her.

Now I felt doubly ashamed, having managed to terrify an already emotionally fragile woman as well.

"It's just a bird," I said.

Still in her squat, Mrs. King inched closer to the window. It was as if she hadn't heard me or had decided she couldn't trust a mere child with detecting impending danger.

"It's just a bird," I repeated, pointing it out for her. "But I think it's sick, it hasn't moved in a long, long time."

Instead of being relieved, Mrs. King seemed even more upset; stood, finally, but began rubbing her hands, gaze fixed now on the bird.

"A sick bird," she said. "A sick bird, today, of all days. Today, of all days, a sick bird." She kept rubbing her hands, kept rubbing them so hard that they began to chafe red.

"It might not be sick," I said. "Maybe it just . . . doesn't feel like flying right now." Did birds ever grow tired of flying? I wondered. I hoped so.

"You have to go outside and see if it's all right," she said.

I was willing—anything to help Mrs. King calm down—but wasn't sure what I was supposed to do. Maybe when I approached it, it would fly away and everything would be like it was before.

"Did you hear me?" Mrs. King said. She grabbed me by my shirt and shook me. "You have to go outside this instant and see if it's all right. Now do as you're told, David. This insolence is unacceptable. Such insolence. And today, of all days."

I closed Mrs. King's bedroom door behind me and let myself outside through the back door connected to the kitchen. There was no one in the house but us—my mother was at the butcher's—and for a moment I considered simply going home and even telling my mother when she returned what Mrs. King had said and done. But I knew it hadn't been really her—not the real her—who'd shaken me. Plus, my mother didn't like me going into Mrs. King's room without her as it was, and if she ever discovered how she'd acted, I'd never be able to hear her play the piano again.

I knew the bird was dying as soon as I was close enough to pick it up. It wasn't that it didn't startle at my approach; it didn't even move its tiny black eyes, just kept staring straight ahead like it was terrified of something it was impossible to look away from. Although it was only a bird, only a common grey chickadee, it had the same look that George's father's horse Missy had had just before she died the summer previous, her body pulled in tight to itself like she was attempting to keep herself from freezing, her eyes dull and faraway, her eyes not Missy's anymore.

"Pick it up," Mrs. King said through the upstairs window. "Show the poor thing it has nothing to fear."

I knew there was no point. Besides, who knew what it was dying of? I didn't want a dying bird that close to my skin. But I did what she asked anyway. I didn't want anyone else to hear her.

I picked it up with two pinched fingers and placed it as gently as possible in the palm of my other hand. The bird felt like nothing, like it was already the decay of feathers and paper-thin bones it was soon going to become.

"Well?" Mrs. King shouted. "What is it doing? Tell me what it's doing."

I saw Mr. Gordon, the man who sold butter and milk, talking to old lady Hampton, who lived directly behind the Kings. I didn't think they could hear us, but I didn't want to find out.

"It's starting to chirp," I lied. Mrs. King was high enough up, she couldn't tell if it was or it wasn't.

"That's good!" she said.

I saw Mr. Gordon place a hand over his eyes and look in our direction.

"I think it was just scared," I said. "It seems better now."

"A cat," Mrs. King said.

"That's probably it. It probably just got scared by a cat and was afraid to move."

"But now it knows it's safe."

"I think you're right. It's really chirping now."

"I can hear it!" Mrs. King said.

"I think I'll take it home with me, just in case that cat is still around."

"I can hear it! I can hear it now! It's just so happy it's been saved, the poor thing can't stop."

"I better go now, Mrs. King."

"Good heavens, David, have you ever heard such a chirping before in all of your life?"

*

Gerald Dawson isn't an ideal corpse. Loretta prefers her subjects family-groomed and feted, part of the appeal of the pictures she takes and collects being capturing how the left-behind living best see fit to send the dearly departed off to their appointment with eternity. On orders of the bill payer, though—Dawson's brother—Franklin collected the deceased's one and only suit hanging in the closet of the room he kept on William Street and personally made the changeover from the work clothes he'd died in, skipping over the optional shave, hair care, and general cleanup. Where Gerald Dawson is headed to next, no one cares what he looks like, at least not on the outside. Loretta pulls her camera out of its black casing and begins to set up anyway. You play the corpse you're dealt.

"This plastic flower in the top button, it is not necessary?"

"No," I say, and pluck out Franklin's attempt at demonstrating that, although body snatchers, we're not entirely heartless. There's no one left to lie to—Franklin and the body both are off to the medical school within the hour—but good liars don't get that way by deciding beforehand whom to deceive.

It doesn't take Loretta long to get ready. In just the eight years or so that I've known her, her tool of trade has metamorphosed from a hulking, glass-plated daguerreotype machine to the seven-inch by about four-inch camera she's been using recently, with a spool inside long enough to hold one hundred exposures. And when the roll is finished, all she has to do is mail it off to the Kodak factory in Rochester, New York, for development, no more having to float each shot individually in a bath of silver nitrate. The camera is expensive, twenty-five dollars, and at ten dollars a turn the reloading fee is dear too, but the ease and efficiency are worth it. Besides, even at triple that, at quadruple that, Loretta can afford it.

"Now, please leave me alone, yes?" she says, and before I can step out of the room, she's snapping away. I don't go far, lean against the wall just outside the door, cross my arms and shut my eyes for a moment while waiting for her to be finished so that, as soon as Franklin arrives, he can load up the body and be on the road to London.

Loretta demands complete silence while she works but, because of the new Kodak, no more than ten minutes in total to get the job done. It wasn't so click-click quick in the beginning. It helped, though, that one of her newest clients provided her with easy access to a steady supply of fresh subjects, even if I didn't understand what she wanted them for.

"But don't the people who pay you—don't they . . . I mean, isn't it their family members whose pictures you're taking?"

"Who is it that says I am being paid?"

"No one, but . . . but why else would you do it?"

Before the daguerreotype machine gave way to the camera, a post-mortem keepsake was out of the question for most people, was very expensive not only because of the cost of the process but because the photographer had to come to his subject. Of course, why anyone would want such a morbid memento had always been beyond me.

"I do it because I enjoy it, yes?"

"You enjoy taking pictures of dead people. Dead people you don't even know."

"That is part of it. I also enjoy afterward looking at the pictures." She didn't wait for me to ask the obvious next question. "I enjoy looking at the faces of the dead," she said. "They are so much more honest than those of the living."

Anyway, intercourse in exchange for corpses, life paid for in full with death. Loretta's and mine was a match made in alchemy, if not quite in heaven. Even then, it took a few visits to Dresden before carnality became part of our covenant. At first I paid Loretta in cash, and only to read to me— Schopenhauer, Goethe, Fichte, all in their own impenetrable Teutonic tongue—because the only topic I could remember Mrs. King broaching more than once was the trip she spoke of wanting to take to Vienna, home of all of her favourite composers. And if the chances of Mrs. King making it there someday were slim before, they were a whole lot slimmer now that she'd been planted in the ground. Some people might have said that frequenting a whorehouse wasn't the best way of honouring the recently deceased, but Loretta wouldn't have been among them. Even if she had known why I'd come to knock on the door of our usual upstairs room more and more.

"In allem was unser Wohl und Wehe betrifft, sollen wir die Phantasie im Zügel halten: also zuvörderst keine Luftschlösser bauen; weil diese zu kostspieleg sind, indem wir gleich darauf sie unter Seufzern wieder einzureißen haben. *Primum vivere, deinde philosophari.*"

I looked up from the fire. "Only the German. Only read the German, please."

Loretta set the book down on her knee, slipped a double-ringed finger inside to mark the page. "But it is here, these is the author's words."

"*Are* the author's words."

"*Are* the author's words. Because more than one. Of course."

Aside from the dollar I paid her, I threw in the occasional English lesson free of charge.

"But these *are* the author's words," she said. "It is Latin, yes?"

"Yes." I grabbed the whiskey from the side table and inched up my drink. I'd taken to lying lengthwise on the bed while Loretta read from the chair by the fire. I held up the bottle. "May I?" Our relationship was still essentially that of buyer-seller, but lately she'd come to share a drink or two with me over the course of our hour together. The whiskey never affected her reading or anything else she did. I didn't like people who couldn't hold their liquor any more than I did people who didn't drink. That didn't leave a lot of room to like too many people.

"The way I read the Latin, it does not please you?" She upended what was left of her drink and came and stood beside the bed, stuck out her glass.

I poured her her whiskey. "You read it fine. Just only read the German from now on, that's all. That's what you're getting paid for." I hadn't wanted to remind either of us why we were really there, but money—who's paying it, who's getting it—stops any conversation you really don't want to have. Ordinarily.

"No."

"*No?* What do you mean, *no?*"

"I mean, until I understand why one language you do not understand is better than another language you do not understand, I stop reading." She stayed standing where she was; sipped, looked at me over the lip of her drink. I knew she wasn't bluffing. This was a woman, I could tell, who wasn't the bluffing type.

"'First one must live, then one may philosophize.'"

"I beg pardon?" she said.

"'First one must live, then one may philosophize.' That's what the Latin you read means in English. Approximately."

She sat down beside me on the bed without asking. Considering what she could have been doing on it to earn her dollar, I suppose she didn't need to. "You know how to read?" she said. "And Latin? You read Latin too? I must say, I am much surprised."

"Surprised because I'm a nigger, you mean," I said, re-splashing my glass.

"Of course not."

"Of course not," I snorted. "Why 'Of course not'?"

"Because you ask me to read to you."

"So?"

"So, why else would you ask me? Of course I think it is because you cannot read. It is only what makes sense, yes?"

I hung a smug smile on my face and nodded into my glass like I knew something she didn't. Because I actually didn't, kept smugging and nodding until I could think of something I did. Before that had time to happen, though:

"My father, he knew Latin like you, too," she said. "A minister, you see. Part of his job."

"Your father was a minister?"

"I am sorry, you do not understand English either? I thought it was just German you need my help with."

I could feel my face stretching into a smile in spite of myself. I poured some more whiskey into her glass. "I suppose I was just surprised to learn that you don't know Latin,"

I said. "What with your father being a minister, I mean. It would seem to come with the territory. Was it because you were a girl?"

She stood up and walked to the fire and warmed an open-palmed hand; switched the hand her glass was in and warmed the other hand the same way. "Oh, no. It was not because he did not try that I do not know. Believe me, he try."

I knew I didn't have to ask, knew that if I waited long enough, she'd tell me what I wanted to know. Finally, still facing the fire:

"But I try harder," she said.

I thought I hadn't heard her right. "Sorry? You tried harder at what?"

She turned around, the glass in her hand empty again. She took the bottle from me this time and refilled her drink and handed it back without bothering to do the same with mine. Toasting herself, "I tried harder *not* to learn," she said.

*

The first time I saw Loretta naked, I thought: You could crack an egg on that stomach, you could fry it on that ass. I'd known from the beginning she wasn't what most men would consider beautiful—it was as if nature had gotten tired three-quarters of the way through the job, couldn't be bothered to make the final effort to mould her nose just a little less wide, to place her eyes just a little farther apart—but until I saw her naked, and what she did with her nakedness, I didn't know that what I had imagined made a woman beautiful, didn't. An expertly painted face or a perfectly formed nose or a tanta-lizingly shaped figure seemed, seeing Loretta readily release herself from the bondage of her clothing and move toward me already lying in bed, simplistic at best, embarrassingly puerile at worst. Climbing atop me, sticking me inside her, unthinkingly moving every muscle in unison to help create the perfect friction for the long final shudder she was after, I found myself being fucked for the first time. I had always thought that was what men did.

I was never a customer—I never once paid for her body, only her translating tongue—so what other men saw and felt when they were in bed with her, I don't know. What I saw was honest desire and healthy greed, the same unmistakable satisfaction I later came to expect when watching her cut into a thick, greasy pork chop or when she snuggles down deep for the night underneath the small mountain of blankets she likes to pile high on top of our bed when it's particularly cold. Loretta's flesh told you precisely what her soul was thinking. Loretta's flesh *was* her soul. Loretta solved the mind–body problem for me once and for all, and she didn't need René Descartes or any other long-winded bore to help her do it.

Finished, then waiting for me to finish, then climbing back off me like a satisfied rider after trying out a new horse, Loretta walked away from me to where she'd left her discarded clothes. She bent over to pick up a stocking and didn't attempt to disguise the fact she had an asshole. I'd never witnessed anything so honest, ever. I felt myself getting hard again and went to her.

Later, Loretta on my mind led straight to Mr. Blake in my brain:

> *The pride of the peacock is the glory of God.*
> *The lust of the goat is the bounty of God.*
> *The nakedness of woman is the work of God.*

It was the first time I'd thought about Him in a long, long time.

*

Of course, there was the matter of Loretta fucking other men for money.

Like most things too important to talk about, we didn't, not directly, anyway. She would simply say she had to go to *work* and I would never ask her how *work* was, and sooner than you'd imagine, anything becomes ordinary, even the extraordinary, such as your one and only beloved performing sexual intercourse with strangers in return for financial compensation. And when it didn't feel normal, it felt nasty, like I was eighteen all over again and discovering who I was by mocking who I was supposed to be. If I was finally going to settle down, it was going to be on my terms, with a Prussian-born white woman who sold her body for money. I wanted to have my cake and to toss it too.

The nearest Loretta ever came to addressing what she did was when she let on she wouldn't be doing it for very much longer, that not only did she have a strategy, it was a strategy she was determined to carry out and accomplish. Taking a stroll with me one spring morning, Loretta insisted we eschew our standard turn around Tecumseh Park in favour of a walk down Hartford Street. I didn't complain; as long as I was with her and moving, I was happy.

She stopped in front of a large, less than impressive house halfway down the street. It sorely needed a fresh coat of paint, new shutters and eavestroughs, and an entirely rebuilt porch.

"What do you think of this?" she said.

"Not much."

"Maybe not now not much, but after fixing, very much."

It didn't appear to be occupied. "You talk like you're thinking of buying it," I said. Loretta still lived above the tavern in Dresden where I'd first met her.

"There is no thinking. I have already bought it."

I was almost as flattered as I was surprised. That she had enough money to purchase a house was one thing; that she would use it to live closer to me, for us, was another. "Congratulations," I said, as much to me as to her.

"Thank you," she said, appraising her new home.

"When do you move in?"

"*I* do not. My tenants, they move in in September. It is not so bad as it looks. I have men do fixing for me beginning next week. I am promised no longer than ten days to make all necessary changes."

As well as surprised and flattered, now I was confused. "You're not going to live here?"

"Of course not. I buy to make money, not spend."

It turned out that, through one of her *work* contacts, Loretta had learned that the Canada Business College on Queen Street was looking to locate a permanent, centralized boarding house for the young out-of-town females attending what was at that time Canada's only business college. At five dollars per week per young lady, Loretta had been quick to see the possibilities.

I joined her in silently admiring her investment. "Congratulations," I said.

"Yes, you have said," she said. She slid her arm through mine and turned us around, back toward the park.

A couple that was our double in everything—age, dress, evident relationship; everything but colour combination—passed us, making no effort to disguise their weary, head-shaking disapproval. Loretta pulled me closer. She was strong enough, she could.

"One more year and I buy one more house. The year after that, two more, I am certain. After that, I make enough money owning houses, I do no other work but own houses and buildings. Buildings for businesses. Many, many buildings for businesses and houses."

"That's a good plan," I said. "An ambitious plan."

"This is no plan. This is what is going to happen."

5

We knew his name before we knew him.

John Brown was a white man with a three-thousand-dollar bounty on his head who'd founded the League of Gileadites to terrorize the legions of slave catchers who'd crawled out of the ground after the passage of the Fugitive Slave Act. Here was another man who knew his New Testament as much as he despised slavery. For as the Lord instructed Gideon, "Whosoever is fearful or afraid let him return and depart early from Mount Gilead," so John Brown required his recruits to swear to "Stand by one another, and by your friends, while a drop of blood remains; and be hanged, if you must, but tell no tales out of school and make no confession." After Brown and some of his men, including two of his sons, butchered five pro-slavery Kansan settlers in retaliation for a sheriff-led posse's destruction of an abolitionist newspaper office and the beating of an anti-slavery senator, Brown was called a freedom fighter by some and a terrorist by others. When he arrived in Chatham in the spring of 1858, we didn't know what to call him.

I may have been only eleven years old, but even I knew that making John Brown feel welcome in Buxton wasn't as simple as fattening a chicken and putting out an extra plate. The Bible said *Thou Shalt Not Kill*, but our heads and hearts said that five fewer breathing slaveholders didn't feel much like a broken commandment. From the moment we found out that John Brown was in Chatham, we were waiting to hear what the Reverend King would say. As usual, he said what we were thinking.

"Of course, he's a dangerous man. Only a fool would deny that. But he is dangerous because he is angry. And anyone who would deny his right to be angry would be an even greater fool."

The Reverend King was talking to Mr. McKellar as they came out of the Reverend King's study. Mr. McKellar was a Chatham lawyer and an early friend and supporter of the Reverend King, one of the few prominent white ones he'd initially had. Ordinarily, no matter the order of business, when the study door opened, whatever had been going on inside was over, at least until the door was closed again. This time it seemed as if whatever they had been discussing would never be over. I was helping my mother in the kitchen put together Mrs. King's dinner tray.

"I'm not in disagreement with you, Reverend, you know that," Mr. McKellar said. "It's just that a man like this Brown—a man like this doesn't believe in compromise."

"We don't know what he believes. We won't know that until we meet him."

"Even then . . ."

"Let's just wait until he calls upon us. We'll have a much clearer idea of his intentions once we've had an opportunity to meet."

Except that John Brown never called, either on the Reverend King or on Mr. McKellar, and no meeting ever took place. There were plenty of meetings—usually at the Chatham home of Israel Shadd, which also served as the offices of the Negro newspaper *Provincial Freeman*, where Brown and his sons were staying—but only coloured men were invited.

Subsequent meetings in the engine house of the Negro-manned No. 3 Fire Company and the First Baptist Church eventually included a few sympathetic whites, but no representative from Buxton was ever asked to attend. The Reverend King never let on that he resented the exclusion, but other people did, no one more than my mother.

"That man up to no good, I tell you that. Friend of the Negro and he don't have the time or sense to pay his respects to the best friend any Negro I ever known ever had? Riff-raff who he associating with instead, that's what I say. Good riddance that the Reverend King don't have to bother himself with him and his peoples none. The Reverend King busy enough already doing *good*."

We were walking home from Clayton House. I'd managed to listen to Mrs. King play the piano for nearly fifteen uninterrupted minutes while my mother gossiped out front with Mr. Johnson, who also sold firewood in Chatham. Apparently the Negroes who lived there were as agitated with John Brown's presence as we were.

"What do you think he wants?" I said.

The story that had spread around Chatham and made it to Buxton was that Brown and his sons were helping to organize a new order of the Masonic Lodge, one for just coloured men, which was why there was so much secrecy attached to the meetings; but no one believed it, everyone knew that John Brown didn't travel all the way to Canada West just to set up a social club. Besides, the Masons didn't allow Negroes to be members.

"I don't know," my mother said. "But it no good, I tell you that."

Some of the men of Buxton sought private counsel with the Reverend King, wanted his advice about whether or not they should attend Brown's meetings, whatever they turned out to be about. I'd see them sitting waiting their turn in the hallway outside the Reverend King's office, each with hat in hand and a worried face that didn't disappear once the conference inside was over. The Reverend King only spoke out publicly once about John Brown and what he meant—or might mean—to the Negro cause, and even then not by name. He didn't have to. We all knew whom he was talking about.

"A spirit of uneasiness is manifesting itself in these times. Hate and a festering sense of undeserved injury, prompting to revenge, together with a despair of attaining its end by lawful means, will goad some on to lawless, desperate acts of widespread rebellion, in which the planter and his property both will perish together."

No man from Buxton joined John Brown's delegation when they departed Chatham for Kansas. When Brown and two dozen other men descended upon the town of Harpers Ferry, Virginia, on October 17, 1859, with the goal of seizing the government arsenal there and calling on the surrounding slaves to join them in an armed rebellion which would, within days, surely, spread throughout the entire South, Osborn Perry Anderson, Israel Shadd's printer's assistant, was all that Brown had to show for his recruitment efforts in Chatham.

And when, instead of the expected tide of Black recruits, it was Robert E. Lee and eighty United States Marines who descended upon Harpers Ferry a day and a half later, thirteen of Brown's men lay dead, seven were captured, while the remaining five managed to escape, Osborn Perry Anderson among them. Anderson later testified how, when one of the men was finally sent outside with a flag of truce, he was promptly shot in the face. John Brown was bayonetted, shackled, and dragged half dead to Charleston, South Carolina, to stand trial on charges of treason, conspiring with slaves, and murder in the first degree. He was promptly convicted and hanged.

So the Reverend King had been right. All John Brown had accomplished was the deaths of several good men and contributing toward the increasing ire of the slaveholding South. The Reverend King had been right, and we had been right to heed his wise counsel. Again.

Sometimes, when George's father would need to go into Chatham to buy an implement or some seed stock he couldn't get in Buxton, George and I would ride along. One Saturday afternoon George and I bought a bag of peppermints to share and walked past Israel Shadd's home on King Street, where everyone knew that John Brown was staying. An old thin white man with a long thin nose and long white hair and a long white beard scowled down from the second-floor balcony of the Shadd house. He stood alone. It wasn't good manners, but we couldn't help but stare up at him as we passed by. The old man paid us no attention. It was as if he didn't even see us, although we were the only ones in the street. He looked like he woke up in the morning furious, as if he'd slid out of the womb with a furrowed brow and a list of several non-negotiable demands.

I knew at that moment that John Brown would either destroy slavery or be destroyed trying. I didn't need to hear about Harpers Ferry to know that John Brown was going to die violently. I have never seen such a beautiful face in all my life as that of John Brown.

*

It hits me hardest when I'm happiest. A good shit; a clean shave; interest calculated monthly that only serves to fatten an already not insubstantial principal—and then a two-by-four to the forehead, because rage's favourite attacking formation is the all-out ambush, and peace of mind has its price, the same as every other human vice.

My father raped my mother. My father owned my mother. By Louisiana law, my mother was my father's to rape.

The same three steps to attempted calm, always the same three steps:

I remind myself that I wasn't the only light-skinned Negro ever born who had the plantation master's dark green eyes and aquiline nose and whom the mistress of the plantation pretended didn't exist.

I reassure myself that no mother ever loved her child more, no son was ever maternally luckier or better cared for.

I console myself with knowing that a doctor I once knew told me that cancer of the jaw is one of the most painful ways to die, that on his deathbed there was nothing my father could do to prevent the pain that was feasting away on every cell in his rotting body, that the only thing he owned in his final hours on earth was his misery.

But no one but a madman or a British empiricist ever had to convince himself that tomorrow morning the sun is going to rise. No one who truly walked in God's light ever had to pray to feel His presence.

My father raped my mother. My father owned my mother. By Louisiana law, my mother was my father's to rape.

Shaving this morning, I spotted another tuft of white hair sprouting over my right ear. Instead of putting my fist through the mirror or going through the same three steps for the three millionth time, I got the scissors from the kitchen and sharpened my razor and soaped my scalp and carefully shaved my head caramel clean. Knives can do things that the alphabet can't.

I rubbed my naked scalp—so smooth, so brown—and smiled at the man looking back at me in the mirror.

*

Loretta has arranged her typical breakfast around her at the kitchen table—pork sausages, bacon rashers, eggs, black pudding, toast, a pot of coffee—and is waiting for the kettle to boil so that I can join her with my cup of black tea and bowl of porridge. Henry's head is already busy in his bowl. Happy as he is to have his morning meal, he's just as eager to get it over with so as to be ready when Loretta decides to drop a sausage end or a crust of bread to the floor. Eight straight hours tight together in bed and here we are gathered together again in the kitchen. And later, after the day is done but before we retire to our shared bed once more, together again this evening in the library in front of the fire. Families are bodies. Familiar, close-by bodies.

Sitting down across from her with my cup and my bowl, now Loretta can finally commence eating. Her side of the table is so crowded with crockery—and everything looks so good, she desires to eat everything at once, just gets started on a dripping slice of just-buttered toast when she can't resist unleashing her knife and fork upon the fat stack of grease-perspiring sausages—Loretta is the only person I've ever seen who eats *sideways*. She bites a piece of bacon in two, makes Henry sit and shake a paw in return for the other half.

"You are welcome," she says. "You are a very courteous dog, Mr. Heinrich."

I sip my tea and watch Loretta eat while waiting for my porridge to cool. Henry stays as close to Loretta as he can without actually sitting on top of her, just in case she wishes to trade another trick for another treat. He and she weren't always so comfortable with one another. Meaning, Loretta wasn't always so comfortable with Waldo, Henry's predecessor.

When I first met Loretta, when I still lived overtop of Sophia's with Waldo, she wasn't even so sure dogs should be allowed in the house.

"You understand," she said, "this animal, if he was starving, he would eat you."

"And if I was starving, I'd eat him, too." I reached down and gently stroked Waldo's head. "We're both hoping it never comes to that."

Time and familiarity eventually accomplished what logic and reasoned argument rarely can. I can even remember witnessing her mind begin to amend. It's a rare day when you can actually *see* an idea.

"One moment, please," Loretta had said.

Our relationship had grown legs. If I wasn't busy with Sophia's or Loretta wasn't reading German to me or we weren't making love—and the latter two usually followed one another—we were walking, eventually ending up in Tecumseh Park. By the time we'd met, I was a confirmed city person and the natural world had become an inconvenience to be overcome. But a well-manicured park is different, is civilized nature. Besides, we were both attempting to save money, and walking, like reading and fucking, is free. The future was something we both believed in.

Loretta drifted from my side in the direction of a young couple pushing their infant in a pram through the park. I stayed where I was, with Waldo, the stray dog I'd recently taken in. Proud new parents are always delighted to provide absolute strangers with the opportunity to marvel over the world's latest little miracle, but mixed-race couples are, unfortunately, just a little too strange.

The day was warm and the baby lay on top of a thin cotton blanket. Except for being dressed in a blue sailor's suit and matching blue cap, it looked like every other baby I'd ever seen, like a tiny, wrinkleless old man. Loretta leaned over the pram with her hands on her knees.

"And who is this little darling?" she said.

"This is Oliver," the woman said. "Say hello, Oliver."

The only thing more ridiculous than parents addressing their infant children as if they're understanding adults is adults who should know better playing along and pretending that's what they are.

"And hello to you, too, Oliver," Loretta said to the expressionless child. "May I say, you look very handsome in your uniform today."

"Say thank you, Oliver."

And this time the baby did respond, with a slight upturn at one corner of his mouth in conjunction with his eye on the same side halfway shutting. At which point everyone but me—even the bearded, cigar-smoking husband—chorused a long "Aww," all in celebration of what was probably Oliver passing wind. Except for the baby she'd lost coming to Canada, we'd never discussed the topic of children, but I'd known Loretta long enough I'd assumed we didn't have to.

I looked at Waldo, sitting patiently, waiting to be on the move again. Dogs do what they're told, will defend you to the death, and will never ask you for money. Why would anyone have a baby when they could have a dog instead? I thought. Loretta bid Oliver goodbye and we continued on our walk.

Waiting what I considered a reasonable interval, "You like babies," I said. I hadn't intended it to sound like an allegation.

"Of course. Everyone likes babies."

"I don't," I said.

"You are mistaken. This is not possible. We are made—yes?—to like babies. It is this way so that we are forced to care for them until they grow up and can take care of themselves. It is children you do not like."

"What's the difference?"

"A baby is a baby," Loretta said. "But a child—a child is almost a person. I have never met a baby I did not like. But persons . . . I have never met many of those that I *did* like. Not, at least, after getting to know them."

Just then Waldo burst into motion, raced off ahead of us. Because he'd been a stray and on his own for who knew how long, and probably owed his survival, in part, to the occasional careless squirrel, I was used to such sudden dashes.

"David," Loretta said, grabbing my arm, "your animal."

Thankfully, any time Waldo had spotted a squirrel he'd wanted to know better, he'd been unsuccessful in making the meeting happen, would, at most, corner it up a tree. This time he kept running. And running. Then I saw what he was chasing.

"Look," I said, Loretta's arm still on mine.

"What? What do I look at?"

I pointed to the sky.

The bird was so high, it took her a moment to understand that that was what I was pointing at. "Your animal is chasing a bird?"

I nodded. Waldo was still running, was almost out of sight.

She patted my hand with hers. "Now this, this is most impressive."

Loretta halves another slice of bacon with her teeth, and before she has time to ask Henry to shake a paw, he's one step ahead of her, is waiting for her to give him hers.

"You are very greedy this morning, Heinrich, but I forgive you, we have quite a busy day today."

Today is March 1—rent day—and every rent day for the last couple of years Henry has accompanied Loretta on her collection rounds. Of course, Loretta could employ someone to do it for her—not just because it's supposedly beneath the dignity of a well-off landowner to travel door to door, but because her property holdings are so extensive it takes most of the day to get the job done—but Loretta wouldn't have it any other way. "I like to *feel* how much money I have made." And Henry is just as happy to spend the day escorting her around town. And stopping off at the butcher shop on the way home for a fresh pork cutlet.

When Loretta pushes her last cup of coffee away from her, Henry knows it's time to go. Loretta stands up, surveys the tableful of dirty dishes.

"Because you are a foolish man who will not do as I say and acquire domestic help, I leave all this for you," she says.

My porridge is just the right temperature now; I'll tidy up the kitchen after I'm done eating and have had another cup of tea.

"You two have a good day," I say.

"Oh, we will, won't we, Heinrich?" Henry's at her side, ready for action. She leans down and scratches him between the ears. "We always enjoy rent day very much, don't we?"

*

One door down from Coopers' Bookstore is the post office. Coopers' is where I buy ink and pens and parchment, but not where I buy books. Coopers' carries books—bibles, bibles, and even a few bibles, right alongside Bowdler's scrubbed and scoured *Family Shakespeare* and a generous sampling of this season's contribution to everlasting literature, such as *The Constant Nymph* and *White Wings: A Yachting Romance*—but not, unfortunately, any books that are suitable for reading. For that I need the post office. For that I need Larwill.

Ordinarily, the tinkle of the bell over the door announcing he has a customer summons Larwill from the rear of the post office with a smile on his face and a spring in his step right up until he sees that I'm the one it's his job to help. Then his face will fall blank and he'll slow his pace and make sure to make me wait for as long as he possibly can while rummaging around in the drawer underneath the counter looking for the nothing we both know he's only pretending to look for. Today, though, the smile stays stuck where it is, even after he realizes it's me, even while he sorts and collects my mail. I can't help but wonder if there's something lodged between my teeth or if I've spilt something down the front of my coat.

Larwill speaks as he sorts. "Mr. King . . . no . . . no . . . no . . . no . . . Mr. King . . . no . . . no . . . no . . . Mr. King . . . no . . . no . . . Mr. King . . . no . . . no . . . no . . . and . . . no. Here we are. Two periodicals and two books for Mr. King, it appears."

He slides across my copies of the *Fortnightly* and the *Quarterly* and the two slender packages containing, no doubt, the two latest instalments in the English Men of Letters series I've been waiting for—Leslie Stephen on Swift, Cotter Morrison on Gibbon—with a smirking courtesy it's like he's daring me to find offensive.

"And will there be anything else today, Mr. King? Or is that everything for you today, Mr. King?"

Of course. Up until this very moment, a surly, exaggerated "Sir" is as close as Larwill has ever gotten to referring to me by name, his only way of not endangering his job yet still shamelessly withholding his acknowledgement of me as as much of a Mr.—of a man, of a human being—as he is. Now all of a sudden I'm Mr. King. Like Mr. King my namesake. Like Larwill's father's one-time nemesis, the Reverend King. Like the recently deceased Reverend King. The King is dead, and Larwill wants me to know just how pleased his demise has made him.

It's harder to impersonate a fool than a wise man, but I do my best.

"No, that will be all, Larwill," I say, like he's just lit my cigar to go along with the final brandy of the evening and I'm granting him permission to retire until tomorrow morning, when it will be once again time for him to serve me my breakfast in bed. I take my mail but turn around at the tinkling door. "Now that you mention it, Larwill, there *is* one more thing."

"Oh, and what is that, Mr. King?"

"I'm expecting the transfer of a very large sum of money in the next few days, and I'd appreciate it if you took special care of it for me when it arrives. It turns out that the bank I would normally have it deposited into can only insure my account up to ten thousand dollars. It seems as if I need to find someone else to hold on to my money for me. Well, if it's not one thing, it's something else, isn't it, Larwill?"

I don't stick around to enjoy the fruits of my labour. The only thing men like Larwill and his father hate more than a nigger is a rich nigger.

*

You never heard the Reverend King himself recount the story of his showdown with Edwin Larwill. Too busy, too occupied with fresh scuffles to be fought and won. Besides, legends don't advertise—it wouldn't be dignified, myths can become mottled. That's what legends have disciples for.

My mother told me—told me more than once—about how Edwin Larwill was a Chatham businessman and local politician who had founded the Free and Easy Club to offset local temperance tendencies and promote saloon society. "That tell you all you need to know right there," my mother would say. "Town leader goin' 'round promotin' *sin*." Told me how, as soon as Larwill learned of the Reverend King's plans to settle the land that was to be Buxton, he got busy drafting and delivering petitions and resolutions of opposition in abundance through his roles as a school commissioner,

a Raleigh Township councillor, and a Member of Provincial
Parliament. Told me how "Larwill was their leader, but it
wasn't just him either," how the letter Larwill wrote in
protest to the Crown Commissioner was signed by hundreds of Chatham's most prominent citizens. Years later I
read the actual letter for myself, was glad my mother never
had:

> *The Negro is a distinct species of the Human Family and*
> *far inferior to that of the European. Let each link in the*
> *great Scale of existence have its place. Amalgamation is as*
> *disgusting to the Eye as it is immoral in its tendencies, and*
> *all good men will discountenance it.*

George's father told me about Larwill too—told George
and me both while we were fishing. About how, while in
Chatham arranging a survey of the land, the Reverend King
was warned by a stranger on King Street not to remain in
town after dark, that his life was in danger. How, instead of
fleeing Chatham, he immediately set up a meeting to con-
front his foes head-on as soon as it could be arranged, how
the Reverend King always said that "'procrastination is the
thief of time.' You boys remember that, you hear?" How another meeting was organized—this time by Larwill's forces—
a couple of months later, and how the Reverend King, after
travelling to Toronto on Settlement business, arrived in
Windsor by lake steamer the night before the meeting as
planned only to discover that *Brothers*, the Thames River
steamer bound for Chatham, had developed engine trouble
and would not be able to sail the next morning, and how the
Reverend King, determined that his enemies would not be
given a single opportunity to believe that either he or his
cause was faltering, immediately rented a horse and buggy
and drove all night, arriving only a couple of hours before the

afternoon assembly. The next part of the story was the part my mother liked to tell best.

"The Reverend King, he knew things might get unruly as soon as he step foot in town, was not just peoples from all over who come to hear what was goin' to be said, but twelve special constables that was sworn in that very morning to keep the peace just in case. Now in them days there weren't no town hall or the like in Chatham, and the meeting commenced in an old barn out back of the Royal Exchange Hotel. And not only was that old barn filled right up, there was men pushin' and shovin' and tryin' to get in at the same time that the speakers was tryin' to speak, and with all that hollerin' and shoutin' it was impossible for a body to hear a single word being said. So finally somebody decide let's move the meetin' to the street and let the speakers have their say from the balcony, and after everybody file out and get settled, the Reverend King is given ten minutes by the chairman to say his piece from the balcony of the Royal Exchange Hotel."

At this point my mother would rest her hand on my knee or my elbow, like she still didn't believe that the Reverend King was safe from harm, like her future and mine and that of the other first thirteen ex-slaves to settle in Buxton was still in doubt.

"But every time the Reverend King try to speak, Larwill's men shout and curse and holler and wouldn't let him be heard. They only settle down when Larwill himself come forward, and that to tell them that because the Reverend King was a Yankee, he had no right to say nothin' to nobody. Well, that crowd, if it was loud before, it was ten times that now, like it can't wait to get its hands around the neck of this here Negro-loving Yankee daring to show his face in their hometown. But the Reverend King"—my mother would lower her voice and lean in closer now, and even if you hadn't heard her tell the same story ten times already, you knew that something special, something miraculous, was about to hap-pen—"he just stood there standing his ground with his arms crossed and let them peoples hoot and holler all they want, moved as close to that rail as he could get, and let them men of Larwill's scream and yell for him to go back where he come from until they get blue in the face, until finally they see he ain't going nowhere no time soon and they just get sick and tired of the sound of their own yellin'. And so the Reverend King, he finally get his chance to speak.

"And he said to them, 'I have come two hundred miles to attend this meeting and you cannot put me down. Besides, I am from Londonberry, and Londonberry never did surren-der.'"

And, unbelievably, some of the men couldn't help but laugh. And after the Reverend King told them he had been born a British subject and was a ratepayer too, just like them, he went on to outline the vision and the goals of the Elgin Association—how education and religious instruction and economic self-sufficiency were the bywords of Buxton, and how a man, any man, was not unlike a crop, any crop, was only likely to grow and thrive if afforded the right mixture of good soil and a fair climate and ample precipitation—and to explain that the Elgin Settlement would add to their tax revenues and increase the value of the land—their land—surrounding it.

"And you know, those men—some of 'em anyway, maybe not all of 'em, but some of 'em—they change a little bit that day. They change not so much by what the Reverend King say as how he say it, the way he show no fear, the way he believe in every word he say."

My mother would take my hand and place it in hers, cover it with her gnarled other.

"Show no fear and mean what you say, son."

Amen.

6

Because it attracted runaway slaves, Chatham also attracted slave hunters. An industrious slave catcher could make a more than passable living tracking down and returning a Southern master's runaway property. The Fugitive Slave Act, which compelled American citizens to assist in the return of escapees, wasn't recognized by the government of Canada West, so slavers' agents who ventured north needed to be extra cunning. A notice posted outside the Chatham courthouse, which George and I had come across when in town with his father to help pick up building supplies for the Freemans' new chicken coop, wasn't unusual:

CAUTION COLOURED PEOPLE!

From information received from reliable sources, we learn that parties are at present endeavouring to induce coloured persons to go to the States in their employ as servants. From the character of the propositions, there is reason to believe foul play is intended.

Let no misplaced confidence in this or that other smooth-tongued Yankee, or British subject either, who may be mercenary enough to ensnare you into bondage by collusion with kidnappers in the States, deprive you of your liberty.

What was unusual was the hand-drawn rejoinder scrawled across the width of the poster in thick strokes of bright white paint:

TROUBLE MAKKERS STAY OUT OF CHATHAM

On the way home, I told Mr. Freeman what we'd seen—he'd given us a nickel each to buy candy while he attended to some other business in town. It was my first firsthand experience of bad people doing bad things, and I was more confused than angry. How could anyone in Chatham possibly believe that people trying to assist slaves were troublemakers? It didn't make sense, I complained. Slaveholders, all right, at least they had a reason—money—to want to preserve the institution of slavery. But what could someone from Chatham gain from keeping Negroes in chains? It just didn't make sense.

While Mr. Freeman listened to me speak, he slowly nodded his head as if I'd just informed him it was going to rain presently and that he'd better bring in the wash off the line. When I was all done, he told George to go in the back of the wagon and make sure that the large roll of chicken wire we'd loaded near the very rear was still tied down properly. I thought he was thinking about how he was going to answer me. When George climbed back beside me and reported that everything was fine, Mr. Freeman answered, "Good," and cracked the reins and was silent again. The sun was going down and the leaves in the trees along the road back to Buxton looked as if they might amber into flame at any moment. I got tired of waiting for Mr. Freeman to make me understand.

"Just bad people, I suppose," I said, and that was that. I caught George with his hand palm down on his knee and slapped it. He pulled it away, but it was too late, I'd gotten him good. He knew it, too, just shook his head and rubbed the back of his hand.

"Ignorant people," Mr. Freeman said.

Ignorant meant not knowing something, I knew that, so Mr. Freeman must not have understood everything I'd told him.

"Whoever did it, they knew what they were doing," I said. "They wrote 'Troublemakers stay out of Chatham.' They were calling the people who were warning the slaves troublemakers." It was wrong to correct one's elders, but I was right. Besides, maybe saying what was true regardless of who said otherwise was how one ended up becoming an elder oneself one day.

Mr. Freeman was in no hurry to answer me, kept his eyes on the horses and the road. I kept my hands balled and at my sides, knew that George was waiting for his revenge.

"Don't pay no attention to ignorant people," Mr. Freeman finally said. "Scared is all they is. Ignorant and scared."

"Why would they be scared?" I said, confused. And angry. It sounded as if George's father was feeling sorry for the bad people who'd defaced the poster. "The runaways, they're the only ones who should be scared. Of getting captured. Of being sent back."

"George, see if that wire still tied good," Mr. Freeman said.

"I already did, Pa."

"Don't talk back, now, go and check it again."

"Ah," George said, but going.

There was no one else on the road, either behind us or coming our way, but Mr. Freeman watched where we were going as if one inattentive moment would send us into the woods.

Eventually, "Scared man is a dangerous man," Mr. Freeman said. "Maybe most dangerous man of all. Who done what they did in Chatham likely don't even know what they scared of. Don't make 'em any less dangerous, though. Maybe make 'em *more* dangerous."

Mr. Freeman, I thought, was a nice man—a good man—but he knew more about what plants could make you feel better when you had an upset stomach and how to get your chickens to lay more eggs than he did about what made people good and bad. Somehow I needed to help him understand.

Trying to figure out how to say it without hurting his feelings, "Got you!" George yelled, whacking me hard, harder even than I had him, on the hand I'd forgotten to protect.

"George," Mr. Freeman said, "sit yourself down and stop that foolishness, both of you."

George slid beside me on the seat and kept quiet, but was smiling like someone had just told him he'd won a hundred dollars.

"Is that wire all right?" Mr. Freeman said.

"Same as it was before."

"Don't sass me, boy, I didn't ask you that, I ask you if it all right."

"It's fine, Pa," George said. "It's not going anywhere."

I scratched the back of my hand. He'd gotten me so good, it itched.

*

Walking, pointing, "A full moon," I say.

"Yes," Loretta says, without looking.

"At least pay me the courtesy of pretending to be impressed."

"I have seen the moon before."

"It's a particularly beautiful full moon tonight."

"It was beautiful before too."

It's not the moon's fault—it *is* beautiful, is a shimmering soft, perfectly round orb expertly suspended somehow high in the sky above us for our, and absolutely no one else's, planetary viewing pleasure. And I haven't had a drop all day.

Sometimes the world is intoxicating enough straight-up.

But Loretta doesn't trust nature. Nothing that hasn't had human hands on it can hope to impress her. Even the faces she collects, it's their reproduction that interests her, not the cold flesh-and-blood source. No living person, not as long as I've known her, has ever held her attention like a single photograph of the dead. *Her* photographs of *her* dead. God died, so Loretta created a new one. When Loretta says, Let there be light, you can be damn well sure there's going to be light.

It's cold and snowing, but it's still disappointing there's no one on King Street except for us and Henry. Time-tested couples don't need words to communicate, so although neither of us has ever said it, we know we both enjoy the act of making passersby at least uncomfortable, and preferably angry, when seeing Loretta and me arm in arm on the sidewalk. What their mouths are afraid to say, or only whisper, their eyes have no hesitation shouting: *The only thing worse than a nigger and a German ex-whore is a nigger and a German ex-whore acting as if they're actually a respectable couple entitled to enjoy the fresh morning air just like any other respectable couple*. That's the cue for Loretta to entwine her arm even tighter with mine, for both of us to lean into each other just a little bit closer.

The bells of the Presbyterian church on Wellington Street, the first of ten identical ringing echoes. The sound of a church bell still soothes me, just like I can't help but salivate every time Loretta fills the house with the warm smell of an all-afternoon-roasting, every-hour-basted roast. Knowing what's true and feeling what's right are rarely the same thing. A wise man once said that if you sit on a fence for too long, you'll end up splitting your pants. Actually, that was no wise man, that was me. But just because I'm no La Rochefoucauld doesn't mean my pants don't need mending from time to time.

"It is time to go home now, yes?" Loretta says.

There's a fresh body upstairs at Franklin's that I know she's eager to get at, but I'm not especially eager to do anything, and walking through the falling snow with Loretta on my arm and Henry by my side is as pleasant a way of doing it as I can imagine. "Ten more minutes?" I say.

Loretta doesn't speak, is thinking, I know. It took me a while to get used to her contemplative silences. When Loretta doesn't know the answer to a question, she makes her interlocutor wait until she does. It can be irritating, like waiting on a judge to deliver a verdict when all you want to know is if you can add a few minutes to the end of your walk; but, on the other hand, when she does answer you, you can be assured it's what she really thinks. Like when she was surprised to spot my mother's bible on my bookshelves and I asked her if, even as a non-believer, she wouldn't have liked to have had the bible her father read from from his pulpit every Sunday, if only as an heirloom. "If I am going to read fairy tales," she immediately answered, "I prefer Grimm's, yes? At least then I get pretty pictures to amuse me, too."

"You hated him, didn't you?" I said, surprised at myself for wanting to hear her say yes.

"Of course not. He was my father. I loved him. I did not like him, but I loved him."

The church bells have stopped ringing, their last notes fading, eventually evaporating in the frozen morning air. Henry stops to sniff something near the doorway of McKeough's hardware store. Loretta and I stop too, let Henry handle the sniffing.

"We will walk for five minutes more, then we will go back. This way we both get what we want, yes?"

I just smile, don't say anything, but not because I'm thinking.

"Yes?" Loretta says.

"Yes," I say.

It's started to snow harder now, and there's no one coming our way, no one anywhere at all, but I tuck Loretta's arm tighter into mine and draw her nearer to me anyway.

A nigger, a German ex-whore, a stray.

A man, a woman, a dog.

David, Loretta, Henry.

Sometimes logic makes sense.

*

I was fourteen when Fort Sumter fell to the South and the men of the Elgin Settlement began to enlist in the Union army. *Attempted* to enlist in the Union army. It would take two long years of continual Confederate victories and increasing northern casualties for Lincoln to finally relent and allow Negroes the privilege of risking their lives for the sake of the Union cause. And even though, by then, anyone who wasn't simple knew that the Civil War was a white man's war meant to settle white men's scores—to keep the Union intact, to keep trade routes open for northern big business, to keep the tariffs in place that were making rich men in the North richer—the men of Elgin met with the Reverend King and asked him to petition the government on their behalf for the right to fight anyway. Emancipation might have turned out to be an afterthought, but it was an afterthought worth killing for.

I told my mother I wanted to enlist soon after Lincoln's first inaugural address, after he assured the nation that "I have no purpose directly or indirectly to interfere with the institution of slavery in the states where it exists." The official age of enlistment was sixteen, but everyone knew that during wartime every government became careless with its arithmetic.

"I'll ask if the Reverend King can find some time for you when he get back from Sarnia," she said. Time to discuss my plans with me, she meant. "Big meeting of ministers going on up there."

I couldn't help but feel a little hurt. Mothers of young soldiers were supposed to weep uncontrollably and plead with their brave young sons not to leave for war—not to counsel patience until the pastor returned home to either give or withhold his permission. Hurt, but not really surprised. The unspoken motto among the settlers, especially the first settlers like my mother, was In the Reverend King We Trust.

Twenty-four hours later, I got my audience with the Reverend King. My mother picked invisible lint off my jacket and straightened and restraightened the tie I'd gotten the year before for my thirteenth birthday, a gift from Mrs. King that she'd selected from her husband's wardrobe and that everyone pretended she hadn't. A muffled piano sonata drifting down the stairs testified to her unseen presence.

"You pay attention to what the Reverend King says, now," my mother said. She'd been at Clayton House when I'd arrived, the rheumatism in her hands and knees slowing her down enough now that another housekeeper had been hired to take over most of the heavier work, my mother making up for her mounting lack of mobility by doubling her dusting duties and supervising the preparation of all the meals and generally making sure that the rest of the house staff kept to their schedules.

At twelve o'clock—not 11:59, not 12:01—my mother allowed me to knock on the door of the Reverend King's study, the hands on the long-case clock in the sitting room praying together perfectly high noon.

"Come in, David," the voice inside said.

The Reverend King stood up behind his desk to shake my hand and offer me a seat in one of the three chairs across the desk from his. Helping to settle controversies, working to defuse conflicts, assisting in building consensus: those three chairs were never empty for long. He folded his hands and rested them in front of him on the desk.

"Tell me why you want to enlist in the army, David," he said.

"To help defeat the South." I was as ready with my answers as I knew he would be with his questions.

The Reverend King nodded his approval. "And it will be defeated, David, and the evil of slavery along with it. God is on the side of the just. And those who would be free must strike the blow."

I nodded back. What else was there to say? And the Reverend King, as always, had said it the best way it could be said.

"And have you given proper consideration to your mother?"

"Yes, sir. I told her of my intentions yesterday."

"Yes, of course. Which is how I know them as well. But have you considered her ailing condition and how she would manage without you—you, her only relative, away from home for God Himself only knows how long?"

"No, sir. I hadn't."

He nodded again, this time like he knew I hadn't but he forgave me.

"Another aspect that you might want to take into consideration is the plight of Buxton itself. Once the government realizes the ignorance of their decision to deny coloured men the right to fight alongside their white brothers, we can expect at least one hundred men to leave us for the war. This means that young men like yourself will be expected to occupy increasingly important roles here."

"Yes, sir."

"And finally, there are your studies."

I at least had an answer for that one. "I thought I could pick up where I left off, when I got back."

"Yes, of course. But even though all of God's children have important work to do in His world, the work He has intended for some of us requires especially long hours of dedicated study and practice, while others can abide His will with less concentrated preparation."

Like George, for instance. We'd ABC'd together, worked side by side memorizing the catechism, and even set sail on the same schoolhouse voyage over the blue Aegean with Odysseus as our captain in his own Grecian tongue, but just that year George had happily left his books and me both behind to take a position as an apprentice in Elgin's new potash factory.

The Reverend King went to one of his bookshelves—the walls of his study *were* his bookshelves; it seemed as if every book that had ever been written was helping to hold up the ceiling—and pulled down a slim black volume. He placed the book face down in front of him on the desk.

"I have known—indeed, I have taught—many bright boys and girls during my years as an educator and religious instructor. And each has benefited in his own unique way—and, according to God's plans, society has also benefited—from the time and effort expended upon his studies."

"Yes, sir."

Aside from his Sunday sermons, if the Reverend King quoted anyone, it was usually from the Bible, usually the New Testament, but one of the few pagan references he allowed room for was Epictetus's "Only the educated are free." Odds were good that the potash factory in Elgin was the only one in existence whose newest employee could read Greek and recite Virgil.

"But yours is a special gift, David. Your swift mastery of any and all assigned materials. Your desire for new intellectual challenges. Your clear leadership abilities both in and outside the classroom. All have compelled me to conclude that your path in life has surely been laid out for you by God's hand. Whether you follow that sanctified path, of course, will be your decision alone." He handed me the book. "I want you to have this, David, something my own father gave to me at a pivotal point in my life, such as you find yourself at now."

It was a copy of Clark's *Commentary on the Scriptures*, essential reading material, I later discovered, for anyone considering entering the ministry.

"Thank you," I said, taking the book.

"You're very welcome, David."

Until that day in the Reverend King's study, I had known him—him, my mother's and my liberator, our resurrector, our redeemer—like someone knows the seasons, like a lake or a river, like sundown and sunrise. Now I knew him as something else. Now he was my mentor.

*

My timing was perfect, Providence once again seeing to it that what had been hard for others was easy for me. It wasn't difficult to arrive at the conclusion that God had chosen me to serve Him and, through Him and His blessed sacrificed Son, the consecrated cause that was the deliverance of my people from the evil of slavery. Why else would I have been eleventh-hour rescued from a lifetime of certain bondage by an abolitionist minister and endowed with talents and inclination enough that this same minister would see fit to encourage me in the enlistment in Christ's army as one of his sanctified soldiers? A, B, C and 1, 2, 3 couldn't have been any more obvious.

It hadn't been as straightforward for the first crop of Buxton graduates. Of the initial seven who were deemed university suitable, only three had parents who could afford to send them. To the Reverend King, this was unacceptable.

He personally canvassed for donations throughout North America and when on Church business trips back to England and Ireland. He solicited funds from every Church sympathetic to the goals of the Settlement, and some, it turned out, that weren't. He appealed for, and received from the Presbyterian Church, a bursary specifically endowed for needy families of promising Buxton students. And he reminded us from his pulpit every Sunday that faith and observance and prayers alone were not enough to do the Creator's will. God loved a self-starter.

"Unless the seed is allowed to grow, to grow and bear the fruit that nature has surely intended it to, one great object of our mission here will be frustrated. I speak, of course, of the training of young men of piety and talents for further usefulness in the Church. Never was there more need for such young men as at present. The slave trade, as we all know, is still carried on along the coast of Africa, notwithstanding the vigilance of the British navy. Nothing but the preaching of the everlasting Gospel will put an end to that inhumane traffic."

Amen, we'd say, and praise the Lord and the Reverend King.

After our meeting in his office, after he'd convinced me not to leave for the war, the Reverend King gave me the same time and attention he bestowed upon every other student whose mind he wished to help hone to an even sharper point, so that when I eventually entered Knox College, no white man, no matter what his background or advantages, would be my intellectual superior. His library was mine now, and after my chores and homework were done for the evening, I'd sit at the kitchen table and read what he'd instructed me to read, to learn what I needed to learn so that one day I could give back to God and society both all that I'd so bountifully received myself.

"Don't you eat that apple core, David. You do, it'll grow in your stomach."

"Yes, ma'am."

Whenever I was studying, my mother—whether cooking or sewing or cleaning—might have been invisible for all the noise she made for fear of disturbing me. Officially, Presbyterians don't talk about the doctrine of the Trinity, but my mother worshipped her very own three-pointed path to personal holiness anyway: I was going to be an educated man; I was going to be a minister; I was going to carry on the Reverend King's work. I was going to be all of these things, and I was her son.

"You still hungry? You want me to make you some warm milk?"

"No, ma'am." Warm milk, particularly the way my mother made it, with just the right splash of molasses, was my favourite, especially on cold winter nights, but it made me sleepy.

"All right, you get back to your studies, your old mother won't bother you no more now."

"You're not bothering me."

"Hush now, you get back to your learning."

I moved my book, the Reverend King's copy of St. Thomas Aquinas's *Summa Theologia*, closer to the lamp. I had two more arguments for the existence of God to memorize before I went to bed. Whatever I didn't understand tonight, the Reverend King would explain to me tomorrow.

7

In the beginning was the word. The curse word.

Profanity was almost as forbidden in Buxton as drinking or blasphemy. "Thou shalt not take the name of the Lord thy God in vain" was for Sunday, but "Curses are like young chickens, they always come home to roost" was an everyday edict. Bad language, moreover, was like bad grammar, was slave talk, the talk of a people denied the education and opportunities that I, for instance, most certainly hadn't been.

"How can a man expect to gain another man's respect if he doesn't first respect himself?" the Reverend King said more than once. Foremost, the white man's respect, he meant but didn't say. I censored my mouth and mind as well as anyone and never said *me* when what I meant to say was *I*.

Taking George and me along with him once to Chatham, Mr. Freeman stopped the wagon near Pork Row to ask directions to the glassworks. A coloured man with one hand resting in the pocket of his unbuttoned vest, the other lazily picking at his long yellow teeth with a thumbnail, said, "Just a cunt hair away, gentlemen, just go back the way you come some and no more than ten doors down, is right there beside Gunsmith Jones' place."

George's father surprised us, didn't thank the man for his help, didn't even acknowledge him with a farewell tip of his hat or a simple "Good day." Mr. Freeman may not have had the schooling that his son and I had, but he limited his cursing to when he was working the field and thought he was alone, and was a stickler for "Please" and "Thank you." You didn't have to know ancient Greek to know good manners.

"What is it, Pa?" George said as his father turned the wagon around. "Do you know that man?"

Mr. Freeman waited for a buggy to pass the other way down King Street. "Did it seem like I knew him, George? Did he seem like the kind of man your father would know?"

We both understood that Mr. Freeman's questions weren't the sort that wanted answers, so kept quiet, although I knew George was as confused as I was. It was funny the way the man had called us gentlemen, the same way we always laughed every time George's own father would ask us if we were taking our wives with us when we'd set out for a morning's fishing at Deer Pond.

We stayed in the wagon while Mr. Freeman went inside the glass-shop. George slid into his father's seat as soon as he was out of sight. He picked up the switch, rested it on his shoulder.

"You know why Pa was mad, don't you?" he said.

I nodded.

George looked at me, shook his head. "Sure you do."

I didn't mind so much not knowing, but the way he was smiling to himself, like he knew something that I didn't, made me cross. "If you know so much," I said, "why did you have to ask him, then?"

George bounced the switch on his shoulder a couple of times. "I wanted him to say it."

"Say what?"

"The word that that man said that made him so mad."

I nodded again, although with even less hope of looking

clever than last time. I wished I was sitting up front in the wagon too.

We saw Mr. Freeman through the glass-shop front shaking the hand of the man behind the counter. George stuck the whip back into place and scrambled out of the driver's seat into the back.

Cupped hand to my ear, "Cunt," he said.

I kept my eyes on Mr. Freeman, still inside the shop but soon to be out the door and on the sidewalk and in the wagon.

"It's the only word it *could* have been."

For the rest of that day and all of that evening—at supper with my mother; head down to my studies; on my knees saying my prayers—the word remained a word, just something someone said that had gone on to where all words went once they're spoken, the ether of endless alphabets, up *there* for the good ones, down below for the bad. I slept the sleep of a child: immediate, deep, empty.

I woke up in the middle of the night with the word stuck in my throat, a tiny tickling bone that wouldn't come clear. Every time I attempted to cough, to get rid of it, the word would grow larger and that much more difficult to dislodge. I knew it was wrong to think of it, never mind actually say it, and I tried to go back to sleep—*prayed* to go back to sleep, albeit without mentioning why I needed heavenly help—but the cool side of the pillow soon grew as hot and damp as the other, and eventually it felt as though, if I didn't say it, I would surely choke to death in my own bed.

"Cunt," I whispered, not knowing what the word meant now any more than I had that afternoon, but knowing instantly that I had sinned; knowing, too, that no matter how dark the night had seemed before, it was about to get much, much darker.

The smell of my mother's pancakes was the next thing I remember. A shaft of sunlight lay on the pillow beside my head, impatient for the curtain in my room to be parted and the day to officially begin. I couldn't remember falling asleep.

"David," my mother called from the kitchen. "Time for you to get up now, son."

*

I could lie and say it simply made sense. That, being a logical being, I'd merely followed the dictates of logic and come to my decision purely logically. Just as any rational being should have. Should have would have could have didn't.

Darwin wasn't the first naturalist to assert that evolution had taken place right underneath our upturned noses, but he was the first to assemble so much evidence that to deny it was only possible by a wilful act of self-inflicted ignorance. And if one accepted the evolutionary kinship of all animals, one not only lost a heavenly father but gained an extended orphaned earthly family, the family of all living, breathing beings. Except that being kin comes with responsibilities— most importantly, that you don't eat your relations, no matter how tasty they might be covered in barbecue sauce. Because if one doesn't acknowledge certain rights that must be granted to all members of the family, there remains the risk that these same sacrosanct rights might be arbitrarily and illogically denied to certain other members. Perhaps, say, the human faction of the family. Perhaps, say, a selected segment of that human faction. Perhaps, say, the coloured segment.

So, one had a choice: either right was might or everyone had the same incontrovertible rights. I didn't have a choice. My last day as a cannibal was November 7, 1881, my thirty-fifth year.

But those are the reasons I quit eating other animals, not why. Why never comes from the head. Why begins much lower in the body and only becomes reasons after first passing through the bowels and the heart and the throat. The brain takes all of the credit, but it's always the last to know what's on its mind.

Twenty years earlier, George and I were on our way to Deer Pond when we spotted one of its four-legged namesakes, except that it wasn't running away from us this time but was lying on its side in the brush. Someone had shot it—there was a neat, blood-rimmed hole no bigger around than a half-dollar—halfway down its long neck, but the shooter must have thought he'd missed and so not done what Mr. Freeman never failed to remind us to do whenever we went hunting: always finish the kill, never let the animal suffer.

George and I crept closer, but the deer stayed where it was. I'd never been this close to a living deer before. Both of its eyes were wide open, but I don't think it saw us. It looked without blinking—not once—in the direction of where its head lay on the ground.

George was standing beside me, pointed at the rising and falling of the deer's rib cage. "It's still breathing pretty good," he said. "There's no telling how long it'll keep going."

If you ignored the bullet hole and the glassy brown eyes, the deer looked like a large, tamed cat sunning itself on the forest underbrush. Then he slowly opened his mouth like he was going to amaze us and speak. Which he did—with a low, guttural groan that sounded like the wailing of a man suffering so much pain he's denied the power of words.

"We've got to kill it," I said.

George looked at me, looked terrified, as if he suddenly realized he'd done something terrible. "I didn't bring my gun," he said.

"We'll have to find a rock."

"It better be a big one."

"Start looking."

It was actually a relief to be out of the deer's sightless sight, to be far enough away that in case he cried again, I wouldn't have to hear it. Not having to look at him or listen to him, I could almost believe he wasn't there and we didn't have to do what had to be done.

"David," George said, and I went to where he was.

He'd found a large, mossy rock with a single jagged side that was perfect, like it was created for killing. We each knew what the other one was thinking.

"I found it," George said.

I would have argued with him, but in spite of being a hundred feet, at least, away, the deer moaned again, another long, wordless whimper. I picked up the stone.

I gripped the rock as tightly as I could and staggered back to where the deer was, almost running, somehow knowing that if I thought about what I was going to do, I wouldn't be able to do it. I willed myself enraged and slammed the rock down on the deer's head. The impact was as hard as stone on stone and as soft as sliding a knife through just-churned butter. I think it groaned one last time, but my ears had been full of the hate I'd needed to kill it. I probably didn't need to, but as soon as I felt the collapse of its skull, I raised the rock again and brought it down a second time, just as hard.

I let go of the stone and half stumbled, half ran, toward the path home, not knowing, not caring, if George was coming or not. But of course he was, was right there alongside me. After about five minutes of silence,

"Do you think it's dead?" he said.

I didn't answer.

"Do you think it's dead, David?"

"It's dead."

George did all of the talking on the way back to Buxton, and because I never responded, by the time we got there I'd tacitly agreed that it would be wrong to just leave the deer to rot and that we should get Mr. Freeman's cutting knife and go back and gut the deer for meat.

"There's enough good venison there to last us a whole year," George said. His growing excitement was better, at least, than what we had been feeling.

By the time we returned with the knife and some rope, I knew I wasn't going to be much help. I picked out a thick tree limb about eight feet from the ground to string and quarter the deer, but that was about all I could manage.

"I'm gonna cut a stick," George said. "Then you can stick it through the ankle tendons and hoist it up the tree."

I sat down on a rock—another rock, not the one I'd used to kill the deer—and watched George work. He didn't ask me to help him again.

George stabbed the animal in its belly and sliced downward in one smooth motion, got right to work with the skinning. His father had taught him well. As he worked to pull off the deerskin, clouds of fur drifted by, slowly floated by our faces, falling snow in July.

As much as George slashed and stabbed and pulled at the deer's hot insides, though, the organs refused to fall, were still attached to the deer's rectum. Then, without warning, the rectum suddenly tore free and sprayed him with liquid deer shit like a blast of winter sleet. All he could do was keep his chin raised, away from the suit of shit he was now wearing, arms outstretched and dripping with the digested remains of the deer's last meal.

I finally stood up from the rock, smiled.

"What the hell are you smiling at?" George said. I knew he'd never been madder because I'd never heard him curse before.

"Let's go to the pond," I said. It was where we'd been headed in the first place.

George didn't move while he considered what I'd said, his chin still lifted and his arms still stuck out at his sides like a shit-drenched scarecrow's.

"Hurry up, let's go to the pond," he said.

I took the lead. I stayed upwind, as far ahead of him along the path as I could get.

*

"Five dollars. Each. Me and you each."

I look at Franklin, then back at the buggy full of Sunlight soap boxes.

"I understand that part," I say. "The part I don't understand is why McKeough doesn't dispose of it himself."

"Like I said, the dump—the town—won't let him, say they're worried it might be poison, want him to send it back, which would end up costing him triple what it would for us just to get rid of it."

It's foolish enough to make sense: Chatham's city fathers concerned that a shipload of soap, however fouled, might contaminate the local garbage. What the hell. It's not like I have to do anything to earn my half but say yes.

"Two things," I say. I've found that if I number my instructions, Franklin has a slightly better chance of successfully carrying them out. "First, you give me my cut now, out of your own pocket."

"Sure."

When Franklin finally realizes I'm not about to continue until I get my money, he burrows deep in his pocket, emerging with three crumpled one-dollar bills and a single ten-cent piece. "Can I get you the rest later?" he says.

I take the bills, fold them, place them in my billfold. "You can bring the other two dollars to Sophia's tonight."

"Sure."

"Second, I don't care how hard that ground is, I want you to dig deep enough to put it all in the same hole. I don't want the entire yard dug up."

"Sure."

I can't think of anything else, yet can't help hesitate, not entirely comfortable with the idea of entrusting Franklin with doing away with a hundred boxes of washing soap. One thing is for certain: there's no danger he's going to forgo his shovel and keep the stash for himself. Franklin never touches the stuff. Not out of laziness or privation, but principled argument. "Soap's just another way for them to make more money off you, the way I see it," he'd said when we'd first begun working together and I'd offered to pay for a visit to the steam house, my nose winning out over my wallet. "And it's not good for you, too, it wipes off all of nature's healthy oils and such. Even too much water is bad for you. It gets in the pores and gives you influenza."

"Okay," I say. "Just have it done by the time I come back tonight to open."

"I'm on it."

"And I don't want to see any of those boxes lying around here, either."

"Sure, sure," Franklin says. "Like I said, I'm on it."

Franklin shows up just before midnight, orders a whiskey and lights a cheap cigar. By the end of every night, even without Franklin's stinking contribution, Sophia's is cigarette and cigar overcast, enough so that even the people who don't smoke, like me, might as well, considering how bad they end up smelling.

Handing Franklin his whiskey, "Everything go all right?" I say.

Franklin straightens on his stool like he'd forgotten a corpse outside in the rain.

"The soap, Franklin."

"Oh, right, that, oh yeah, no problem. Which reminds me." He pulls two moist dollar bills out of his pocket and places them on the bar. I decide to let the money dry off for a while.

Meyers looks up from his week-old *Times*. "Do you know, just this month, in Braemar, in Aberdeenshire, the lowest-ever English temperature was recorded. I was just telling Mrs. Meyers not two nights ago . . ."

Mercifully, Franklin interrupts him, is the only one who ever addresses Meyers directly, and then only to ask, "So, who's dead these days, Meyers?" at which point Meyers will obligingly turn the pages of his *Times* looking for the most famous formerly once-alive he can find.

Coming up short, "It appears Louis Pasteur is mortally ill," Meyers says, pronouncing it "Lewis Pastor."

Franklin sips his whiskey, pets his greasy billy-goat beard. "I've heard of him. A bishop, I think he is. Way high up in the Church of England, I think."

Meyers reads on. "Must be a different Pastor," he says. "This one used a microscope to discover germs, apparently."

"Germs," Franklin spits, sucking hard on his cigar, blowing a cloud of fresh stink my way across the bar. "Some bigwig government type, I bet. Just one more rich sonofabitch out to bleed the workingman dry any way he can."

I decide now's as good a time as any to get another couple of bottles of whiskey from the back.

Henry opens his eyes when I open the door but doesn't bother to get up from his blanket. Not because he's disappointed that I only own an after-hours saloon and haven't furthered modern medicine, but because he knows we've got hours to go before we can go home. Besides, Louis Pasteur may have been Dean of the Faculty of Science at the University of Lille, but it was a man called Bigo who worked at a factory that made alcohol from sugar beets who put Pasteur on the trail to tracking down germs in the first place. Because Bigo wanted to know why so many of his vats of fermented beer were turning sour, Pasteur got busy with his microscope and became the Patron Saint of Hand Washing. Just in case anyone needed any further proof that civilization began with distillation.

"Boss," I hear Tom say out front, and I know there's trouble; Tom would never leave his post otherwise. The whiskey can wait. I lock the door to the backroom behind me.

"Boss, you best come upstairs."

I grab a roll of twenty-dollar bills from the cash box underneath the bar. I don't know what sort of problem it is—a bad drunk, a nosy neighbour, a prying policeman—but there aren't too many kinds of trouble that money can't solve.

On the way up the stairs, following Tom, "Who is it?" I say.

"No *who*—a *what*."

Before I can ask what kind of what, we're standing outside in the rain. The money is tight in my right hand, but there's no one I can see to show it to. Reading my mind, Tom raises his lamp, limps into the middle of the yard. I follow until he stops and lifts the lantern still higher for me to see. Peering through the cold, hard rain left and then right, "Tom?" I say, and he motions with his head at the ground directly in front of us.

What *used* to be the ground.

If an artist needed a model for a depiction of the lake of fire, and if fire was white and bubbled and smelt like fresh lemons, Franklin would have achieved something truly remarkable.

Unfortunately, what he was supposed to do was get rid of a hundred boxes of soap.

"My God," Franklin says.

"I say," Meyers says.

Until now, I hadn't noticed either one of them behind us. I look at the lake of bubbling soap again. It's at least six feet square and who knows how many deep.

"Went to relieve myself and nearly walked right through it," Tom says. "Thought you should know, Boss."

"But what is it?" Meyers says.

"You're going to deal with this, Franklin," I say.

"Yes."

"Tonight."

"But David, the rain—"

"Tonight, Franklin."

"Don't get me wrong, it's not that I'm personally afraid of a little weather—I'm not made of sugar, I know that—but it seems to me that the rain is what in fact has caused this very problem in the first place, and if we wait—"

"*Tonight*, Franklin."

The four of us stand in the rain, watching the gush and gurgle of the lemon-scented lava of the world's only back-yard volcano.

"And Franklin," I say.

"Yes?"

"Give me the other five dollars."

Franklin fishes in his pocket, counts what's in his hand, holds out a palm full of silver coins, rainwater, and a single soggy dollar bill.

"Seems like I'm a little short," he says. "Any chance I can get the rest to you later?"

*

Loretta's asleep and I'm not and it's all Saint Hippolytus' fault. Henry's asleep too, at the end of the bed, but animals have nothing to feel guilty about. That's their reward for never knowing how happy they are.

When Henry and I arrived home from work tonight, Loretta was already here, the fire fortified, both of her knitting needles wagging, and halfway through her second glass of schnapps. A shame that the older one gets, the more the despised clichés of one's youth turn out to be true, but a sight for sore eyes to see her snug as a bug in her chair and smiling at me without speaking, an expression that always says the same thing: *You're home—wherever else you've been today and tonight, whatever else you've been doing, this is where you belong, home.* I took off my hat and coat and watched Henry wag her hello.

I read, Loretta knitted, Henry dozed, and whatever combination of cold and menace the world could conjure up, we were warm and safe inside, at least for one more night. When I returned from the kitchen with our refilled drinks, Loretta had gotten up to stretch her legs and was flipping through the book I'd left on my chair, Saint Hippolytus's *The Refutation of All Heresies*. Seeing Loretta handle a book is like seeing a dog sitting beside a cat. I handed her her drink and she gave me back my book.

"Very big, this one," she said.

"It has to be," I said, sitting down. "The good saint gave himself a big job. Nothing less than discrediting every pagan Greek writer who he felt had been a bad influence upon the doctrines of the early Christian Church."

Still standing, and not before tasting her schnapps, "And what possible pleasure is there in studying such a thing?"

I laughed, because she meant exactly what she said. "Because in the course of six hundred pages of being consistently wrong, he inadvertently preserved many otherwise unrecorded quotations from many men who were right."

"And this amuses you?"

"It's an irony I can certainly appreciate."

Henry yipped, and we both sipped our drinks and watched him twitch in his sleep in front of the fire.

"Mr. Pythagoras, your Mr. No Meat. He is one of the ones this man records?"

Fifty years ago, vegetarians were known, if at all, by their most illustrious exemplar, Pythagoras, who was advocating the avoidance of slaughtering animals—and not just human ones—six centuries before Christ was up to saying something almost as altruistic. I smiled and thumbed to where I thought I remembered the short section on Pythagoras was located, thought I'd appear extra clever and answer her question with a choice injunction against the killing of all living creatures. But before I could find the right quote:

"This saint, I suppose he would find you ironic, too, yes?"

Still skimming and flipping, "I don't follow you," I said.

"Look around you."

I looked up from the page I was on with that impatient look people wear when trying to illustrate just how patient they're attempting to be. I shook my head. "What am I supposed to be looking at?"

Gesturing around the room with her glass, "A man who does not eat the flesh of animals has covered an entire room with their skins. This is ironic, yes?"

My library is colour-coded, a different shade of binding for each different genre. *The Refutation of All Heresies*, for example, is bound in red—wine-red calfskin. But it's a book, it's different, it's . . .

"It's different," I said.

"Now it is I who do not follow."

"Any good library's best editions are always bound."

"Of course. My father did the same with his. With skin of animals."

"You're missing the point."

"I see." Loretta settled back down and picked up her needles and went back to work.

And now Loretta's asleep and I'm not. And I don't count sheep, and I don't care how many angels can fit on the head of a single pin. But if Saint Hippolytus happens to be listening, here's another big job for you, maybe your biggest yet: Tell me, Saint, whose hands are ever really clean?

8

All men by nature desire to know.

Aristotle wrote it, I read it, and wouldn't you know it, he was right. And because the copy of his *Metaphysics* that I first encountered it in belonged to the Reverend King, I copied out this and whatever other snatches of wisdom I wanted to remember into a hardback black leather notebook that my mother surprised me with for my fifteenth birthday, "For the special schooling you doing now with the Reverend King." When, every Wednesday afternoon at three, the Reverend King would shake my hand at his study door and usher me inside for our weekly tutorial, my mother would somehow always manage to be nearby, broom or rag or mop and pail in hand, incapable of looking any prouder unless it had been my study door, the Reverend David King's, I was disappearing behind.

As long as I kept up with the reading I was supposed to be doing—the *Iliad* to sharpen my tongue, *A Brief Outline of the Evidences of the Christian Religion* to buttress my mind, *The Genuine Epistles of the Apostolic Fathers, St. Clement, St. Polycarp, St. Ignatius, St. Barnabas; the Shepherd of Hermas, and the Martyrdoms of St. Ignatius and St. Polycarp, Written by Those Who Were Present at Their Sufferings* to nourish my faith—I was allowed to take home with me whatever books I wished from the Reverend King's crowded shelves. And after we'd reviewed to the Reverend King's satisfaction whatever I'd been assigned to learn that week, there would always be a few minutes left over at the end to discuss my supplementary studies, any questions, comments, or confusions I might have come up with. One Wednesday, I had a few of all three.

"He says," I said, reading from the Reverend King's own copy of the *Nicomachean Ethics*, "'But is there any one thus intended by nature to be a slave, and for whom such a condition is expedient and right, or rather is not all slavery a violation of nature? There is no difficulty in answering this question, on grounds both of reason and of fact. For that some should rule and others be ruled is a thing not only necessary, but expedient; from the hour of their birth, some are marked out for subjection, others for rule.'"

I looked up, closed the book. At the end of our hour together the Reverend King would allow himself a rare moment's ease, rest one long leg over the other and settle back into his desk chair while listening to me talk, occasionally clarifying or explaining something, but mostly just enjoying my enthusiasm for the new world of books and ideas he'd helped me discover. This time he stayed where he was, at straight-backed attention behind his desk, rubbing his chin with his right hand like he was trying to determine if he'd shaved that morning. The room, which ordinarily smelt like old books, smelt instead of axle grease. His chair must have just been oiled.

"It's Aristotle who provides the foundation for Aquinas' entire theology," he finally said. "As you know. As we've already gone over. That's where his importance for us lies."

I knew it was time for me to go—if the Reverend King had a meeting that ended at four o'clock, odds were he had somewhere else he had to be or someone else he had to meet with at four-fifteen—but I wasn't done. "But he's—I mean, it seems to me—that Aristotle is saying that some people are naturally slaves and that others are naturally masters."

"Yes, and he's obviously wrong." The Reverend King stood up, my usual cue to do the same.

"But if Aristotle—"

"All you need to know of Aristotle, David, you already know. I think it's best now if we turn our attention to next week's material. Duns Scotus was a particular favourite of mine when I was studying at Edinburgh. I think when you read him, you'll understand why."

The Reverend King walked to his study door, stood there with his hand on the handle waiting for me to gather my books together. Once I had, "But Aquinas . . ." I said.

"Yes? Aquinas what?"

"But Aquinas, he didn't believe that some men are born to be slaves."

The Reverend King looked as if I'd just asked him if he himself believed the same thing. "Of course not. Saint Thomas Aquinas was a Christian."

I smiled, shook the Reverend King's hand, told him, "Thank you."

"You're welcome, David. And if you happen to see Mr. Brown on your way out, please tell him to come right in. The poor man's entire tobacco crop has been laid waste this year, I'm afraid, and he and his poor wife with another little one on the way, too. There simply must be something that can be done to help him."

*

Lead arms and legs; a fog-lost mind; smoke-blown days: only when I'm ill do I understand what happy people must feel like. Happy people like my mother. Yes, my mother.

My mother, born a slave, but whose father was a talented carpenter who paid his master two hundred dollars a year for the right to work his trade and manage his own affairs. "Weren't no better carpenter in all southwest Louisiana than your grandfather," she'd say. "And Master Williams, he know it, too, he knew he make more money letting him go about his line of work than if he stuck him off in some field all day." Thank God for small favours from business-savvy slave owners. And give you this day your daily bread, and whatever crumbs lie left over, please allow me to keep them to feed and clothe and house my own family.

My mother, stooped and shackled her final years by rheumatism, for whom even the previously most ordinary movements—twisting the lid off a jar of preserves, handling a broom, holding a glass of water—were never not accompanied by a lightning bolt of bright white pain dependably trailed by a thundering of muted moans and winces and sighs, but who was grateful until the day she died to do what she barely could, just thankful that the Good Lord still saw fit to give her a task, no matter how small, to carry out as her own.

The last year of her life she used a stick—*attempted* to use a stick—the slightly increased mobility it afforded offset by the difficulty of bending and curling and keeping ten tortured fingers how and where they didn't want to be. Once, coming home and seeing her before she saw me, I stopped in the road and watched as she used her stick, not to help her move, but to flail at some yellow leaves that had fallen onto the stone path that ran to our front door. Slowly, with both hands and with obvious pain, she'd wind up—six inches, at most, from start to follow-through—and whack away one or two offending leaves with her makeshift broom, then quickly replant the stick's end into the earth to steady herself until, secure again, she'd take another swipe at a couple more defiling leaves. I watched until she'd hobbled her way down the entire length of the walkway, until every leaf was gone. I watched her limp inside the house, sore but satisfied.

On the walk home from Sophia's last night, the tiredness I'd ignored behind the bar became an achiness in my joints and a shortness to my breath that I couldn't disregard once I'd slowed down long enough to let my body admit what it was feeling. Henry and I went immediately to bed, a good night's sleep as good a cure for what ails you as anything.

Most of the time. Today, all day, lead arms and legs, a fog-lost mind, the day smoke-blown and drifting, drifting toward time for me to get back behind the bar, influenza-ill or not. I've never missed a shift in eight years, never lost a single night's income. I woke up near dawn to let Henry piss and for me to do the same, then slept straight through to the afternoon.

When Henry got me up—cold nose to my hot face, time to go, David, time to go to work—I felt for my legs and, surprise, there they were. I stood up from the bed and waited to tip over, but didn't. Not entirely right, no—putting on my pants a dizzying dance; my mouth as dry as my nose was wet—but right enough, anyway, to get through the night and then home again and back to bed. And with enough strong tea and an only slightly earlier than usual closing time, I did.

This morning, still shaky, still sniffling, still sore in places I'd forgotten I had, I spent the day upright at least, resting in my chair until it was time to go to Sophia's. I watched the tree in the front yard through the window for almost the entire afternoon without once being bored. The dry toast I forced myself to eat stayed inside my stomach. Henry never left my side, never once complained I wasn't my fun old self anymore. This must be what happy people feel like, I thought. It's not the same as being alive, but it's not bad.

*

For all the time I spent with Mrs. King—which wasn't much, although, compared to everyone else, it was a lot—we didn't do much talking. Sometimes she embroidered, mostly she played the piano, eventually she mainly sat at her small bedroom window watching the world get by just fine without her. But even when she didn't speak, I knew she liked having me there. Or at least didn't mind, which, coming from her, was probably the same thing.

If Mrs. King did offer anything more than an intermittent "Sonata Number 7, D Minor, it's sometimes referred to as the Tempest Sonata," it wasn't because of anything I asked. When Mrs. King did undertake to talk at paragraph length, it wasn't so much with me as at me, a gentle *ex nihilo* monologue one couldn't help but feel would have been delivered whether she was with company or not.

Recital temporarily over but fingers still on the keys, the piano's last melancholy notes still alive in the air, she'd look up like she'd suddenly remembered something that, unless she repeated it aloud, she'd forget again, perhaps forever.

"Once things become settled, I'm going to go away. I'm going to go away to Vienna for a long, long visit. I plan to attend a different musical event every evening, so it won't be surprising if I occasionally sleep late in the morning. But no one could possibly object to that. Once they review my schedule, how could they possibly object to that? Once things become settled, I plan to visit Vienna and attend a different musical event every evening. People forget: beauty is such very, very hard work."

I didn't know what "Once things become settled" meant, but I did know that she never mentioned the Reverend King in her travel plans. In fact, the only time I can recall her ever mentioning him by name was once when, mid-sonata, she abruptly stopped playing. I listened along with her to the sound of nothing until, eventually, I heard what she must have heard, the heavy steps of the Reverend King coming into the house and then going into his office, office door shutting behind him.

"What's wrong?" I said. "It's just the Reverend King."

Mrs. King folded her hands in her lap; turned slowly on the piano bench toward the window. As if addressing it instead of me, "The Reverend King doesn't approve of Beethoven," she said. "The Reverend King says that Beethoven isn't good for my health."

I don't remember precisely when Mrs. King stopped talking or when I quit visiting her, but I can remember the first time she wouldn't play the piano.

I'd been working at my Latin all Saturday afternoon and was looking forward to both the walk to Clayton House in the fresh fall air and the clearing of my head of the delicate differences between *municpeps* and *municipalis* and *municium*. Hearing Mrs. King's music was like what happened inside the snow globe Mrs. Brown had given my mother one year for Christmas. Once you shook it, the snow would wildly whip about its watery insides for a few moments until eventually, tranquilly, falling past the tiny painted picture of a quiet country church. When Mrs. King played the piano, it was the same old clutter stuck inside your head, but everything would be lifted up and rearranged, and when she was done, your brain felt rested and refreshed, although you knew nothing had really changed.

I did what I always did, opened her door without knocking, but slowly, so I wouldn't startle her. I'd never had to ask her to play the piano because she always seemed to be playing, the muffled music of Clayton House morning, noon, and night. This time Mrs. King wasn't at the piano or in her chair with her knitting needles, or even in bed, which she sometimes would be even in the middle of the afternoon. Those times I'd stay standing just inside the doorway and ask after her health, to which she'd always answer, "I'm fine, child, just a little tired is all," and the next time I'd come by, there would be music again.

This time Mrs. King wasn't doing anything, only sitting in her chair looking out the window.

"Good evening, Mrs. King," I said.

Mrs. King didn't answer, so I invited myself in, sure she simply hadn't heard me. Standing beside her chair now, "Good evening, Mrs. King," I said.

"Please just leave it on the table," she said.

I glanced around the room, not knowing what she wanted me to do. "Put what on the table, Mrs. King?"

"I'll eat it later," she said. "I promise I'll eat it later."

She thought I was my mother. I was standing right next to her, but she thought I was my mother. "Why don't you play the piano?" I said.

Mrs. King kept staring out the window, so I looked too. Whatever it was she was seeing, she was the only one seeing it. Either that or she was seeing the same thing I was—nothing.

"Please play the piano, Mrs. King." It seemed very important that the room stop being so quiet.

"I'm not hungry right now," she said. "I promise I'll eat it all later."

"There isn't any food. I don't care about any food. Come to the piano and play, Mrs. King, just play for a little while."

"Just leave it on the table. I promise I'll eat every bite later."

The room was so quiet, I thought my eardrums would burst. "Please play, Mrs. King," I said. "Please just play the piano."

But Mrs. King just kept looking out the window. I closed her bedroom door, slowly, behind me.

9

I didn't have anyone else to talk to about it, so I talked to George. This is what best friends are for.

Actually, I had already spoken to someone—the Reverend King—about what was bothering me, but his answers sounded less like explanations and more like reasons to stop asking questions. It was like the time I was ten and played in the poison ivy. Nothing—particularly not scratching, the only thing that seemed to offer even temporary relief—could stop the itching except for the smelly medicine that George's father finally mixed up. Only this time there wasn't any medicine.

"Leviticus, chapter 25, verses 44 through 46," I said. "'You may purchase male or female slaves from among the foreigners who live among you. You may also purchase the children of such resident foreigners, including those who have been born in your land. You may treat them as your property, passing them on to your children as a permanent inheritance.'"

I looked up from the bible opened across my knees. I was sitting atop the big hill. George was standing at pond's edge, casting and recasting his fishing line. I'd waited for him on the steps of the potash factory. I knew he'd listen to me if I agreed to let him go home first and get his fishing pole. Being an apprentice at the factory put more money in his pocket but a lot fewer fish on the end of his line.

"Well?" I said.

"Well, what?"

"Well, doesn't that bother you?"

"Why would what anyone did in Egypt two thousand five hundred years ago bother me?"

Instead of answering, I flipped until I found the passage I had bookmarked in Exodus with a piece of torn newspaper. "How about this? Does this bother you? 'When a man strikes his male or female slave with a rod so hard that the slave dies under his hand, he shall be punished. If, however, the slave survives for a day or two, he is not to be punished, since the slave is his own property.'"

I watched his face for at least a flicker of anger, either because of the scriptural sanction for the sort of beatings his own father had endured for so much of his life or because I'd had the impudence to remind him of them. Either way, annoyance was better than indifference.

George kept casting.

Now *I* was angry. I flipped again, the accumulated bookmarks sticking out of the bible fluttering in the July breeze. I stopped at Ephesians. "This is from the New Testament," I said.

George thought he had a bite—teased his line a little, waited—then realized he didn't. He cast again.

"I said, this is from the New Testament."

"I heard you the first time."

We both knew that both books were holy but that the New Testament was holier. I read what was written.

"'Slaves, obey your earthly masters with deep respect and fear. Serve them sincerely as you would serve Christ.'" I didn't wait for George to ignore me. "'As you would serve Christ,'" I said.

"I think you've got me confused with someone else. I can see *and* hear just fine."

"So say something, then."

"If I had anything to say, I would."

"The Bible condones slavery and you've got nothing to say."

"What did the Reverend King say?"

"It doesn't matter what the Reverend King said. I'm asking you what you think."

"And now I'm asking you: what did the Reverend King say?"

I picked up a small rock, tossed it in my hand. "He said that what some translators call slaves were actually servants."

"Well, there you are."

"But what he didn't say is that even if they worked as household servants, that doesn't mean they weren't bought, sold, and treated worse than livestock."

Still sitting, I lobbed the rock into the other side of the pond, away from where George had cast his line.

"Cut it out," he said.

"It wasn't even near you."

"It doesn't matter, you'll scare away the fish."

I watched the circles the rock made in the water grow larger and larger until they weren't circles anymore, were only water again.

"Besides," George said, pulling in his line, "you've heard the Reverend King, the Bible is just man's words. And man isn't perfect—God is."

"So some parts we're supposed to ignore and other parts we're supposed to believe."

George pretended like he was concentrating on his line but couldn't resist nodding—once, leisurely, indulgently—as if I were a pesky child who'd finally agreed to settle down.

I couldn't stand his calm, I couldn't stand his certainty. I picked up another rock, a bigger one. "So let's ignore 'In the beginning God created the heaven and the earth,' then.

Let's ignore 'Thou shalt not kill.' Let's ignore 'I am the son of God.'" I pitched the rock into the water not two feet from where George was standing. It plopped. It splashed the cuffs of his pants.

"I told you not to do that," he said.

"So what?"

"So you shouldn't have done it."

"Why not?"

"Because you shouldn't have."

"Why not?"

"Shut your mouth, David."

"Why should I?"

"Shut up."

"Why?"

George dropped his fishing pole and charged up the hill, giving me just enough time to raise my fists in front of my face. I'd never been in a fight before—neither had he, as far as I knew—but we'd both seen the same outdoor boxing match his father had taken us to in Chatham, so I stood ready for him to stop running and put up his hands. That was how real fighters fought.

He caught me in my stomach with his shoulder and didn't stop moving until I was on my back and he was on top of me, a knee wedged deep into the dirt on either side of my chest. He needn't have worried about me going anywhere—his shoulder had forced me to forget how to breathe. I couldn't speak, let alone fight back.

He sat on me with his fists clenched at his sides, watching me imitate a dying fish. When he saw air finally going in and coming back out of my mouth, he stood up. I stayed on the ground and watched him pick up his fishing pole and patiently gather in its line.

He put his pole over his shoulder and started down the

path home. I waited until I knew there was no chance I'd overtake him before I got up.

*

So I was confused. So I was skeptical. Mostly, I was excited.

Before my next birthday, I'd be a university student. In Toronto. With unrestricted access to Canada West's largest and best libraries. Plus, I was going to buy a slate grey fedora, just like the one I'd seen a white man wearing once in Chatham.

I copied out the same sentence from Pascal into my notebook to soothe myself whenever the occasional doubt pinched my conscience, made me question the appropriateness of my training for the ministry.

The knowledge of God is very far from the love of Him.

Maybe I didn't know God as well as I used to—as well as I would have liked to—but I was still very, very fond of Him.

Mr. Rapier said that there were musical concerts every week in Toronto. There was even an orchestra there that performed monthly. You cannot believe the beautiful sounds a full orchestra is capable of, he said. It is truly something one must experience for oneself.

And so that was one more thing I was going to do.

*

Loretta and I are doing what we usually do after she's spent the night, except this morning it's me who can't get the water in the bathtub hot enough. I may have been the fourth man in Chatham to have indoor plumbing, but that doesn't mean the sink doesn't get stopped up from time to time or the tank doesn't run out of hot water quicker than it's supposed to. Progress breeds new problems, necessitating more progress, which breeds new problems, necessitating more . . . I shut my eyes and lean back in the tub, intent upon absorbing whatever's left of the cooling water's warmth.

I rub my hand all over my head, still not used to the smooth ride it gets no matter where I let it wander. The first time Loretta saw me newly sheared, she laughed; not as if she thought I looked ridiculous, but as if she thought it was funny that I would do what I did. When she wordlessly rubbed the top of my skull like a Buddhist his wise worship's belly, I laughed too.

"This is one more reason for you to go back with me," Loretta says. Back to Germany, she means.

Without opening my eyes, "I can take a bath in Chatham," I say.

Loretta flicks a fingertip of cold water at me from the plugged sink. She's at the mirror, applying her powder and paint. "Baden-Baden," she says. "It is the most famous spa in Germany. The springs there were known even during Roman times. The baths, they were uncovered in near-perfect condition only forty years ago."

Heraclitus may have been right, maybe you can't step twice into the same river, but to stand where Lucretius or Seneca or Horace possibly stood, just one more bone-weary traveller aching for ancient healing waters, is almost incomprehensible. Incomprehensible and impossible. To shut down Sophia's in order to travel to Europe for a month or more would cost me . . . a lot. And what exactly do I need a holiday *from*? Prosperity? Security? A life, finally, exactly as I'd always wanted it, a life no one born where and what I was should have had any right even imagining? My mother never took a holiday. Neither did the Reverend King. My life *is* a holiday. I change the subject.

"It's supposed to storm tonight," I say. "Why don't you stay in town?"

Loretta spends most nights with me, and invariably has business to attend to the next day around town, but still keeps a small residence in Dresden. She says she'll move to Chatham only when she can afford to buy the biggest, most expensive house in town.

Loretta applies a last layer of lipstick, turns from the mirror. "Who is it that says this is so?"

I don't answer, only smile. She knows it's at her expense but can't help joining me. "And what is it you find so amusing?"

"You," I say.

"And what specifically is it about me that is humorous?"

I close my eyes again, ease back even farther into the tub. The air in the bathroom is almost as warm as the water by now, but I don't want to get out, am not ready not to feel almost weightless yet. "If I told you, you might change. What fun would that be?"

"Tell me," she says.

"Nein."

That's all the teasing Loretta can take. I can hear the scoop of a handful of cold, whisker-filled water that's coming my way, but don't have anywhere to go, can only sink beneath the surface of the bath. I stay under for as long as I can, but as soon as my head hits the air, I get what I have coming.

"Okay, okay," I say, standing, holding up both hands. "You win." I grab a towel from the rack.

"Of course I win. Never start—"

"—a war with a German, I know."

"Good. You are learning. Now, what is it that is so funny about me?"

Drying myself off, "It's a compliment, actually."

"Yes?" When I don't answer, only smile again, she immediately dips her hand back into the sink, ready and willing to catapult a fresh assault of dirty water. "Now is when I should take your photograph," she says.

Loretta has been after me to have my picture taken for years. At first I couldn't be bothered to sit still long enough, although now, with her new camera, that's not a concern. I suppose I don't like the idea of being her only still-breathing model.

I hold up a conciliatory hand, use the other to keep towelling off. "It's just that, somehow—and I really don't know how you do it—you manage to sound like absolutely no one else I've ever heard speak before, while at the same time making yourself more clearly understood than anyone else I've ever met either."

Hand still loaded, "That is all?" she says.

"That is all."

Loretta finally surrenders her liquid artillery back into the sink, grabs the end of my towel and wipes her hand dry. "Of course," she says. "It is because I am German. A German says only what needs to be said."

When I met her, Loretta talked with a German accent, thought with a German brain, acted with a German will, but was rarely ever *German*, only in the last year or so referring to herself as being anything but her, Loretta. Approaching thirty, maybe, or perhaps the news of her father's death. Around this same time, too, the first talk of her returning to Germany for a visit, specifically Rocken, her birthplace.

"The return of the prodigal daughter," I'd said.

"Do not be foolish. I simply wish to make all those who made me suffer when I left there suffer tenfold upon my return." Loretta claims she never dreams, and I have no reason to doubt her. Loretta doesn't need nighttime's dark hints and shadowy hunches; Loretta's mind is hers.

"The best revenge is a well-lived life," I said, trying again.

This one she thought about for a moment. Eventually, "Of course," she said.

By the time I've dressed and appear in the kitchen, the water for the coffee is boiling on the stove and two plates have been set on the table. Henry, smelling Loretta's sausages bubbling in the frying pan, has quit his customary spot in front of the library fireplace and is sitting at attention in the middle of the kitchen floor, waiting for either a lucky accident or a kind handout. When Loretta decides to cook, Henry isn't, like his master, a strict vegetarian anymore. Henry likes it when Loretta decides to cook.

"One soft-boiled egg for Mr. Pythagoras," she says, placing just that in its tiny silver cup in front of me. "And for Mr. Heinrich and myself"—Loretta sets down her own cupped egg then thuds an enormous sausage from the grease-popping pan onto her plate, along with a fat plop of dumplings— "something just for us, *ja*?" Something just for them, plus an already prepared, neatly arranged tray of fresh rolls, three kinds of preserves, and various cheeses for all of us to share. Loretta eats like a German too.

After Henry has been hand-fed his designated share of the sausage link and dismissed back to the library ("That is all, Mr. Heinrich, be a good boy now and lay down elsewhere"), Loretta proceeds to cut and spread, to spoon and swallow, to fork and chew, in the process not neglecting to go over in detail her entire day's itinerary. There's no need to go over mine. Mine is the same today as it is every day, the same as it's been since the first day I opened up Sophia's.

"Even after I pay this man, this Hanna, to take care of the roof, I still do nicely. This time next year, I already make back what I spent, and after that it is all profit." Loretta celebrates the success of her most recent investment by spreading her roll with an extra-thick measure of peach marmalade.

The way she studies me while she chews tells me what she's going to say next. Every time she purchases a new rental property, it's always the same topic. "I know of another house, on Prince Street, near the park, that would be an excellent investment for you. Why not we should look at it this afternoon, after I am finished at the bank?"

"Because I like the house I have now," I say.

"Do not be difficult, David, it is tiresome. You know what I am saying. It is foolish for a man with the capital you possess not to let it work for you."

"I don't need my money to work for me. *I* work for me."

"Yes, and work too hard, too. There is no reason for you to be at that place of yours every single night. Not anymore. At the very least, you need to hire someone to work for you occasionally."

"Work alone is noble."

"You sound like my father."

"It's Thomas Carlyle, actually."

"A minister, no doubt." Unless it's to read to me, Loretta makes it a point of pride never to pick up a book.

"A British writer," I say.

"He sounds like a minister to me."

Because she's right, he does—sounds like the Reverend King, actually—I pick up the coffee pot and pour Loretta a refill.

"See?" she says. "Whenever you do not know what to do, you play at being bartender. It is reflex, you cannot help it."

"I know what I have to do," I say, stacking Loretta's plate on top of mine. "I've got to clear this table, then I'm going to fix the bathroom drain, and then I've got to take Henry for his walk." Hearing the *w*-word, Henry trots back into the kitchen and sits in the doorway, ready to go when I am.

"Excuse me, but I am not finished, please," she says, taking back her plate.

I don't let her slow me down, pile cup and silverware and saucer and whatever else I can grab on top of my own plate. Loretta absently butters half a roll while watching me work, like a physician observing a patient exhibiting all the telltale symptoms of an exotic disease.

"You are a strange man," she says.

I pretend to ignore her, dump my first batch of dirty dishes into the sink, return to the table for another load.

"You work hard—you work very, very hard for many, many years, just like me—to make a life for yourself, and then, once you have made it, you choose not to live it."

"That doesn't even make sense," I say, not bothering to look up, wiping down the table, careful, though, to keep my rag clear of Loretta's continuing feast.

"You know what you are, David?"

I rinse my rag out at the sink, keep my back to her.

"You are spilt religion."

I don't know what she means, but I'm enormously insulted anyway. I hang the rag over the pump, turn around. "You're having a very un-German day," I say.

"I am sorry?"

"That's the second thing you've said in the last two minutes that's entirely illogical."

"Oh." She seems relieved, folds a piece of cheese in two and places it in her mouth. "No, you just do not understand."

"Really. Enlighten me."

She can see that I'm angry now, so smiles, knows she finally has my attention. "It is quite simple, really."

I watch her chew, swallow.

"You are a Christian without a Christ."

Now it's my turn to smirk, although my smile doesn't feel right on my face, feels like a new shoe you desperately want to fit but know deep down doesn't.

"And that doesn't make any sense either," I say.

Loretta rises, wipes her mouth one last time with her napkin before letting it drop to the table for me to pick up.

"Doesn't it?" she says.

*

We met the summer I turned seventeen.

Every illicit passage I read in place of what the Reverend King assigned me to study intimated earthly enchantments I had never known. Every reprieving spring breeze reminded me I had a body as well as a soul, wasn't just a shivering spirit waiting around for celestial translation but was also a corporeal creature with dirty, idyllic desires of its own. Every time I told myself it was forbidden, was out of the question, to put it out of my mind, instead of ears waxed shut with cooling, calming silence, an obstinate echo never failed to answer back: *Why?* And: *Why?*

If it was going to happen, though, there was no chance of it happening in Buxton, that much was certain. If I wanted it, if I really wanted it, I needed to go into Chatham to get it. Alone. I couldn't even risk telling George.

I told my mother I had to ride into town on Mr. Freeman's horse to pick up a parcel for him from the hardware store. I told George and his father I needed to borrow their horse to ride into town to pick up a parcel for my mother from the drugstore. Two wrongs made it right, and it was the first time I'd ever been alone in the city.

It was Saturday afternoon, and the streets being so busy with honest commerce made it easier not to imagine that every set of eyes was watching me, knew and disapproved of what I was doing. I stopped to stare in store windows and tipped my cap to elderly strangers and even purchased something so as to better resemble a real shopper, a candy apple on a stick from the same general store George and I always used to visit when we'd accompany his father into Chatham. The hard candy coating tasted like cherry shellac, and the apple itself was mushy, nearly rotten, collapsed in my mouth on the very first bite. I threw it away and headed south along King Street. *Procrastination is the thief of time*, the Reverend King liked to remind us.

I had a plan. First, I needed to find someone who could make the transaction for me. Second, I had to ensure that, whoever he was, he didn't know I was from the Settlement, because if he did, the Reverend King would know what I'd been up to before I had time to get back to Buxton. I walked to where the majority of the Negro saloons were and lingered far enough away that no one would think I was trying to get inside, but close enough that I could spot an especially drunk patron upon leaving, just the kind of person who'd know how to get me what I wanted and who wouldn't be morally opposed to doing it. I pitched rocks up into the billowing branches of a weeping willow tree and waited. It was Saturday afternoon, workingman's payday, so I didn't have to wait very long.

A man weaved out of the saloon while attempting to light his cigarette like a newly vertical infant chasing after an elusive butterfly, until he saw the fifty-cent piece in my hand. The man stopped, carefully lit up, shook and dropped the dead match. He was skinny but had a bulge over his belt like he'd swallowed a small pumpkin, whole. His eyes were mostly red, as if he'd been up all night, and there was a scar on his right cheek that moved when he spoke.

"You're just a kid," he said.

I didn't answer, held up the coin between my thumb and forefinger. I'd planned on this very sort of objection, was proud of myself to have been so prepared.

The man blew a smoke ring and looked me over. Although he was coloured, there was little chance he had any close contact with anyone in Buxton, but the way he stared worried me anyway. I was contemplating running—he'd had a hard time walking, there was no way he'd ever catch me—when he said, "Go around back, and don't say nothin' to nobody unless it's me, understand?"

I nodded, and he reached for the fifty-cent piece. "Not until I get what I came for," I said, sticking it in my pocket.

I thought he might try to take it from me—I'd allowed for that possibility too—but the man laughed instead, then coughed, then laughed and coughed at the same time.

"Just don't talk to nobody," he said, and went back inside the saloon.

Later, back in Buxton, in bed that night, I couldn't sleep. Not because I felt guilty or was worried I'd be found out, or even because I was excited at the idea of what I'd chanced and done and gotten away with.

I couldn't sleep because I felt like someone different, as if the person who'd ridden off that morning wasn't the same person who'd ridden home that night. I got up from bed and went to my desk and lit the lamp, opened the book of ancient Greek epigrams that Mr. Rapier had bought and brought back for me from Toronto.

> *Drink down the strong wine: Dawn's but the span*
> *Of a finger.*
> *And shall we wait for the lamp that brings Good night?*
> *Drink, drink to joy, dear friend:*
> *for soon we'll have*
> *A lonely night for sleeping, and that's for ever.*

It was true and I knew it, and not just because I'd read it in a book, but because I knew it. And behind the big hill at Deer

Pond, underneath the heap of dead leaves and fallen branches where I'd hidden it, there was still over half a bottle of whiskey left.

I'd wanted wine, as in the epigram and in all the poems I read, but when I complained to the man in Chatham, he'd said, "Wine's for old ladies and priests. A man's drink is whiskey, boy. You're a man, aren't you?"

"Of course I am," I said.

*

Lies, lies, lies: there *was* such a thing as heaven on earth. All it took was a pint of cheap Chatham-bought whiskey, a book of ancient Greek poetry, and an unobserved drinking and reading spot high atop the big hill overlooking Deer Pond. Add a dash of the not-insubstantial earthly pleasure of doing what you're not supposed to be doing, as well as wilfully disregarding much of what you are, and you've got yourself a can't-miss recipe for real-life rapture that bypasses Judgement Day altogether and gets right down to all the good stuff. Just shake and stir, and be prepared to shake and stir.

Watching me get drunk, however, was as far as I could persuade George to join me in breaking one of the Reverend King's most sacrosanct edicts, and even that had taken some convincing. It was a good thing I'd paid such close attention to the Reverend King's patient elucidation of the Socratic method; you never know when you're going to need to induce someone to do something they don't want to do.

"Has he ever said that it's wrong for a person to be in the presence of alcohol?" I said.

"You know he has."

"Really? I thought that what was forbidden was to *drink* alcohol."

"That's what I meant," George said.

"But that's not what you implied. You implied that it's prohibited to simply be in the presence of someone who's drinking alcohol."

We were walking through the bush in the direction of Deer Pond. George had agreed to accompany me but had made it clear he was turning right around as soon as I pulled out the pint bottle of whiskey hidden in my coat pocket. The moon was freshly risen and burning white, but we didn't need it to get where we were going. Our four feet alone had worn a path over the years that would deliver us safely there.

"It's still not right, and you know it's not right," George said, holding a thin branch back for me until I passed. George's father had taught us to always hold down a branch in deference to the person walking behind you on the trail.

"Not right to consume alcohol in Buxton," I said.

"That's right."

"But we won't be in Buxton. Deer Pond lies outside the limits of the Elgin Settlement."

George didn't reply; didn't need to. Even though all I could see was the back of his head, I knew what the other side looked like: purse-lipped and slit-eyed, angry at me for doing wrong, angry at me for making it sound right. It was a look I was becoming used to.

We let the sound of the mud slopping against the soles of our shoes do our chatting for us. By the time we were almost at the pond, "Woods' isn't in Buxton, and it's off limits," George said.

An Englishman named Woods had recently purchased one of the first settlers' farms on the Middle Road, just beyond the Elgin boundary, and opened a grocery store there that sold whiskey. The Reverend King immediately called a meeting of all of Buxton's residents and entreated them to shun Woods's store until he ceased to sell intoxicants, reminding them how masters in the South would encourage their slaves to drink away their few hours not spent toiling in the fields and so remain subservient because they knew how alcohol made men lazy and violent and lustful. I'd stood at the back of the crowd that had gathered on the church lawn and couldn't help but be impressed. Not by what he said—I'd never suffered under a manipulative master, I'd never known a morally degraded slave—but by the effect his saying had on every assembled listener. The entire crowd nodded their heads in unison whenever what the Reverend King said required agreement, just as they all shook their heads as if on cue when whatever he said was intended to inspire disgust. Talk about drunken subservience. And not an ounce of liquor acting inside a single one of them.

Before I had time to cleverly formulate another argument clearly illustrating how if X then Y, then therefore Z, we arrived at Deer Pond. We did the right thing—quit talking—without having to remind ourselves or each other, as sure a sign as any that you're actually doing what's right. I went and sat where we always sat and George went and stood where we always stood. The moon used the water as its mirror.

I looked at the pond from atop the small treeless hill while George stood at its edge skipping stones, *thip thip thip glug* after each new toss. The April air was cool enough that the coat I was wearing wasn't just to conceal the whiskey, but the earth was thawing, you could feel it, you didn't need a calendar to know it was spring.

A single *thip, glug*.

"I heard that," I said.

George shrugged his shoulders. "Out of practice," he said, looking for another rock. Since he'd graduated to full-time status at the potash factory, our visits to Deer Pond had become as rare as my secret trips into Chatham had become common.

I pulled out the bottle but didn't open it, waited to see what George would do, a jumpy hunter feeling out his jumpier prey. When he didn't motion to leave or even say anything, I slowly cracked the cap.

"Do what you want, I don't care," he said, sidearming a new stone, an extra *thip* added to his toss.

"Nice one," I said. I raised the pint and pulled, made an effort not to show how terrible the whiskey tasted. It didn't matter—George was looking for a good skipping stone.

I drank and George threw. I got gently drunk and George never missed. But most of all, the earth breathing easy again, new sap and fresh dew and even the sweet rot of dead leaves forcing you to feel alive. I lay face down on the hill, breathed. "Come here," I said.

George stopped throwing but didn't move any closer. "You're drunk," he said.

"No I'm not." I pressed my nose deeper into the dirt, inhaled hard. The earth cleared my head of the whiskey yet made me feel drunker.

Glug.

"I'm going home," George said.

"So I'm drunk." I tossed the bottle and what was left inside it into the woods. "Come here anyway."

The surrendered whiskey made the impact I'd hoped for; George stayed where he was, but at least he wasn't leaving.

"Come here and smell this," I said.

"Smell what?"

"The earth. Spring."

"You *are* drunk."

I knew what he was thinking—*This was why the Reverend King was right, this was what drunken people did, lay around on the ground smelling dirt*—but I refused to get mad, there was too much at stake. "If I wasn't," I said, "I wouldn't have known."

"Known what?"

"I can't tell you, you have to see for yourself."

"By smelling a hill."

"Just do it, George, get down here."

"I'm going home."

"I threw away the whiskey."

For a moment, just the hum of the blood in my ears and the rustle of the slight breeze in the trees.

"Will you come back with me if I do?" George said.

"Yes. Now come here."

"You'll come back straightaway?"

"Yes, I already said yes. Now lie down like me, push your nose right down to the ground, it won't work if you don't."

I gave him some privacy, shut my eyes while he lay down a few feet away from me on the hill.

"Now breathe," I said.

"I already was. That's why I'm not *underneath* the ground."

"Just do it once—just do it once right—and I won't ask again."

He didn't say anything, so I knew he was contemplating either getting up or doing what I wanted. I heard him take a deep whiff, like the way the doctor made you inhale when he was listening to your heart. He whiffed again, more deeply than before.

"It's good," he said.

"Now do it with your eyes closed."

This time he didn't hesitate. "It's like—it's like it's spring in there," he said.

"Everything is being born again."

George inhaled one more time. He rested his head on its side, stared in the direction of the pond.

"Well," he said, "it's spring, anyway."

*

You can't regret what has to happen. It's not reasonable, is like being upset with a child for growing out of his Sunday shoes or castigating an old man for falling asleep in the sun. Born to grow, grow to die. And if unassailable logic and sage proverbs could cure a sick soul, we wouldn't need God or whiskey.

I *needed* to flout my doubt. It wasn't enough to be bored with my studies, it required that I call into question how anyone could find them compelling. Falling in love with illicit tomes, someone other than just me had to know what they were and why they were so wonderful. Someone—anyone—but my mother. For her I still believed that the sun revolved around the earth and that farther along we will surely understand why.

> "'If all be true that I do think,
> There are five reasons why I drink:
> Good wine, a friend, or being dry
> Or lest we should be by and by—
> Or any other reason why.'"

I waited for George to say he hated it. Nothing could have been finer—except, perhaps, him fearing it.

"It's Latin, sixteenth century," I added.

Human beings three centuries dead celebrating intoxication seemed almost as impossible as the idea of the very same people having sex or going to the bathroom.

"Is it your translation?" he said.

I'd picked him up after work at the factory on the way to Clayton House to collect my mother. Her rheumatism was so bad now she shouldn't have been travelling anywhere farther than from bed to her window chair, but the more her fingers froze and the less her legs would obey her, the more determined she became to fulfill her duties. "The Good Lord give everyone something to do," she'd say when I'd plead with her to at least take a day's rest. "And if He didn't want me to take care of the Reverend King like I do, I expect He wouldn't let me do it, then." The way she struggled just to hobble around enough to oversee the new cleaning and cooking staff was reason to believe that He was very seriously considering her imminent retirement.

I pulled the copy of *Benjamin's Epigrams* from my satchel. "It's from here," I said, holding up the book like a revival preacher his faithful bible.

"Oh. I thought you'd translated it. For practice. For Knox."

I opened the book and read it while we walked. Finished, "Does that sound like something I'd read at Knox College?" I snarled.

We were at the gate of his property. "How would I know?" George said. "You're the one going there, not me."

"Why don't you just listen this time, then," I said, reopening the book to the same epigram.

George half waved and walked up his sidewalk instead. "Not today. I'm tuckered. And hungry. You wouldn't believe how much you need to know about a furnace before they even let you get near one."

When I got to Clayton House, my mother was waiting for me on the front step as usual. She didn't like to keep me waiting when I had important studies to attend to when I got home. I kissed her on the cheek and entwined her arm tight with mine and we started our snail crawl home.

The fact that she was silent told me she had something to say. Ordinarily, I would have been hearing about how Liza put too much salt in the bread dough or how Harriet has to be told every single day to sweep under the beds, not just around them where everyone can see.

"The Reverend King say you not been at your special meetings with him two weeks runnin' now," she said.

"I haven't been feeling well."

"Seem to me you been feeling well enough to be sittin' up half the night readin'."

"I've been studying." And I was—Lucretius, Horace, Heraclitus—just not the things I was supposed to be studying. "I just haven't had the time to see the Reverend King. But I've been doing what I need to do on my own."

She made a face like someone had slapped her. The shot of pain she must have felt only jiggled my arm still entwined with hers, the gentle tug on the fishing line that belies the torture going on below. I pulled her tighter to me, but she grimaced like it did more bad than good, so we stopped for a moment instead. I let go of her arm, let her stand on her own.

"Is it your legs or your back?" I said. Or your aching wrists or your warped hips or your swollen ankles or . . .

She shook her head, saying no to the pain as much as to my question. I looked away to allow her a moment of privacy with her agony.

The scent of fresh tree sap; the softness of a surprisingly warm breeze; the sight of so much bright new green where, just two weeks before, there'd been only grey skeleton limbs: all failed to cheer, only jeered, in fact, my poor mother's poor broken body.

Carpe diem, I thought.

I turned back to my mother, the pain only now partially subsiding.

Of course fucking *carpe diem*. If your hands can close tightly enough without pain to do it.

"Don't let the Reverend King down, son," my mother said.

I hugged her, as gently, as tightly, as I could. "I won't let you down," I said.

My mother squeezed me back, stronger than I would ever have thought she could. "The Reverend King, he has such high, high hopes for you, son."

10

Everything is unimaginable until it happens. The pitiless, punishing logic of inevitability. Your own mother, for instance, the woman who gave you life, dying. And the stupid symbolism of one damn thing after another, like the smoke rising from every chimney in Buxton, sooty souls eagerly departing this broken, useless planet.

Although she was entirely bedridden by now—either propped up in the daytime amidst a cocoon of pillows and cushions or carefully laid out for the night—it was hard to feel too sorry for her unless she was sleeping. She wouldn't *allow* you to feel sorry for her. She rarely complained. She never expressed self-pity. She was actually most concerned with not being too much of a bother to others. Others being me, of course, as well as all of the Settlement women who were always there whenever anyone was ill or injured. The people of Buxton were good at circling the wagons, even in cases like my mother's, where little could be done but making things as comfortable as possible until God in His infinite sadism decided He'd seen enough suffering and eventually allowed his forlorn child to stagger home.

"Are you sure you wouldn't like some breakfast? Maybe just some bread with honey. Mrs. Hamilton brought some by yesterday, from her own honeycombs."

"I thought I told you to go to school, now, David. You going to be late."

"I'm not going to be late. And it doesn't matter."

"*Doesn't matter.*" My mother slowly turned her head to the left as far as the pain permitted; just as slowly, just as painfully, lifted it upward as far as possible to look Mrs. Jackson, who was arranging her pillows, in the face. The rheumatism, not unlike Grant's army, had changed strategy, had stopped attacking this limb or that joint in favour of all-out assault. It was as if the rheumatism had moved from her bones to her blood, had finally captured her entire body. "Boy gonna be a minister someday, and he says it don't matter if he goes to school today or not."

Mrs. Jackson did what she knew she was expected to do, smiled and shook her head along with my mother.

"I didn't say I wasn't going to go."

"So get," my mother said, raising her arm, its wooden stiffness all the more an admonition.

And I'd go, because I knew the women of Buxton would take as good care of her as anyone could, and because I knew my going to school meant to my mother that I was one day closer to graduating and going on to Knox College and becoming the Reverend David King. It sounds vain—it sounds sinfully vain—but I think she even minded dying less because she could imagine that someday I was going to become the one thing she wanted more than anything, maybe even more than her own restored health.

So I would go to school and pretend to pay attention, and study what I really wanted to study at home, beside my mother's bed while she sat staring out the window or dozing; and, after she'd fallen asleep for the night, in my room, where I didn't have to hide my copy of Erasmus or Montaigne or Cicero inside a book large enough and hallowed enough to escape suspicion.

But every night I would awake to the sound of my mother whimpering in her sleep. Her mind at rest, her body said what it wanted to say in the waking hours that her will wouldn't allow. She sounded like the dying deer George and I had come upon in the woods as boys. She sounded like what she was—a wounded animal asking for release. In the beginning I'd go to her and gently wake her, thinking I was helping, but the look of confused fear on her face upon first realizing where she was eventually convinced me she was better off asleep, no matter how fitfully. Besides, the pain would always wake her long before dawn anyway, eager to inflict another long day's suffering.

And every day, the news from the war was better than the day before, the Confederate side collapsing, falling in on itself under the ceaseless pursuit of the North, retreating and retreating until, it was becoming clear, there simply wouldn't be anywhere left to run.

*

Right up until the moment the Reverend King opened the door to his study for our Wednesday afternoon tutorials, I always knew what recently unearthed scriptural contradiction, what theological inconsistency, what intellectual illogicality I was going to raise and rail against and inevitably discredit. But then he'd shake my hand and escort me inside and calmly entwine his fingers before setting his large hands down on his enormous oak desk, and all I'd want to do was please him. By the time I got home I'd be so mad at myself for not doing what I'd promised myself I was going to do, I had no choice but to be furious with him. Next time, I'd promise myself, next time . . . Until, of course, next time.

This time, "Yes," he said.

"So, basically, Luther's essential importance is that he challenged the authority of the papacy by holding that the

Bible is the only infallible source of religious authority and that all baptized Christians are a sort of spiritual priesthood. According to Luther, salvation was a free gift of God, received only by true repentance and faith in Jesus as the Messiah, a faith given by God and unmediated by the Church."

"Yes. That's correct."

Evidently, boredom was contagious, or at least the tiresome strain that was afflicting me. I still studied whatever the Reverend King instructed me to study—Church history, theology, anything that would assist me in excelling at Knox College—but only with my mind, which is fine for gathering knowledge but entirely inadequate if what you are after is the truth. I'd discovered the distinction from Plato, from reading *The Republic* while my mother moaned in pain in her sleep in the other room.

I stared out the window behind the Reverend King. It was nearly May; the sky stayed lit a little bit longer every day. I had nowhere to go, only home to sit with my mother, but I felt my body crave to be anywhere but where I was. I might have felt guilty if the Reverend King hadn't been examining his folded hands like he'd never noticed them before. There were ten minutes left in our hour, but I didn't have anything to say, ask, or comment upon. Maybe we'll break early today, I thought.

"The part I have most difficulty understanding is the timing of this . . . impudence."

I looked from the window to the Reverend King. "Pardon?" I said.

"Never mind your studies, which are, as you are aware, at such a pivotal stage of their progress. But with your own mother suffering so, did not the obvious selfishness of your actions give you pause to reflect?"

I studied his face for a clue to what he was talking about. All I saw was anger scarcely held in check by disgust.

"You're going to make me tell you what we both already know," he said. "I see. This is what the depths of your dishonesty have led us to." Before I had time to understand, never mind answer or even object, "Number one," the Reverend King said, using the thumb on his left hand to keep count, not a heartening sign, "you were seen in Chatham buying liquor, not once, not twice, but on three separate occasions. Number two, you were seen consuming this same liquor—I assume it was the same liquor, although if it was otherwise, at this point I wouldn't be surprised—in the woods of Buxton. Third, you kept a portion of this liquor in your poor mother's own house." He left his three fingers extended and accusatory for me to ponder.

I had honestly thought no one would ever discover what I'd been up to. I'd been so careful, expert even. I should have known better. The Reverend King's eyes were everywhere.

"I—"

Boom! The flat of the Reverend King's hand collided with the top of his desk—the desk, and my ears, the worse for it.

"I, I, I," he said. "Precisely. That's correct. You do not know the degree of truth of what you say."

I resolved not to try to speak again.

"Your selfishness is sinful to a degree I sincerely never expected you capable of. And your mother, your poor, poor mother, did you never consider the shame she would feel if she were to discover that her only son, whom she has such fine, pure hopes for, was a drunkard?"

"I'm not a drunkard."

Boom! Boom! This time loud enough I was afraid that one of the members of the domestic staff would hear.

"You have not seen as I have—first-hand, with my own eyes—how masters use alcohol as a tool to subdue the will and extinguish the spirits of otherwise hard-working, morally upright, good Christian men and women, who become little more than debased animals under the spell of the evil effects of hard liquor. Is this the condition you would willingly, voluntarily, inflict upon yourself?"

"I'm not a slave," I heard myself say.

For a moment—the slight narrowing of his eyes, the slow constricting of his fists—I was afraid that my face might take the place of his desk. He must have seen what I feared. He inhaled and exhaled equally deeply through his nose; carefully reintwined his fingers, locked them in place on the desktop.

"This can never happen again, David," he said. "Never. Your academic and professional future. The sanctity of the Settlement. The welfare of your mother. All of these things depend upon you pledging never to consume another drop of liquor."

I didn't think. I didn't have to. "I promise you," I said. "I swear." I felt tears dripping down both of my cheeks, but I didn't feel embarrassed, only cleansed of my sins.

The Reverend King looked surprised. "It's not me you have to swear before," he said. When I didn't say anything, "*God*, David," he said. "It's God you need to swear before."

I shook my head, understanding now.

"Let us pray," the Reverend King said. "I will pray with you, David."

And we did.

A tear slid over my upper lip while the Reverend King prayed for us both. I licked it away. It tasted hot and salty.

*

I stayed away from Chatham. I condemned my mind to my school work. I even began to voluntarily read the Bible again, snubbing the company of my growing outlaw library for a better class of ideas and stories intended to slake the spirit, not inflame it. If it had been any other season but spring, and if my mother hadn't decided to stop eating, I might have had a chance.

It helped that the very next Wednesday after the Reverend King had confronted me with my aberrant ways, he handed me a large grey envelope with my name on it, care of himself. In the upper left-hand corner was the crest of Knox College; inside, another set of forms to be filled out by me and mailed back to Toronto as part of my application package. I'd expected still-simmering anger or at least understandably lingering irritation, but all I received was forgiveness. *Practise what you preach* could never be mere words to me again.

I spent every evening at my mother's bedside, sometimes talking, sometimes reading Scripture to her, but mainly just being there. Even when she was first bedridden, she would have liked nothing more than hearing how the Reverend King was arranging the financial component of my education, or what sorts of things a minister-in-training studies, or even simply the details of what Mr. Rapier had written to say the student accommodations at Knox College were like.

"If my hands didn't trouble me so, I'd make you a nice new cover for your bed next year."

"I don't need a new cover, the one I've got now is fine."

"And a sweater, a nice warm sweater. It gets cold up there, you know."

"It gets cold down here too, and I haven't frozen yet."

"You make fun all you want, but you make sure to wear your hat all the time you outdoors once you're up there. You can't afford to be missing no time learning just because you go and forget your hat at home."

Even though using her chamber pot was the only physical exertion she was capable of—this for a woman for whom a twelve-hour day keeping Clayton House spotless and smoothly running was never anything but an honour—and she still moaned me awake most nights, talking about what

my life was going to be like or listening to what the neighbourhood women had to report about the ever-increasing
number of Union victories kept my mother's eyes clear and
her spirit strong.

Then, slowly, as slowly as the buds on the bare tree limbs
began their green bursting, my mother lost her appetite.

The doctor from Chatham, whom the Reverend King
had paid to come all the way out to Buxton, told us what was
coming, said there was nothing that could be done, that my
mother's body would sooner rather than later begin to simply
shut itself down until it eventually just stopped. But understanding what was happening didn't make watching it any easier. That look again. That same not-themselves-anymore look
in their eyes that every dying animal I'd ever seen had had.
And not in a dying bird's eyes or a dying deer's eyes, but in my
mother's eyes. My dying mother's eyes.

Even the little hot tea and honey she could be coaxed to
drink didn't seem worth it, didn't merit the pain that swal-
lowing brought. Every hour of every day now, it looked as if it
hurt her just to breathe. It *did* hurt her just to breathe.

Instead of trying to talk now, I read. She was too weak to
tell me what she wanted to hear, so I just started with Genesis
and kept reading. And read and read, until one night, near
dawn—I'd taken to reading through the night, to keep myself
company, if not her—I read:

> For that which befalleth the sons of men befalleth beasts;
> even one thing befalleth them; as the one dieth, so dieth the
> other; yea, they have all one breath; so that a man hath no
> preeminence above a beast; for all is vanity.

I set down the bible on the side table beside a cold, untouched cup of tea. I turned down the lamp until the room
was dark.

"Jesus," my mother moaned.

I took her hand, as tenderly as I could, but it didn't matter. Her hand spasmed; she screamed; but she didn't wake.

"Oh, Jesus," she yelled. "Help me."

I let go of her hand and got down on my knees. I put my elbows on the bed and prayed for the pain to stop, for God to please stop my mother's pain. I told Him He'd never had a more faithful servant and that she deserved to be at peace.

With the warmer weather, all of the windows were open, even at night. The cruel caress of drape-fluttering, soft spring breezes. The inconsiderate taunting of busy, twittering sparrows. The obscene freshness of another perfect spring morning. All while I prayed to God to please let my mother die.

"Oh, Jesus," she said.

With first light, I got up from my knees. I sat back down and waited for the initial shift of Buxton women to arrive.

"Oh, Jesus," my mother said.

She wasn't speaking to me, but I was the one who was listening.

*

"Just push it in, like this, see? Push it in all the way until you get right to the end. And then pull it all the way back out. That's all there is to it."

"Just one?" I said.

The cigarette stuck in the corner of the man's mouth rose with his bisected grin. "Sure, just one. You don't want to overdose, do you?"

"Of course not," I said, taking far too much umbrage for someone purchasing morphine in the dirty backroom of a Chatham saloon. "But how many shots would someone have to take to have an overdose? Just to be sure I don't, I mean."

The man placed the loaded hypodermic needle in the cigar box with the four others I'd already paid for. "Just do like I said: one shot, nice and clean, throw out the needle as soon as you're done. Nobody needs more than one shot."

No doubt. I'd done a little research. The German pharmacist who'd first isolated pure morphine from opium named it *morphium*, after Morpheus, the Greek god of dreams.

The man walked me to the back door and clicked open the padlock with the key dangling from a brown shoelace tied to his belt. "You need more after these are gone, you come and see me, okay?"

"Sure."

The man stuck his head out the door like he was looking to see if it was raining; didn't see anything or anyone coming, moved aside to let me leave.

Before he could shut the door, "If someone did overdose," I said, "they wouldn't feel anything, would they? Any pain, I mean."

The man grinned again, the cigarette on his lip nearly vertical this time. "If they felt anything, they'd feel like they'd gone straight to heaven."

I untied George's father's horse. I headed back to Buxton, back home.

*

It was easy. Killing my mother was easy. I kissed her brow and simply let the morphine give her what nothing else could. I allowed the women who had cared for her so well while she was ill to look after her just a little while longer now that she was dead. George came to the house directly from work as soon as he heard the news, but I convinced him to go back to the factory, that I would need his support more tomorrow, at the funeral. I carried the empty needles in a satchel to Deer Pond and buried them behind the big hill. From its summit I watched the sun go down and the stars come out and the pond turn black. When I got home, one of the women told me that the Reverend King wished to see me, no matter how late I returned.

He met me at the door of Clayton House. All the members of the house staff, each of whom my mother had personally selected and supervised, were tending to her body and the preparations for tomorrow. Still, it was odd to have the Reverend King himself answer his own door. He'd been to our house earlier in the evening to offer his condolences, so I assumed he wanted to discuss the eulogy. Whatever he wanted to say was fine with me. I'd already said my goodbye.

When he didn't accept my hand to shake, I knew something was wrong. When he wordlessly led me to his study, I couldn't help but suspect the worst. But even God's eyes can't see what's not there. Or hardly there. Only three of the tiniest, virtually imperceptible pinpricks on the back of my mother's right bicep even hinted at how she'd died. By the time we were seated across his desk from one another, though, I'd reconciled myself to my naïveté. That it was impossible that he knew didn't matter. He'd always known everything else, so of course he knew about this. Surprisingly, I didn't feel scared or even nervous, only curious, as if what was taking place were happening to someone else.

"I . . ." The Reverend King paused, made a triangle of his hands, balanced his chin gingerly on top. He appeared to be reconsidering what he was about to say. He refolded his fingers and rested them back on top of the desk. "I have hesitated whether or not to allow you an opportunity to explain your actions. Because we both know that what you have done is incontestably, inexcusably wrong. Even now—even in your present, undeniably debauched state—I know that you know, David, that which is right and that which is wrong. Even if you have failed to act upon this knowledge."

I wasn't sure what option he had, in fact, ultimately decided upon, but it didn't matter. "The pain was too much," I said. "I couldn't allow it to go any further. I couldn't." There wasn't any guilt attached to my confession. If I hadn't known before that I was right to do what I had, I did now.

The Reverend King silently nodded, although whether in even partial understanding I couldn't tell. It didn't matter. Either way, I knew he was going to turn me over to the Chatham police, probably as soon as the funeral was over.

"And do you hold that this pain justifies your act of weakness?" he said.

"Weakness?" I said, tasting the word's worth in my mouth. "What I did wasn't weak."

"What would you call such an act, then?"

"I don't know." I thought about it for a moment. "Merciful," I said.

The Reverend King lowered his eyes. Without looking up, "I don't believe you mean that," he said.

"I do. I do mean that." I'd never meant anything more.

He raised his eyes and stared hard into mine, searching to see if I was telling the truth. Deciding that I was, "Then you don't understand what the word means."

"I think I do. I think I understand it as well as anyone possibly can."

The Reverend King's eyes were still on mine, but he wasn't looking for anything anymore, he'd seen and heard all he needed to. "I can forgive you your ignorance, but not your arrogance. You may stay on for the funeral tomorrow, of course, but I'll ask you to take your leave of Buxton within the week. The Settlement of Elgin will buy back your mother's house at the price she originally paid, plus interest, and the money will be forwarded to you in full. Anything you don't wish to take with you will be distributed among those wanting something to remember your mother by."

That I'd just discovered I was soon to be homeless wasn't what was on my mind. "You're not going to tell the police?" I said.

"Out of respect for your mother, and because I still hold out hope that you will one day conquer your drug lust and be the man I know you can be, I see no reason for your future to be clouded by a criminal record. Of course, you understand that there is no question of your finding support for your education, financial or otherwise, from these quarters. If, however, in, say, a year's time, you can convincingly demonstrate that you have freed yourself from the clutches of this sickness that has claimed your will and—"

I laughed.

The lack of sleep; my mother's death; the future behind bars I'd been forced to envision for myself: for whatever reason—I laughed. Which only further confirmed the Reverend King's belief that I was a hopeless morphine addict. In spite of which, "I'm not a drug fiend," I said.

The Reverend King straightened in his chair, linked his fingers at desk level again. "I am not going to refute your lies, David. You were seen purchasing morphine in Chatham. You were seen returning with morphine to Buxton."

"I bought it, yes, but—"

"But what? But you did not plan to use it? But it was for someone else, perhaps? For the sake of your mother's soul and the merciful Lord who rescued her from her long, long suffering, stop your lying, David. Can't you see what this filth has done to you, how it has rotted away your very mind and conscience?"

"You're wrong."

"For the love of Christ, David, stop your lying."

"You're wrong," I said. He was wrong. The Reverend King was wrong.

*

My mother was buried in the cemetery in Buxton the same day that Lee surrendered to Grant. I mourned the one and celebrated the other by riding into Chatham and getting too drunk to ride back. There wasn't any point in pretending to be pious anymore anyway. If I was honest, I'd be guilty of murder. If I lied, I'd be excommunicated from Buxton and blocked from going to university.

The Reverend King was fond of quoting, *You shall know the truth, and the truth shall set you free.*

That was one more thing he was wrong about.

*

As promised, the Elgin Association paid me in cash for my mother's house and decided to allow me two weeks to vacate, but I didn't need them, put what little I wanted to keep of my mother's belongings in storage at George's house and took a room at the Griffin House in Chatham, a new hotel where Negroes were welcome. George's father returned to Mississippi almost as soon as the armistice was announced, so George had plenty of extra room. Now that the war was over, the exodus immediately commenced the other way, north to south, back to familiar seasons and forgone friends and family members. At the first light of the false dawn that was Reconstruction, even free-born, Elgin-educated Negroes were abandoning Buxton, hurrying to take up positions as much-needed teachers, ministers, doctors, and even politicians in the reshuffled Southern states.

Mr. Rapier, one of the Reverend King's first six graduates, returned to Alabama after the war and became its first
coloured congressman. He and I used to have contests over
who could recite from memory more lines from *The Aeneid*.
Because I won more often than I lost, he didn't tell the Reverend King when, later, I nagged him into bringing me
back a copy of Lucretius's *On the Nature of the Universe* from
Toronto, where he was attending Knox College, where everyone knew that all of the smartest boys from Buxton went on
to study. Almost all of the smartest boys.

Making his steady rise to the top of the pile at the potash
factory, George had decided to stay behind in Buxton. George
was like me: might have been born in the South but became
himself in the North, a field of white forever a field of snow-
flakes, not cotton balls. All of Buxton turned out for my
mother's funeral, but George's words were the only ones I
heard.

A tide of warm hands and moist cheeks reminded me that
my mother was going to a better place, that no one who knew
her would ever forget her, that Jesus had called her home.
The Reverend King shook my hand and told me my mother
was a good woman. Back at Clayton House, where the reception was held, George waited until all the others had paid
their respects and were busy filling their plates with the cold
buffet lunch that the women of Elgin had prepared.

"You should eat something," he said.

"If I was hungry, I would."

In fact, in spite of myself, I was. I'd discovered that nothing cut through a whiskey hangover like a cold roast beef
sandwich dressed with plenty of horseradish, but at the moment, doing what was good for me seemed wrong. The throb
in my temples and the churn in my stomach, on the other
hand, felt absolutely right. George looked at the loaded-down

plate in his hand like a thief caught with his fingers in the till.

"It should get eaten, though," I said. "A lot of people went to a lot of trouble putting it all together."

George nodded, pushed around his ham with his fork. I watched Mr. Freeman bending over to hear better what Mrs. Hampton, the Kings' nearest neighbour, was saying to him from her chair. Mrs. Hampton had been "old lady Hampton" since we were boys. Now we were men, and she was still old lady Hampton.

"When is your father leaving?" I said.

"Soon. As soon as he hears from his people down there that they're ready for him."

"If they're his people, they're your people too, aren't they?"

George took a bite of his ham. "I suppose."

Now that the service was over and the body was in the ground and everyone was together inside eating and chatting, if one hadn't known what had been going on that morning, the spirited conversations taking place throughout Clayton House might have seemed like a communal lunch intended to celebrate the imminent end of the war. And if more people were talking about the death of slavery than that of my mother, who could blame them? The Confederacy's demise meant, finally, freedom for all our people. My mother's death didn't mean anything.

"Are you going to stay on in your mother's house?" George said.

He knew I wasn't. I knew he knew. I told him no anyway, that I'd already sold it back to the Settlement. The Reverend King had assured me that my expulsion was no one's concern but his, mine, and God's, and that as far as the villagers knew I was simply making a fresh start after my mother's death. George knew better. Even without anyone telling him what had happened, he knew better.

"Where are you going to go?" he said. He used his fork to drag his green beans from one side of his plate to the other.

"I don't know."

He divided his beans into two, then three, then four separate piles. "I suppose you can go anywhere you want now. Do anything you want."

It took me a moment to understand what he meant. "I'm free now," I said.

George stabbed a green bean and stuck it in his mouth. "We're all free now."

I liked living in Chatham.

I liked the crowded shops and the congested streets in the daytime. I liked the loud saloons at night. I liked waiting out a hangover sitting in the shade on the bank of the Thames watching the steamboats glide by in the afternoon. I liked it that no one knew who I was and that I wasn't expected to know who anyone else was. I even liked the polite insolence that frequently met my questions, or sometimes just my face. Partly, I knew, the result of having a black face, but partly also the result simply of mixing among strangers, of living in a city whose citizens weren't united by a proud historical pedigree or a higher moral purpose, of being just one of many thousands of people whose primary societal obligation was to try to not bother anyone else too much.

My first night at Griffin House, once I'd unpacked my clothes and my books, I decided to go for a walk. The porter, a Negro from Detroit not much older than me, told me the name and address of a saloon I should visit if I liked good whiskey and pretty women. After walking for over an hour in the after-dinner dusk, not minding terribly that I wasn't sure where I was or where I was going, I stopped in front of a house where an old white man in a rocking chair was sitting on his porch. It wasn't near being warm yet, but people were beginning to reappear, slowly recovering from winter's long assault.

"Excuse me," I said. "I'm looking for Eugenie Street."

The man didn't bother to stop rocking. "It's a free country," he said.

I kept going, couldn't help laughing. That sonofabitch, you know, he wasn't wrong.

*

I wasn't particular about how I kept myself in cheap whiskey and expensive mail-order books. Not at first, anyway. I made bricks at the James Cornhill Brick Yards, flour at the Kent Mills, barrels and casks at the Chatham Pump, Stave and Barrel Factory, candies and biscuits at Chatham Confectionery Works. The only thing I wouldn't do was anything agricultural, not so much a reasoned decision as a spiritual injunction. No matter that no omnipotent overseer reigned over the fields anymore, the picking of crops was somebody else's job as of the day the South surrendered, my people having spent more than their fair share of time sowing the soil for someone else's reaping. The closest I came to bringing in a harvest was the six months I worked at the Thames Cigar Company. The Turko-Russian War was every newspaper's number one news story, and the owner of TCC decided to capitalize on the public's interest by renaming several of his products after the war's most famous figures. I helped manufacture the Czar, the Sultan, the Ali, the Suliman, and the Iron King. "Be a King, Smoke an Iron King," the advertisement in the *Chatham Planet* said. There must have been a lot of men who secretly imagined they were kings—the Iron King was our most popular brand by far.

Most factories wouldn't hire Negroes, but because I could spell and count and compose a proper telegram to suppliers,

I generally worked at white-owned businesses. If they'd had their preference, of course, a white man would have been in my place, but because few white men who could spell and count and compose a proper telegram wanted a filthy, exhausting, tedious factory job, an exception could be made in my case. Once I'd demonstrated my usefulness, it wasn't unusual for the man who'd hired me to inform me, usually come payday, that he was pleased I'd managed to fit in as well as I had. Handing me my pay packet, "You're a credit to your people, David, a real example of what they can accomplish if they put their minds to it. I'm just glad I was able to offer you a helping hand when I did." I'd take the money and remind myself that this fucking fool had never read Plato's dialogues or even a single aphorism of Lichtenberg's and that I was the superior, not to mention happier, human being because I had. You find your worldly compensations where you can, and self-righteous condescension is in no way the least satisfying.

I could have gotten a job at a Negro-owned business. There were restaurants, grocery stores, barbershops, even shoe stores that sold exclusively to Chatham's darker-skinned citizens. But white-run businesses were bigger and paid better. And to be honest, working alongside whites turned out to be easier than the time I spent at the all-Negro mills and warehouses on the Boyd Block, where the bulk of the coloured businesses were located. At worst, whites would ignore you, leave you alone with your lunch, never call you by your name, only by "Hey." Eventually, though, in tiring time, just one more overworked, underpaid *Us*. *Us* as in *Us* and *Them*. No matter where you ended up working or whom you ended up working with and for, always *Us* and *Them*.

Negroes didn't trust me. A white man might ignore you, might not even acknowledge you as a fellow man, but even if I didn't want allies when I worked among my own kind, only to do my job and collect my pay, I didn't want to be mistaken for a spy. Yet every time I preferred a book as a lunchtime companion, every time I didn't want to wager that week's pay at a Friday night dice game, every time I said "isn't" instead of "ain't," "you" instead of "youse," my skin turned another degree paler. I was invisible to the white man, I was a white man to the coloured man. I chose to be a ghost instead of a devil.

I did my job and made my pay and went my own way. When a better-paying job became available, I took it. When my rooming-house room became too small for my growing library, I moved. Every night, I read myself to sleep, except for Saturday night, when I got drunk at a saloon and let whiskey and a strange woman put me to sleep in a bed not my own. My mother was dead, I might as well have been dead to everyone in Buxton, and if I died in my room, the only reason anyone would care would be because of the smell my corpse made.

One Saturday night, instead of going to a whore after the saloons closed, I went to a man on Lacroix Street who gave tattoos, mostly to sailors stopping off in Chatham during their travels down the Thames.

"What do you want it to say?" the man said, dabbing alcohol along my forearm, preparing my flesh for his instrument.

For the past several weeks I'd been reading *Paradise Lost* when I wasn't selling my time to the biscuit factory, surprised but pleased to learn that Satan had most of the best lines. Alone late one night in my small, under-heated rooming-house room—motherless, friendless, my back still sore from a long day's heavy lifting—*Better to reign in hell than serve in heaven*, I read.

"*Non Serviam,*" I said.

The man stopped rubbing, looked at me. "You better write it down."

When he was done, there were ten raised letters stencilled across my right forearm, a long scar of language that reminded me of George's father's scars. Except that my scar was self-inflicted. And my scar meant that I was free.

*

The day begins with Loretta shaking me awake. The day begins in the middle of the night, sunlight still hours until showtime.

"You must stop this," she says. She's leaning back on both elbows, squinting down at me in deference to the table-side lamp she's lit.

I concede a second opened eyelid. "What is *this*?" I say.

"You know what you do."

"What—snore?"

"Hah. I wish it was snore."

I close both eyes with the intention of deciphering what she means, but immediately drift back to . . .

The day begins with Loretta shaking me awake, this time hard enough to qualify as a soft punch, or at least a serious shove. I join her on my elbows to prove I'm really alert and concentrating.

"Okay," I say, "enough. What do you want me to stop?"

She takes an angry moment to accept that I really am oblivious to what she's so obviously aware of. "Bathroom sounds. In the bed. This is not the place."

I take my own moment—to translate "bathroom sounds in the bed" into English—and, after doing the alphabetical arithmetic, am more surprised than chastened. It's Loretta, after all, who has to be occasionally reminded to close the bathroom door behind her. It's Loretta, not me, who needs to be asked to please cut her toenails when she's sure she's alone. Besides,

"How can I stop something if I don't know I'm doing it?" I say.

"You do not know." It's an accusation, not a question.

"I'm asleep, how would I know?"

"I do not know," she says, putting out the lamp and flipping over her pillow, punching it in the middle—once, hard—before laying her head down, facing away from me. "But this is unacceptable."

Unacceptable, maybe, I think, staying flat on my back, the most flatulence-frustrating position possible, but inevitable. I've grown tired of spending the majority of my time the last two days in the bathroom waging a silent contest with my taciturn bowels, but I get up from the bed and go anyway. Henry, nose tucked deep into his curled front legs at bed's end, looks up long enough to see me slip into my slippers then disappears back beneath his limbs. Henry doesn't get constipated. It's not the first time I've been envious of a dog.

I lock the bathroom door and light the lamp on the wall and turn the wick until I get an adequate reading light. I used to keep copies of the *Fortnightly* and the *Quarterly* in here; now it's Gibbon's *The Decline and Fall of the Roman Empire*. The object is not to notice what you're doing, to force your bowels to say what you want them to say by pretending not to care if they stay quiet forever. Eight pages of how "The Doctrine of Future Life contributed to The Rise of Christianity" later, my bowels still aren't talking to me. Arrogant organs. They say that Lincoln suffered from lifelong constipation, that he required a powerful purgative delivered to the White House once every week. They also say that Lincoln suffered from extreme melancholy. I'm not a doctor, but . . .

Since I'm already here and have nothing else to do, I decide to shave—the top as well as the front of my head old habit now—then manage to get dressed without waking Loretta. Henry seems puzzled by the early hour but jumps out of bed and follows me downstairs nonetheless, liking his odds of being served an early breakfast. I first light the fire in the library and then the stove; put the kettle on for me and get Henry's food out of the cold room. The rice and carrots and corn and peas and squash are already mixed up, but I give them a fresh churn anyway, ladle out half a bowlful.

Except for a single serving of porridge every morning, the vegetables and rice we both eat is the only cooking I do, Loretta the sole semi-member of the household who uses the stove for more than the kettle and another fire to help keep the house warm. Cooking is for cooks. I'm not anyone's servant, not even my own. I buy my bread from the baker, my milk from the milkman, my vegetables from the vegetable seller. Let someone else till the soil and serve the food this lifetime.

I pass the hours of darkness into dawn in the library, riding along Gibbon's looping Latinate sentences, trying to hold on while following the fortune of his hero, human reason, as it falls, as it will always fall, before the usual list of ancient enemies. Meyers won't be opening his drugstore door for another hour, but I could use a longer than usual walk this morning. My blocked bowels could use a longer than usual walk this morning. Henry is always game for extra walking, the more the better, even if his bowels never need any extra encouragement. No wonder people believe that animals don't have souls. Small compensation for not being born perfect.

It's not even nine o'clock in the morning and there's an old man voluntarily freezing just for the opportunity to be mesmerized by the sights and sounds of the man who lives a quarter-mile over from me milking his cow for his family's morning milk. Old men who can't work anymore like to stand around and watch young men who can. Their entire adult lives are one long moan about how they *Gotta go to work*, about how *Work is killing me*, about how they can't wait for the day to be over so they can finally get home from work. Then, the day after their last day on the job, they're poking around the house looking for something to fix, or else are roaming the neighbourhood in search of someone lucky enough to be patching a hole in the roof or digging a new well. Servitude is habit forming, the same as whiskey and tobacco. Fresh air and plenty of exercise can maim a man too.

My anger keeps me warm and occupied all the way downtown. Meyers is just turning around his CLOSED sign to the OPEN side when I leave Henry beside the lamppost out front. There's a new display in the front window he's obviously put a lot of time and consideration into. Such a variety of shiny bottles affixed with such healthy names and happy promises (Dr. Pierce's Golden Medical Discovery, Dr. Dalzell's Nasal Douche, Kickapoo Indian Sagwa, Dr. Hercules Sanche's Oxydonor, Pink Pills for Pale People, Thayer's Slippery Elm Lozenges, Galvanic Love Powder, The Invalid's Friend and Hope, Princess Lotus Blossom's Vital Sparks), it's almost a shame not to be sick.

Meyers is always glad to see me come through his door, happy for the opportunity to impersonate a respected member of Chatham's professional class and not be just one more King Street shopkeeper with a personality so impossibly grating he's reduced to doing his socializing at an illegal, underground saloon owned and operated by a former slave. Meyers still sells simples and chemicals, which he uses to compound and dispense medicine, still spreads his own plasters, and duly prepares pills, powders, tinctures, ointments, syrups, conserves, medicated waters, and even perfumes. But since the big American companies have started offering up cheap patent medicines that pharmacists previously had to make by hand, he's had to pick up the sales slack, has started to stock confectioneries, spices, tobacco, paint, even groceries and liquor. Poor Meyers has even had to install a soda fountain.

Self-delusion is man's greatest gift, but it's difficult to success-fully masquerade as a dignified man of medicine when just a fraction of your working day is given over to exhibiting your vast knowledge of artificial flavours and carbonated water to every snotty six-year-old armed with a nickel.

Meyers doesn't know what I'm here for and I'm in no hurry to enlighten him. Asking for constipation medicine is simply embarrassing. It's not even the pills themselves or what they're made for that are the problem. It's only that, I know Meyers knows I shit—well, ordinarily—but I don't like the idea of needing him in order to do it.

"And how is Mr. King today?"

"Just fine."

"Jolly good."

I nod in appreciation of my surfeit of goodness and fine-ness. Now if only I could crap.

Meyers nods right along with me, last man nodding wins.

"I wonder," I say, "if you have anything for . . . I mean to say, lately, I haven't been . . ." I discover I'm pointing at my-self, clearly indicating that there's something definitely wrong with either my heart, my lungs, my stomach, or perhaps my genitals.

Meyers nods again, but this time just once, and with solemn purpose, as if he actually knows what ails me and has just the thing to cure me of it. Before I can tell him to forget it, not to bother, he's left me alone for his backroom. I con-sider simply leaving, but instead walk to the door to check on Henry. He sees me see him and wags. I smile back.

"Here we are," Meyers says, holding up a small brown bottle. "Just take one of these a day until you're feeling more yourself."

I want to say, *Meyers, you fool, you don't even know what's wrong with me, how can you possibly prescribe something for me?* but because that would entail having to tell him what actually is wrong, I just take the bottle and drop it in my coat pocket without so much as glancing at it. Meyers adds the cost to my tab in his accounts book.

"Quite a remarkable little pill, actually," he says. "Called Blue Mass. The key ingredient is mercury—that's what gives it its real acting power. The late President Lincoln was a devoted user, I understand. Can't ask for a stronger recommendation than that, can one?"

I don't know what to say.

"Thank you," I say.

"Why, you're most welcome, Mr. King."

*

I couldn't prove it, but when I received a letter from Anderson Abbott—Dr. Anderson Abbott—inviting me to come and visit him at his new home soon after he moved back to Chatham, the year after the war ended, I knew that the Reverend King was behind it. I'd met Dr. Abbott only twice, when he'd returned to Elgin for short visits during his time studying in Toronto, but I'd only been a boy, little chance he would have remembered me, or remembered me well enough to want to see me again ten years later. But I pressed my suit and shined my shoes and showed up on the appointed day anyway. If the Reverend King believed he could accomplish with his proxy what he hadn't been able to do in person—get me to admit I was a chronically lying, spiritually lost drug addict— it would be a pleasure to have his appointed messenger deliver him the news that I was a man of unassailable integrity and conviction, even if what I was convinced of wasn't entirely clear.

The Reverend King was clever, I'd grant him that; he knew whom to have check up on me. Dr. Abbott was who I was supposed to have been if everything had gone according to plan, God's and otherwise. Although his father had been a free-born Negro, the family had fled Alabama when the Mobile city council passed a law requiring all free Blacks to post a bond signed by two white men guaranteeing their good behaviour and to wear badges proving they'd been bonded. The family eventually immigrated to Toronto, where Dr. Abbott was born, but, wanting his son to have the best education available, Mr. Abbott sent him away to study at the already renowned Buxton school, where he was among the Reverend King's first six graduates. From there to Knox College, of course, but, instead of going on to study theology, matriculating in medicine at the age of twenty-three at the University of Toronto, becoming Canada's first native-born Negro doctor. Soon after enlisting in the Union army as a surgeon, he was appointed overseer of two different Washington hospitals for the duration of the war. The Reverend King would keep the entire Settlement informed of each graduate's achievements and honours, but made a special point of ensuring that I was personally aware of every step, no matter how small, along the way of Dr. Abbott's exemplary professional ascension.

"You put me in mind of Dr. Abbott when he was a young man," he'd said.

It didn't matter how, it was an honour just to be compared, but, "In what way?" I said.

The Reverend King looked at me for a moment. We were in his office, going over that week's supplementary reading assignment. "Tenacity," he finally answered.

I was flattered, but confused. The Reverend King could tell.

"When confronted with a problem or a task, no matter how difficult, neither of you will repine."

I was still flattered, but just as confused, so simply nodded and put my head back down to the page. There was work to do.

The letter said that Dr. Abbott lived on Maple Street, so I didn't have far to walk from my rooming house. Even though I was standing out front and had double-checked the address twice, I still wasn't convinced I had the right house. It didn't make sense somehow that someone that I knew—someone *coloured* that I knew—could live somewhere this large or this nice.

There were green, cooling vines crawling up all three brick storeys and an enormous maple tree shading the majority of the front lawn. The windows on the upper floors were bare and mirrored back the bright July sunshine, each windowpane its own four-square sun. I turned the brass bell handle and Dr. Abbott himself opened the door.

"David. Please, come in."

We shook hands inside.

Paintings hung from every wall, landscapes and religious scenes and portraits of people Dr. Abbott must have known. There was a mahogany side table just inside the door supporting a vase of freshly cut flowers, from his own garden no doubt. A cylinder-top writing table and bookcase appeared more ornamental than operational.

"Let's go into my office," Dr. Abbott said, and I followed him to the rear of the house.

Men and things sometimes shrink, seem disappointingly reduced in size or status once one has grown up. Not Dr. Abbott. He was still taller than me and still walked with perfect posture and an unhurried step and still looked like, if he hadn't decided to use his long fingers and dinner-plate-sized hands to heal the sick, he could have easily survived as an executioner without having to resort to anything so crude as a noose.

"Please, David, sit down."

Unbelievable. The floor-to-ceiling bookshelves bursting with many of the same titles; the placement of the desk directly in front of the window; the dual reading chairs stationed at the exact same angles on either side of the fireplace—it was as if he'd imported the Reverend King's office directly from Buxton to Chatham. The only thing substantially different was significant, however: an anomalously ornate carved gilt table with a marble top supporting a decanter full of what appeared to be whiskey alongside an ice bucket and several glasses. Most Elgin residents remained lifelong teetotallers.

He must have seen me staring. "Would you care for a drink?" Dr. Abbott said.

The Reverend King had to have told him about my expulsion from the Settlement, so I knew he'd expect me to feel embarrassed and refuse his offer.

"I would, thank you, yes," I said. Even though I didn't. Even though whiskey in the afternoon seemed as inappropriate to me as spare ribs in the morning.

"I was hoping you'd say yes," Dr. Abbott said, pouring our drinks. "I usually see patients in the afternoon, but I've cleared my schedule so we can talk, and I don't like to drink alone."

Handing me my whiskey, he saw that I'd spotted another decorative deviation, a plaid shawl laid under glass like a museum piece. He sat down in the chair opposite mine by the unlit fire. The leather embroidery of his seat made a soft hissing sound.

"Mrs. Lincoln gave that to me," he said, sipping his drink. He said it without emphasis, as if he were describing a medical fact.

Since he'd brought it up, I felt permitted to take another, longer look. "Not Mrs. *Abraham* Lincoln," I said.

Dr. Abbott smiled. "Yes, that Mrs. Lincoln."

We sipped our drinks. Wherever he got his whiskey, it wasn't from any saloon in Chatham, at least not any I'd visited in the last year. It tasted like it existed for more than just getting drunk.

"It's the shawl President Lincoln wore on his way to the first inauguration. It was part of the disguise he wore on that occasion to help escape assassination." This last word hung in the air between us like a bad odour. We both drank to pretend it wasn't there.

"You must have been important," I said. "Your job, I mean. You must have done important work during the war."

"No more than any other man who was willing to die for our cause. And those who did."

My face flooded furious, and it had nothing to do with the whiskey in my belly. "I wanted to fight, but the Reverend King wouldn't let me," I said. Instead of seeming defiant, I only managed to sound petulant, like I was still complaining about how someone had taken my favourite ball away from me when I was eight years old.

Dr. Abbott nodded into his drink, but I couldn't tell if he believed me or not. "I seem to recall that the last time the Reverend King wrote to me during the war mentioning your progress, he said you were preparing for entrance into Knox College."

"Yes," I said.

"But you didn't go."

"No."

"Why?"

Between work, whiskey, and generally growing used to doing whatever I wanted, I'd done a good job during my first year in Chatham of forgetting I'd ever lived anywhere else or had any other ambition. I swallowed what was left in my glass. "May I have another, please?"

"Of course."

I splashed more whiskey into my glass like I'd seen bartenders do on Saturday night when things would get so busy there wasn't time to measure out an even shot. "I didn't go because the Reverend King wouldn't let me."

"I'm sorry, David. Are we still talking about the war?"

I sat back down with my drink. "Of course not. I'm talking about Knox College. The Reverend King withdrew his support of me. His promised support."

"Why would he do that?"

"Dr. Abbott, please don't condescend to me."

"I beg your pardon?"

"I know that you know what happened between the Reverend King and me. At least, what he believes happened."

"David, I can assure you, I don't."

"Then why did you invite me here today?"

Dr. Abbott looked at me as if I were simple. "Because I wanted to know why you didn't continue your education. The Reverend King always emphasized what high hopes he had for you."

"Please, Dr. Abbott, I asked you to please not—"

Dr. Abbott held up his hand. I stopped talking. "When I came to Chatham to set up my practice and I eventually paid the Reverend King a visit, he said nothing of you."

"Nothing."

"Nothing. In fact, I thought it peculiar—as, as I've said already, he was very proud of you and rarely failed to mention this. So I finally asked him about you—that I expected you were in Toronto by now, and I wondered how you were getting along—and that's when he told me you had been living in Chatham. And when I asked him what you were doing, he said he did not know. And then, when I asked him why you weren't attending the university as had been planned, he said I would have to ask you and that he did not wish to speak of the matter any further."

He had to be telling the truth. I could hear the Reverend King saying the words he was only repeating. I couldn't stop hearing them.

"I suppose I don't wish to speak of it any longer either."

Dr. Abbott looked at me over his glass like he was giving me an opportunity to change my mind. I didn't.

"Thank you for the drink," I said, standing up. Dr. Abbott did the same. "I have to be going."

Dr. Abbott walked me out of his office the way the Reverend King used to do. I hadn't noticed his medical degree on the wall on the way in. There were also framed documents verifying his status as president of the Chatham Literacy and Debating Society and president of the Chatham Medical Society.

I stopped at the door. "I hope you don't think I was being rude. When I said I didn't wish to talk about what we were talking about."

"I respect a man's reasons for speaking or not speaking."

"It's only that . . . things aren't always as simple as they sometimes should be."

"They rarely are," Dr. Abbott said, smiling, straightening his medical degree—lifting, then dropping, then lifting again its bottom left corner with a careful forefinger. "When I offered my services as a surgeon to the Union army, I was called to Washington for examination. I believed it was merely a formality, as I had been told it had been for the other surgeons who'd already been accepted for service. Much later, a member of the examining board who became a friend of mine told me that the Surgeon General had pledged never to allow any Negro the title of surgeon in his army as long as he was entrusted with that position. According to my friend, there was also a Dr. Cronyn, the president of the examining board, who was asked by the irate Surgeon General: 'I say, Cronyn, how did you come to let that nigger pass?' And Dr.

Cronyn replied: 'The fact is, General, that nigger knew more than I did. I could not help myself.'"

*

The sky is beginning to crumble crimson, so I know it's time to go to work. Except for the first Saturday of every other month that George comes to visit, I haven't seen the sun set in nearly ten years. I'm not complaining; my early Chatham years, my factory years, were a workday blur of surly early mornings. But such a favourable day today for making some significant reading headway—the snow falling lazily outside, the fire crackling busily in here, the fading late afternoon sunlight—my body just doesn't want to do what my brain keeps telling it to, to get up and put my coat and hat on and walk through the snow to Sophia's. So pleasant the scene, in fact, it seems almost enough to sit here with a volume, any volume, on my knee and spend the evening simply admiring the walls of books that surround me.

I'm not vain about much, but there's no better private library in Chatham than mine. Which is akin, I realize, to claiming credit for being the most moral man in Hades, but someone has to be number one, and I'm him. Thanks, in great part, to Mr. Richard A. Stevens, Esq.

When I had this house built—I'd bought the land first, with the initial trickle of money I'd accumulated after opening Sophia's—the bookshelves were designed for more than just a few books: I wanted a library large enough to double as a personal challenge. Qualitatively I was fine, owned maybe two hundred good editions in total, each volume individually purchased with the understanding that you eat what's in front of you and don't ask for more until your plate has been scraped and scoured clean. But good intentions rarely make it past the age of forty. Halfway to the tomb, it doesn't matter so much anymore that you're not likely to get though all eight volumes of *The Decline and Fall of the Roman Empire* or that Boswell's *Life of Johnson*'s two thousand pages are probably a thousand more than you're ever going to read. Life's sundial suddenly way past noon, time's ticking shadow makes it absolutely essential to acquire every book that's ever been written that's worth reading, if not to actually read, then at least to call one's own. I promised myself on my fortieth birthday that I would not die without a copy of Plutarch's *Lives of the Poets* left among my worldly possessions. When the time came for indifferent strangers to haul my lifeless body out the back door of my home, I wanted it made perfectly clear that I was a man who had possessed the best that has been thought and said.

So when Thompson mentioned one night at Sophia's that one of his firm's clients in London was having them administer an estate sale on her behalf that included the entirety of her late husband's substantial library, there was only one thing I needed to know.

"Was the husband a minister?"

"A professor. Of philology, I believe."

"I'll take it."

"I beg your pardon?"

"I want to buy the library."

"But you haven't seen it. It's customary in the occasion of estate sales for—"

"Make this happen for me, Thompson. This is something I need you to do."

"Yes, but David—"

"Make it happen, Thompson."

Thompson's tab wasn't then the leviathan it is now, but was well on its way. Any smart businessman is happy to have his clients owe him money. Why else would banks be in the business of handing out loans? Jesus didn't put his sandal to the backsides of the moneylenders because he couldn't negotiate a competitive interest rate.

Thompson did what needed to be done, and I got a thousand books with the nameplate *Ex Libris Richard A. Stevens, Esq.* embossed inside the front cover of each. After a week of sorting and separating—no one but a professor of philology needs to own more than a single volume of philology—I was left with nearly eight hundred first-rate books, heavy on the Greeks, strong in all the major Germans (most in the original, but some in translation), and with a surprising emphasis on nineteenth-century English verse. If it hadn't been for Mr. Richard A. Stevens, Esq., introducing us, for example, I might never have made the acquaintance of Keats and Shelley. It's still one of the nicest things anyone has ever done for me.

Sometimes, though, I worry I'm not living up to my half of the relationship, that I'm letting my old friend Mr. Stevens down. So, regardless of whatever books I happen to be spending time with—at the moment, Carlyle's *Sartor Resartus* interspersed with Huxley's *Evidence of Man's Place in Nature*: full-moon, full-throated raving magic interspersed with hard and dry daybreak common sense—I always keep an attentive eye, literally, on my library shelves, shelves squirming with books bought with good money and better intentions but many of which haven't been picked up since the honeymoon day of their purchase—and sulking, I know, feeling abandoned and forlorn and screaming their silent yearning to be taken down and dusted off and opened up and brought back to life.

When I was sixteen and read Bishop Berkeley's *The Dialogues of Hylas and Philonous* for the first time, the evidence for God's existence I was supposed to ferret out and commit to memory as per the Reverend King's instructions was secondary to the wallop of logic that delivered me there,

Berkeley's meticulously convincing claim that material objects exist only through being perceived. For several days afterward, every time I found myself somewhere other than at home, a part of me would suffer a pinprick of panic that my mother's and my house was in danger of disappearing because I wasn't there to perceive it. Thankfully, a week later I was too busy trying to keep Kant's *Critique of Pure Reason* distinct from his *Critique of Practical Reason* to be worried that our house might vanish into the intellectual atmosphere whenever I left for school in the morning.

But a book unread is dead. You can call yourself a collector and stand the leather-bound volumes side by side, row upon row, floor to ceiling and wall to wall, but all you're doing is building an impressive cemetery, a graveyard of words where no one comes to visit and it's hard even to remember who's buried there. For a book to breathe it needs to be held, paid attention to, lived with, the same as any other living thing.

But don't worry, Mr. Richard A. Stevens, Esq. I've got both eyes on all four walls. Your books—my books—our books— aren't going anywhere.

*

I never saw Dr. Abbott again—our circles weren't the sort to intersect—but he was the one who taught me how to hate my life.

Up until our half-hour visit together, I'd been happy being no one, content to make a little money and read a few books and drink a lot of whiskey, and quite pleased with myself, in fact, for being wonderfully free to do all three in whatever measure I desired. For some reason, though, lifting twenty-pound bricks all day or hacking the leaves off tobacco plants for fifteen cents an hour didn't seem like quite as satisfying a life plan anymore after inhabiting, however briefly, Dr.

Abbott's heady world of accomplishment, self-esteem, and simple but civilized pleasures. All of a sudden, callused hands and a sore back and a small rented room littered with empty whiskey bottles and half-understood books weren't a satisfactory substitute for a university degree and framed community honours and a glass-encased gift from President Lincoln's widow.

But, I began to burn, it wasn't supposed to be this way. I'd been raised for better things, just like Dr. Abbott. Raised by the Reverend King for better things. But because he'd broken the promise of financial support he'd made to me, I was marooned on my little island of freedom, was never going to sail away to university or live in Toronto or have an impressive home library like Dr. Abbott. Of course, I could have put away what little pay was left over at the end of each week and maybe, if I eliminated such superfluities as food and shelter, by the time I was fifty years old I'd have saved up enough money for my tuition. Or I could take up the Reverend King's benevolent offer of returning to Buxton on my hands and knees, ready to redeem myself with the lie that I was a wholly reformed ex–opium addict. Or simply tell him the truth, that I'd murdered my mother, and, by the way, about that money for my education I'd been promised . . .

So I wouldn't be a man of the cloth. So I wasn't going to be a scholar. So I was fated to work in a biscuit factory for the rest of my life. And if anyone asked me what I did during the War Between the States to help liberate my people from the bondage of slavery, I could tell them I read a lot of theology books.

If I didn't entirely disbelieve in God yet, it was only because I still needed Him to despise.

Him and his earthly advocate, the Reverend William King.

12

Saturday night was for drinking and whoring, Sunday for resting and recovering. And then, too soon, Monday, and five more days of doing what I was told until, at the end of each, it was time to go home to whatever tiny room I was renting and read myself to sleep. Pissing away an entire day simply coaxing your body back to pre-hangover health wasn't, I soon learned, the wisest way to make use of one of the one and a half days a week when your hours were all your own; but wasting time is what a young man does best. Now that I didn't attend church anymore, my Sundays needed filling up anyway.

A whiskey hangover is best endured outdoors. Idling underneath a shady tree long enough that the afternoon sun periodically nudges you to move a few inches toward a more soothing shadow is a good way to re-acclimatize your debauched body to nature's healing essentials of time and quiet and fresh air. My favourite mending spot was underneath an old elm tree in Tecumseh Park that overlooked the Thames River.

Cool earth for my bottom, smooth bark for my back, I'd watch the river flow and the birds drift by and even the occasional fish poke its head above the water's surface. And doze, inevitably doze, waking up to not quite feeling good, but not as bad as before, which was something to be thankful for, which was a start.

The only human beings I was ever happy to see—the elm sat alone on a small, grassless hill, so the majority of the arm-in-arm couples and ball-playing children were compelled to keep their happiness to themselves—were those on the decks of the steamships that would occasionally float by. Three, sometimes four levels full of people I'd never seen before and would never see again standing at the rails, some of the men smoking, some of the women peering through their looking glasses, men and women both sometimes observing a coloured man they'd never seen before and would never see again sitting leaning against an elm tree looking at people he'd never seen before and would never see again. Thames River Infinite Regress Reverie.

Once, I even saw the steamer *Lorena*.

During and after the Civil War, hundreds, probably thousands of newborn Southern girls were named Lorena, as well as several pioneer settlements and even the steamship that one Sunday afternoon passed through Chatham by way of the Thames River. All of them got their names in honour of the heroine in an old ballad called "Lorena" that for some reason became a favourite of the Confederate soldiers.

The song was the usual sentimental sap that passes for art among people who, if they put in their stomachs what they put in their minds, would all be dead of malnutrition:

> *We loved each other then, Lorena,*
> *Far more than we ever dared to tell;*
> *And what we might have been, Lorena,*
> *Had our loving prospered well!*
>
> *But then, 'tis past; the years have gone,*
> *I'll not call up their shadowy forms;*

I'll say to them, "Lost years, sleep on,
Sleep on, nor heed life's pelting storms."

As the War Between the States dragged on, the song grew even more popular among the increasingly battered Southern troops. One Confederate veteran swore that, by the time of the South's surrender, he'd heard "Lorena" more often than "Dixie." The same man also claimed that "Lorena" was banned by at least one Confederate general. Some of the men who heard it or sang it, it seemed, would grow so nostalgic for their homeland, the South, they wouldn't be able to stop themselves from deserting.

Maybe it was the hangovers, but those steamers passing by, and all those people aboard them, somehow always made me feel homesick. But I knew that didn't make sense. After all, I was already home.

*

Thompson isn't leafing through *Leaves of Grass* or ecstatically scribbling in his notebook or even scratching at his scalp while angrily slashing out what he's already written; appears, in fact, almost pleased with himself, sips at his whiskey while slumped in his seat surveying the room with no particular purpose, slight smirk etched into his relaxed face. It's probably just another false alarm, but I fill my coffee mug with water and wander over to his table anyway.

"Evening, David."

"Thompson." I sit and sprawl in the seat next to him. If I'm going to get him to tell me what I want to know, it's important he not know that's what I want. "I see Coopers' has got a sale on," I say.

Coopers' Bookstore is more stationery and writing instrument purveyor than bona fide bookseller, bearing out its retail locale on King Street right between McKeough Hardware and Miller's Dry Goods. Thompson is a fellow antiquarian—or was, until he lost his barrister's job last year and I began gradually relieving him of his above-average personal library in settlement of his burgeoning bar tab, eventually acquiring even his prized copy of Whitman's own self-published first pressing of *Leaves of Grass*—but if we don't buy our books at Coopers', it is the only place in town where you can purchase Stephens' ink and genuine Waterman fountain pens.

Thompson's grin grows wider, although he's not smiling at me or at anyone else that I can see. "Wonderful," he says.

"Fifteen percent off all writing supplies is wonderful?"

"Absolutely wonderful."

It's not even midnight—Thompson hasn't had time to get drunk yet. Besides, Thompson isn't a happy drunk, isn't your everyday, everything-is-all-right, everyone-is-okay drunk. That's why *Leaves of Grass* is his bible, even in the cheap, mass-produced form he's had to settle for since he became broke. All of the inexhaustible optimism and bounteous new world vigour between two covers that anyone could ever hope for. That's the idea, anyway. Old world-weary Dr. Johnson opined that "nothing is more hopeless than a scheme of merriment," and he was dead a century and then some before irrepressible Walt was alive and spreading the yawp of his bardic good news. But, then again, Dr. Johnson was disfigured as an infant by scrofula and suffered throughout adulthood from dropsy, emphysema, gout, and insomnia, while dear old Uncle Walt stood six feet tall, weighed two hundred pounds, and, unless he was dining with strangers, preferred to drink directly from his water pitcher and his bottle of rum. Most philosophy is seventy-five percent chemistry.

"Tell me what you need and I'll pick it up for you tomorrow," I say. "I have to go anyway."

Thompson clasps my shoulder—hard—his face a Halloween pumpkin burning with candlelit eyes and a jagged smile. "I don't need anything anymore, David. That's the thing, that's the very thing."

Now that I know what I wanted to, I wish I didn't, don't have a clue what I'm supposed to say or do next. There have been a couple of close calls previously, but I've never seen Thompson this elated, this ecstatically confident that he's finally done what he's been attempting to do for years, what he confided in me late one night that I wished he hadn't.

"A clean goodbye. A flawless farewell that will leave absolutely no question unanswered. Executed properly—executed perfectly—just think how pure it would be. Just think of it, David."

"Is that it?" I say, nodding at the sealed, unmarked envelope lying in front of him four-square on the table. It's not what I should say, I know, but it is what I do say.

He leaves his hand on my shoulder, his grip not getting any looser, and joins me in looking at the envelope like we are admiring a treasured photograph of his first-born child. "Yes," is all he says.

I lift my mug and wish there was more than one magician adept at turning water into wine. "Stay here," I say. "Don't go anywhere until I get back, all right?"

"No," Thompson says, still staring at the envelope. "I'm not going anywhere."

I shout upstairs to Tom that I need him to sling drinks for a while, but before I can grab a bottle and two glasses, Meyers' face is no more than six inches from mine on the other side of the bar.

Holding up my hand, "Tom will get you whatever you need in a minute," I say.

"Very good," Meyers says, "splendid, splendid. But I say, you seem to have a bottle handy right there, David, so perhaps you wouldn't mind . . ." He holds out his empty glass like Oliver Twist begging for more gruel, just begging to have his bowl slapped from his fat hand to the ground.

I surprise myself—don't snap at him or even worse—pour him a drink, in fact—and, without stopping to watch the reaction on his face on my way back to Thompson's table, tell him that it's on the house.

It's not every day, after all, that someone you know composes the perfect suicide note.

*

Thompson with his never-without Whitman is proof that it doesn't have to be the Holy Bible for a man to find shelter from the storm of life in a holy bible. Whatever keeps you warm and dry on the inside.

As a young man, I employed the usual young-man methods—whiskey and women—to numb the dumbness of the labourer's life I was leading and apparently was always going to lead. In the ancient battle between dissipation and desperation, however, Monday morning at six a.m. always wins. Supplementing my debauchery with hours of hard reading helped, but beauty and intelligence are almost as ephemeral as liquor and lust, life's abundant ugliness and stupidities as instantly sobering as any dawn alarm clock. I tried switching subject matter—from the delights and discoveries of literature and philosophy to the long, purportedly consoling view of history—but names and dates didn't dull the pain of trading my existence for a weekly pay packet as I'd hoped. Just the opposite, actually. As far as I could tell, the study of history was essentially the recorded particulars of how one country robbed another country. I didn't need to read books to learn about exploitation, self-interested rationalization, and inevitable resentment; all I had to do was show up for work at the factory.

And then I met Mr. Blake.

Mr. Blake had already been dead for nearly fifty years, but it took Alexander Gilchrist's *The Life of William Blake* to raise him from his grave of anonymity. An article in the *Fortnightly* piqued my interest enough for me to order Gilchrist's *Life*, biography having become a recent favourite form, reading about someone else's troubles a pleasant change of pace from living my own. Except that Mr. Blake, I learned, didn't have any troubles. Or rather, he had them, plenty of them—was poor, artistically scorned, professionally ignored—he just didn't suffer them.

Instead of seeing the plaster falling off the walls, Mr. Blake saw angels on the bedposts. Rather than bemoan his deathbed poverty, he spent one of his last shillings on a pencil to continue sketching. As opposed to those who might agonize over an inability to shoehorn their heretical beliefs in full sexual freedom and racial equality and anti-materialism into comfortable contemporary Christianity, Mr. Blake merely shrugged and said, "I must create a system or be enslaved by another man's." Mr. Blake was the true anti-Christ. Not as in an evil-doing devil, but as in a suffering-eschewing, life-affirming god whose number one commandment was *All deities reside in the human breast.* And as far as I was concerned, a small-*g* god was better than no god at all.

I read and reread Mr. Blake's poems until they weren't his anymore, weren't even poems, were what I thought and how I lived and who I was.

"You better put that book away, David, I don't pay you to diddle-daddle."

"I'm on my lunch break."

"Then you should be eating lunch."

"I'd rather read."

"Reading no book isn't going to help you get those boxes filled up by the end of the day."

"Right now I'm not filling up boxes. Right now I'm on my lunch break."

"You *were* on your lunch break. While we were talking, it just ended. You better put that book away and get back to work."

Listen to the fool's reproach! It is a kingly title!

Mr. Blake: a good god and an even better teacher, sagacious salves for every wound and irritation the world could possibly inflict.

I called him—*call* him—Mr. Blake because when I was a young boy, the Reverend King introduced my mother and me to a man leaving Clayton House, the man and the Reverend King having just concluded a lengthy meeting in the Reverend King's study. "David, this is Mr. McKellar," the Reverend King said.

I sent my little brown hand up to meet the big white hand coming down to me.

While my mother showed the man out the front door, the Reverend King said to me, "People whom we respect, we always call them Mr., don't we, David?"

"Yes, sir," I said.

Even if he wasn't a god—even if not a small-*g* god—the Reverend King, whatever else he was or wasn't, he wasn't such a bad teacher, either.

13

It's not as if I wrote them down—that would have meant I was keeping track, that might have implied I cared—but each time I was able to junk another Biblical injunction, I couldn't help but be pleased. It transpired, for instance, that you *could* serve two masters, if not actually concurrently. Because if the Reverend King had provided the promise of a better life, Burwell actually delivered one. And Burwell was certainly everything that the Reverend King wasn't. Which is just the thing required if you're a thief and a smuggler and an enterprising grave robber.

I first heard his name from a man who heard it from another man that if a man was interested in making some quick and easy money, he should tell the first man who would let the second man know who would be sure to put the interested man in touch with a man called Burwell. I was twenty-eight years old, and ten uninterrupted years of hard, honest labour had netted me approximately seventy-five dollars in savings and a far less approximate awareness that hard-working, honest people tend to die alone in small rented rooms with worn-out bodies and washed-out souls. I told the man I was interested who told the other man who set up a meeting with Burwell.

Considering that, whatever it was we'd be doing, I was fairly certain it wouldn't be legal, I was surprised when instructed to show up in the Market Square on Saturday at nine a.m. There wasn't a busier time or place in Chatham than Saturday morning in the market. I'd been told to wait near the wagon set up nearest to Wellington Street West, which I did, pretending to find the bushel baskets of apples and onions and tomatoes as interesting as I could. After another and then another young Negro added their own mute admiration of the vegetables, the farmer—the man, any-way, who'd been sitting in the buggy seat with his back to us—climbed down and joined us at the rear of the wagon.

"Take a few, lads," he said.

The other two Negroes seemed as puzzled as me, didn't know if he was referring to the produce or to what we were there to be paid for. The man laughed, enjoying our confusion.

"The farmer charged me enough to borrow his wagon, we might as well take a few apples home with us." Then the man, Burwell it would seem, did just that, loaded down the pockets of his jacket with as many apples as would fit. He was white and clean-shaven and wore silver spectacles, but his leathery-looking skin, and something about his eyes—the way they narrowed when he spoke—suggested someone who'd spent the majority of his life outdoors, who'd only recently taken to the relative ease of city life. There were spider veins, broken capillaries, up and down his nose.

"I'll put my cards on the table, lads. What I'm looking for is someone not unlike myself, someone smart enough to take advantage of an opportunity when it presents itself." Burwell watched the assorted Saturday morning crowd wander past, tipped his hat at a blue-bonneted, busily made-up matron and her two equally fussily attired young sons. The three of us stood there with our pockets full of apples, watching him.

"What I ask of my employees, lads, is simple: loyalty and common sense. What I can offer in return is just as straightforward: four dollars per man for a couple hours' work per night, sometimes once, sometimes twice, sometimes more than that, every week." His accent wasn't Scottish—wasn't anything—but the way he used "lad" reminded me of Scots I had met.

The other two Negroes looked at each other. They were ready to start immediately. Today. Right now. Starting at *what* wasn't important.

"Could you please be a little more specific?" I said.

Now the two Negroes looked at me: white men don't like uppity niggers, and Negroes don't like uppity niggers who could cost them a chance at four dollars' pay for two hours' work.

Burwell took another apple out of the basket and wiped it on his thigh. He rubbed it until it shone. "No," he said, crunching into the apple. He managed to chew and smile at the same time.

"So when do you plan on telling your employees exactly what it is they'll be doing?"

Another bite, another crunch. The same condescending smile. "I don't."

"You don't."

"That's right."

"You don't plan on telling your men the nature of the job you're hiring them for?"

"That's right." Burwell kept crunching, steadily working his way around the circumference of the apple.

"Look here," one of the Negroes said. "This here man don't speak for us. We two"—he thumbed himself and the other Negro—"is good workers and we don't need to know nothing we ain't supposed to know."

"I'm sure you don't," I said.

"Don't smart-talk me, boy," the Negro said.

"Don't worry," I said. "I wouldn't want to confuse you."

The Negro may not have understood what I meant, but he knew enough to know it wasn't intended to be flattering. He took a step toward me, and I let him get close enough that I was able to kick his back foot from underneath him and send him backward to the ground. I knew that the other Negro would be on me as soon as his friend went down, but before I could turn on him, an enormous, practically round white man with a horseshoe moustache, who looked like a walrus smuggled into a too-tight blue pinstriped suit, stepped out of the passing crowd and twisted the standing Negro's arm behind his back.

"Thank you, Ferguson," Burwell said, taking the last bite out of his apple.

The Negro I'd sent to the ground sprang up but, seeing Burwell's man tighten his hold on his friend's arm, stayed where he was. "We gonna settle this," he said.

"Use your head," I said, nodding in the direction of the busy thoroughfare. "There are women and children here."

"What the fuck I care about women and children? We gonna settle this. Now."

I reached into my jacket pocket and gently tossed him an apple. "Have an apple instead. It'll help keep the doctor away." Undoubtedly wishing he hadn't, he caught it anyway.

Burwell clapped his hands, twice, with hands raised and even, like a child. He'd put his apple core in his mouth in order to applaud, but instead of removing it and throwing it away, he pulled it inside his mouth like a snake its doomed victim and chewed, swallowed.

"You two can go," he said, pointing at the other two Negroes.

His leviathan of a bodyguard, if that's what he was, released his prisoner's arm and lumbered over to where Burwell was, placing his body between his boss and the two dismissed applicants. Before he crossed his arms over his chest—with slight difficulty, his chest being his stomach and vice versa—he pulled back his suit jacket to reveal a sheathed knife on one hip and a holstered gun on the other.

While his friend rubbed his sore arm, "Fuck you, fuck all of you," the other Negro said, throwing the apple I'd tossed him straight down at the earth. It made a soft thud. The two of them walked away arguing.

"I'll tell you tonight," Burwell said.

It took me a moment to realize he was speaking to me and not his henchman. "You'll tell me what tonight?"

"What your responsibilities will be. It's the sort of job where it's simply a matter of it being easier to show one than to tell one."

"What makes you think I want the job?"

Burwell selected a pre-rolled cigarette out of a tin in his vest pocket, lit it. Eyes constricted to near slits from the smoke of his own making, "Because I get the feeling you're a man not unlike myself," he said.

He offered me a cigarette from the open tin. I rarely smoked, and even then only a cigar when I was drinking, but I took one anyway. I put it in my mouth and let him light it for me.

"A man smart enough to take advantage of an opportunity when it presents itself, in other words," I said.

Smoking, smiling, "Among other things."

For an instant we were two old friends enjoying a shared smoke amidst the sights and sounds of a simple spring morning in the market.

"Are you a religious man?" Burwell said.

"No."

"Good."

A squawking wagon pulled past, the last day on earth for a wagonload of chickens.

"Do you know where the cemetery is?" Burwell said.

"Yes."

"Good." Burwell dropped his cigarette to the ground, didn't bother to toe it extinct. "I'm Burwell and this is Ferguson," he said.

"David," I said. I waited for someone to offer a hand to shake, but the two of them stepped into the crowd instead. Into their backs, "When do I start?" I said.

"Tonight, two a.m.," Burwell said without turning around.

"Where? Where at two a.m.?"

"You said you knew where it was."

And then they were gone.

*

Just like any other smart businessman, Burwell believed in diversification. Unlike most, though, he also strongly believed that his employees should be diversified as well, one helping hand rarely knowing what the other hand was up to. I worked the graveyard shift—literally—and never with another strong back to lessen the load on mine or another pair of vigilant eyes to watch it. Instead of complaining, I did what had to be done, and Burwell noticed, gave me enough work at good-enough pay that it wasn't long before he was my sole employer. The Reverend King used to emphasize that every man needed a trade, needed to acquire at least one in-demand skill he was good at that he could always fall back on, and I was good at stealing corpses.

My specialty was the hook and pull. The key was to dig at the head of a recent burial using a wooden spade—wooden spades being much quieter than metal ones—and, after you'd reached the coffin, crack it open and place a rope around the deceased's neck and carefully drag the corpse to freedom. The medical schools, Burwell emphasized, wanted their bodies fresh and with the organs and flesh intact and untouched, weren't in the habit of paying for week-old rotting specimens or specimens with a pierced lung or a speared heart. Unlike some of my colleagues, I was also careful never to steal any-thing—no jewellery or watches or gold fillings—as this would have left me open to a felony charge if I'd gotten caught. Steal-ing a corpse, Burwell pointed out, was only a misdemeanour.

As lucrative a profession as it could be, however, grave robbery did have its downside. For one thing, as medical schools multiplied, bodysnatching was becoming so common that it was not unusual for relatives or friends of someone who had just died to watch over the body until burial, and then to keep watch over the grave after burial, to prevent the corpse from being stolen. For another, iron coffins were more and more employed by anyone well-off enough to afford one, or else the grave was protected by an expensive framework of underground iron bars. And there was always the threat of mob justice. In 1882, for example, a few years after I'd gotten my start, hundreds of Philadelphia Negroes stormed that city's morgue. Six bodies that had been taken from their graves at Lebanon Cemetery, the Negro burial ground, had been discovered on the back of a wagon headed for the local medical college. The newspaper said that, at the morgue, one man asked all the others to bare their heads and swear on the bodies of their dead family members lying before them that they would murder the grave robbers as soon as they were found.

Of course, I never raised a single dead Negro from his grave in my life. I may have been a mercenary, but I was a mercenary with morals. And just as long as I came up with enough bodies, Burwell allowed me the luxury of my ethics.

As to what else he was up to, you'd hear things, there'd be hints: smuggling (U.S.-way and this way both, depending on the tariff); moneylending; even simple thievery (a wagonload of canned peaches is never just a wagonload of canned peaches). But Burwell and Ferguson were the only ones I spoke to, and only about how many corpses were required and where I needed to deliver them. And even then, my only actual communication was with Burwell, Ferguson remaining as silent as he was sizable.

"Doesn't he *ever* speak?" I asked Burwell once, Ferguson safely out of earshot.

"When he has something to say."

"I'd like to be around when that happens."

"Don't be so sure."

Initially, my only job was to get the body and deliver it to Burwell, who would hand it over to his contact at the medical school. After about a year of doing what I was told, and doing it well, Burwell entrusted me with making the handover as well, at an extra two dollars per body, not including what it cost me to feed and water my horse plus the wear and tear on my wagon, not to mention running the risk of making the trip to London with one or more recently exhumed cadavers in the back. Still, it was worth it. I was saving money at a rate that simply wasn't imaginable before, even figuring in my monthly indulgence of five dollars' worth of brand new books ordered directly from Reed's Bookstore in New York.

It got to be that the only contact I had with Burwell was to surrender the cash I'd receive in London on delivery of the bodies, which he'd then hand right back over to me at a rate of fifty cents on the dollar. Naturally, the thought crossed my mind that, doing all the work and getting only half the profit, there were ways of increasing my take, such as skimming the top by miscounting a body or two, or even cutting out the middleman altogether and going into business for myself. The thought must have crossed Burwell's mind too. Probably long before it did mine.

"Five, ten, twenty, twenty-five, thirty-five. Thirty-five, twenty-five, twenty, ten, five." It was always the same: we'd meet wherever he sent word he wanted to meet, and I'd have to get down from my wagon and go to him in his; then he'd count out the money I handed over, twice—forward and backward—only to repeat the process when he paid me out my share. It was raining and October and dark, nothing besides Burwell and Ferguson and me but dull stars and black trees and a frozen moon. All business between us took place outdoors, in the open, no matter what the season or the weather. The entire time I knew him, I never knew Burwell to belong anywhere. He never had any home address that I was aware of, there wasn't any saloon or restaurant he was known to frequent, there wasn't even an office or a pretend place of business to carry out his dealings.

Done counting, "You never cease to surprise me, lad," he said.

"How's that?" He and Ferguson were out of the rain in their canopied buggy. I pulled my hat down lower so that the rain would roll off the brim easier. I was almost up to my ankles in field mud.

"Every count you bring me is always correct. Every dollar is always accounted for."

"That's the idea, isn't it?"

"From where I stand. Someone else might say, not from where you're standing."

"You sound disappointed I'm honest."

"You misunderstand me, lad—I didn't say you were honest. You just haven't stolen from me."

The rain was dripping off the tip of my nose now as much as it was the brim of my hat. I just wanted my money and to go home and be warm and dry. Priorities are remarkably easy to unearth when you're cold and wet and fatigued and tired of spending time with the recently deceased.

"And I'm not going to," I said.

"You haven't forgotten where you came from," Burwell said.

"Believe me," I said, "I've tried. Now can I have my pay?"

"Certainly, lad." The stack of bills I'd handed him was still in his left hand. Once again, left to right, then back, "Five, ten, fifteen. Fifteen, ten, five." He held out the money with a smile that said as soon as I reached for it, he'd pull it back.

"You're short," I said.

Ferguson, who up to now had seemed content to stare at the rain, turned his head. He still had the whip in his hand.

"Oh?" Burwell said. He squinted at the bills as if they'd deceived him. He began to count again. "Five, ten—"

"Cut this shit out, Burwell, and just give me my money. You know as well as I do, you owe me seventeen dollars, so just give it to me so we can both go home."

Now Ferguson was staring at me with the same bored annoyance he had at the rain. The rain that had managed to make it past their canopy dripped from the ends of his moustache like the liquid remains of a pail of dead fish he'd just consumed in two easy swallows.

Burwell smiled at me again, this time like a parent who can't help but be amused by a badly behaved child. "Seventeen. Of course. I must have miscalculated. Forgive me, lad." He shuffled the bills and offered over the revised amount.

I took the money and climbed in my wagon and shook the reins. On the way home, I stopped myself—twice—from taking out what he'd handed me and counting it. If he wanted it to be fifteen, it was going to be fifteen.

I'm going to have to keep an eye on that sonofabitch, I thought. Because he sure as hell is keeping one on me.

*

We're getting ready for bed and Loretta wants another log on the fire. I say it's fine—it's oranging warm and all the heat we'll need until morning. Besides, the fire in the library will burn all night.

"Heat rises," I say.

"For heat to rise, first there must be heat."

I step out of my clothes and I'm ready for sleep, my long underwear my second skin for at least another month. Loretta has to get undressed in order to get dressed all over again, this time for the night. Winter is just another thing that's more difficult for women.

Loretta unbuttons and pulls down and peels off until she's standing naked with her backside to the fire.

"If you're so cold, get ready and get into bed," I say. I'm already under the blankets. Not that I object to the view.

"I am warming my centre."

"What you're going to do is set your ass on fire."

Just for that, she pushes her rear end a little closer to the heat.

"I'll tell you what I'll do," I say. "Get in here and I'll let you read to me for a while." A naked woman, a few pages of Goethe, a cold night and a warm bed: what more does a man really need?

"This is how you try to succeed in getting a woman into your bed?"

"I'm not too concerned about getting her into bed. It's what she does once she's here that I'm thinking about."

This at least elicits a smile. Loretta's arms are covering her breasts, but only for warmth, not out of modesty. Never out of modesty.

"Let me tell you what I will do," she says. "I will read to you if you let me take your photograph."

I punch a burrow in my pillow and slip my head inside. "I don't need a photograph. I already know what I look like."

"This answer of yours, it is no longer amusing."

"Maybe, but it's not any less true."

"What about others? Myself, for instance? What if I want a photograph of you?"

"You know what I look like too. Even more than me, actually. You see me all the time."

"If you die before me, what then? I have nothing. This is not acceptable."

"That's what we have memories for."

"People can forget. These memories, sometimes they do not work."

"Then I suppose they weren't worth remembering, then."

Loretta silently pulls on her long wool socks, the night's outfitting beginning. I know I won't be hearing any German tonight.

*

Pride, arrogance, conceit—call it whatever you want, only never underestimate the supposedly sinful as a reliable indicator of healthily sprouting self-worth. Grave-robber solvent for the first time in my adult life, I tended to body first, instinctively knowing that soul would somehow follow. No ancient Greek sage may have said it, but if you're feeling blue, buy a brand new pair of shoes.

Which I did—an imported pair of Randall, two-piece, russet riding boots from Detroit, the leather soaked in oil and jacked to expertly soften, then stretched over a crimping block to create just the correct turn—as well as a closetful of clean white shirts and perfectly tailored pants along with two dressing-table drawers neatly stacked with warm cotton underwear and socks and even abundant handkerchiefs, a different colour for every day of the week. Just clothes, just soon-to-be rotting rags fulfilling their final worldly function swathing their equally rotting owner on his final, six-feet-beneath sleep; but if clothes don't make the man, they can certainly make the man feel better about what kind of man he's stuck with being. I may have raised the dead for a living, but my shoes always shone and my pants were never without a sharp crease.

Fearing that I might be growing just a little bit smug—sitting about so smartly attired in my bigger, better rooming-house room (more room for more and more books; a window overlooking more than the wall of the house next door; my own small kitchen), a book of Latin verse resting on my knee, while sipping, not gulping, good whiskey—I took solace in remembering something I'd read a long time ago, so long ago I couldn't remember where: "How can a man expect to gain another man's respect if he doesn't first respect himself?"

Quickly realizing that I'd never read any such thing—had, instead, heard the Reverend King say it, say it over and over—I then took solace in knowing that, although he taught me to know it, it was me and me alone who'd made it possible for me to live it.

Creatio ex nihilo. I should get *that* tattooed on my other arm, I thought.

The only trouble with limbs covered in personally significant Latin inscriptions, however, was that virtually no one you met knew what they meant. It wasn't everyone, after all, who read Horace and Virgil in their difficult dead tongue. Like me.

Because the Reverend King had taught me.

*

Ostensibly to stretch my legs and rest my eyes, I stroll to the front window to see what the world outside is up to. As usual, not much. Waning winter's first thaw, fresh garbage in full bloom: empty whiskey and medicine bottles, rusty cans and rotting vegetables, a single, laceless black boot. White snow then dirty snow then yellow slush then this. Nature tries its best to make the world nicer but always returns it naked. I return to my chair and my book.

Moments made mellow like this, I can almost imagine myself accompanying Loretta abroad, black and white parading together in public not quite the colour clash it is over here. Reading all day atop the sunny deck of some luxurious steamer; quietly dining every evening with Loretta at our own private table; toasting the full moon and the foaming sea and our shared good fortune at starry midnight. Our actual time in Europe is a little less lucid, but would certainly include plenty of actual places where actual great men were born and lived and died, as well as, after docking at our first stop, as many first-rate London bookstores as I could talk Loretta into visiting. I've never been inside a proper bookstore before.

But too much leisure feels dirty. Even today's half day of rest will, I know, by the time the sun begins to sink, sour, the pleasant indolence of afternoon curdling into sinful sloth by evening's first dimming. "'For Satan finds some mischief still/For idle hands to do,'" the Reverend King would remind us from the pulpit. My mind knows it's illogical—foolish, Loretta would say—to feel guilty for enjoying oneself, but my soul knows it's a sin. *Soul*, that's right. Did you think a soldier who loses a limb ever really believes it's gone?

Besides, I can't run the risk of being bored. Because being bored isn't possible—isn't permissible. I might have remained a slave if the Reverend King hadn't bought my freedom for me and brought my mother and me north, let us be thankful. I call no man sir and own my own home and have a woman I love and a friend I trust, let us give thanks. I stand free and rich and beloved high atop the shattered bones and extinguished hopes of every Negro who never knew any of these things, so how could I possibly be complacent or ungrateful or bored? To be bored would be an insult. To be bored would be immoral.

I mark my place in my book and remove my spectacles.

"Come on, Henry," I say, "let's bring in some wood," and Henry is up from his spot in front of the library's fire before I've even finished my sentence. When Henry's eyes are closed, he's not wondering whether or not they should be open. When Henry sleeps, he sleeps; when Henry's awake, he's awake. Too bad I'm not a Hindoo—maybe next time I could come back as a dog. But I'm not a Hindoo or a Buddhist or a Moslem or even the thing I was born to be. I'm . . .

"Let's go, Henry," I say, slapping my thigh. "We've got things to do."

14

One day Burwell informed me that not only did he require four bodies and not the usual one or two, but he also needed me to pack them in ice. I wasn't to worry, though: the ice and the wooden crates that the bodies were to be stowed in would be supplied to me as soon as I gave notice I was in possession of all four samples. *Samples* was what we called bodies, just in case someone not so . . . scientifically advanced as us somehow overheard what we were saying.

"There's nothing wrong with my samples," I said. A first-rate tailor prides himself on the cut of his suits, an expensive defence lawyer on his high acquittal rate, a successful grave robber on the quality of the corpses he delivers. A professional is a professional.

"Easy, lad," Burwell said. "No one said there was. These samples need to travel a little farther than usual, that's all. And it won't take you any more time, if that's what you're thinking. Will likely take you less time, if I know you. Once they're packed, your job is done, Ferguson will take over from there."

"Ferguson's never met our man in London."

"Don't concern yourself, they're not going to London."

"Where are they going, then?"

Burwell smiled, studied the spring air, deciding, I could tell, whether or not to let me know the truth. Ferguson, sitting beside him in the driver's-side seat of the wagon, stared straight ahead as usual at the horse's behind. A significant portion of Ferguson's life, it seemed, was spent studying Burwell's horse's ass-end.

"A good bit south of here," Burwell said. "Hence the need for the ice."

"How much south of here?"

"Kentucky."

Climbing on my horse, "No," I said.

As was our meeting-place custom, it was just after twilight and nowhere at all; technically, near the Bloomfield road, but just bush and untilled fields for as far as could be seen. I'd gotten there first and was sitting on a rotting tree trunk waiting for them to arrive. I was always waiting for them to arrive.

Burwell allowed a closed-mouth smirk, like I was a naughty child he didn't want to encourage but simply couldn't help being amused by. "It's not as if *you* have to travel to Kentucky, lad. Your job remains essentially the same. As I said, you'll hand off the samples to Ferguson and he'll take care of the rest. Simple as simple could be."

Which was another reason I didn't want the job: I'd yet to be alone with Ferguson and his three hundred pounds of silence, and I intended to keep it that way. But it wasn't the main reason. Before the Civil War, slavery had given Southern medical schools a significant advantage in procuring bodies, because masters could sell the corpses of deceased slaves, and Southern schools rarely failed to use this as a recruiting tool. The Medical College of Louisiana, for example, promised incoming students that "subjects for dissection will be provided in any number free of charge." I knew because a professional knows his profession. And this particular professional wasn't about to send a single Canadian body—regardless of the colour of its dead flesh—south of the forty-ninth parallel. Let Dixie dig up its own dead.

"I said no, Burwell." I said no, but I remained where I was, on my horse, the reins loose in my hands.

Burwell rubbed his bare chin as if contemplating some great mystery. "I don't see it," he said.

"What? You don't see what?"

"How I can allow you to refuse."

"How you can allow me to refuse?" I'd intended it to sound like I thought what he said was amusing, but all that happened was I repeated him.

Burwell finally released his chin from his hand and shook his head, the matter apparently settled. "No, I just can't see it, lad. This is a transaction upon which much potential future business depends, a potential new market that could prove extremely lucrative for all of us. You're the only one besides me who knows of our dealings, and I simply couldn't take the risk of even one more individual saying something he shouldn't say."

"What about Ferguson? He could blow the whistle, he knows as much as either of us." I was furious, and not entirely at Burwell. I reminded myself of when I used to bargain with my mother to be allowed to stay up a little later than my normal bedtime.

Burwell smiled again—indulgently, almost benignly. "Lad, there's no risk of Ferguson ever talking."

"Just because he never says anything doesn't mean he won't talk," I said. As angry as I was, I wasn't unaware that Ferguson was listening to every word we were saying. Not that he seemed to notice, much less care. If he didn't blink occasionally, he could have been a mammoth flesh statue dumped in the driver's seat.

"Well put, lad, well put. But it's not by *how* he can't speak but *why* that I know I can trust him."

The flame was beginning to go out of the sky, but not so much that Burwell couldn't see the confusion on my face.

"Show him," Burwell said, and before I could determine which one of us he was speaking to, Ferguson turned to me and opened his mouth as wide as possible. He looked like a terrified horse braying at a rattlesnake but with nothing to sound for it. Ferguson didn't have any tongue. His eyes stayed open and on me the entire time I stared at the dark hole where his voice should have been.

"All right, that's enough," Burwell said, and Ferguson snapped his mouth shut.

"How did he lose his tongue?" I said. Now I sounded like a five-year-old asking how the sun ended up in the sky.

"The regular rate, David, and within forty-eight hours. Four samples are a lot, I know, but think of all that nice money you're going to make." Pulling down his cap, and to Ferguson now, "Let's go," and Ferguson tugged on the reins and the wagon moved off.

It was dark now. Burwell was going to get his bodies. I raced home, although there wasn't any reason.

*

Tom lives outside of town, halfway between Chatham and Buxton. He couldn't have chosen a more appropriate location to call home if he'd tried. It's only a coincidence, of course—Tom could never be bothered to correlate his geographical *where* to his biographical *who*—but it's fitting all the same.

When he asked me to stop by and see him—last night, while we were closing up—naturally I asked him why. I've known Tom for almost as long as I've had Sophia's, and I've never had any reason to visit him, nor him me.

I like Tom. I know I can trust Tom. Which are two things I can't say about most people I know. But I'm not my black

brother's keeper any more than I am that of any other what-
ever-shaded sibling. The older I get, I'm not sure I even know
any black or white people anymore. I only know for sure that
I know Loretta and George and Henry and a few foggier and
foggier others who only still breathe way back inside my
brain.

"I want to give you something," he said.

"Can't you bring it with you to work tomorrow night?"

Tom shook his head. "I wouldn't care to do that, no."

"What is it?"

"You come and visit me tomorrow. Around noontime?"

"If you want me to."

"I do."

"All right."

Tom is standing on his front porch when I ride up, coat-
less and with a steaming tin cup of coffee in one hand, a cigarette burning in the other.

I climb down from Franklin's horse and tie the rein to the
porch. I sold my last horse the same week my house was finished being built. The day I moved in, I knew I wouldn't be
going anywhere far enough away that I'd ever need to travel
by horse again.

"You can put him around back if you want, out back with
Sister," Tom says.

"It's a nice-enough day," I say. "He'll be all right."

"It is that," Tom says, taking a sip of coffee followed by
a long pull on his cigarette while enjoying the view from his
porch, the towering trees and more trees surrounding every
side of the cabin. Tom's nearest neighbour is more than a
mile away, and in spite of the snow-covered branches of the
trees and the puddles of ice and the hard, frozen ground, the
wind is only wintertime cool, the country air all the fresher
for it. Everywhere you look is clean and quiet and empty of
anything that isn't supposed to be there.

Splashing the little that's left in his cup over the side of the porch, "Suppose you better come in," Tom says. He steals a last puff from his cigarette before stamping it out on the porch underneath his boot, holds the door open for me, and closes it behind us.

Inside is pretty much what I'd imagined: a table and a single chair; a small, neatly made bed; a few time-scarred pots and pans hanging by nails over the fire. If you had taken one of the original cabins built at Buxton forty-five years ago and simply moved it out here, it would be hard to tell the difference. The room is warm and dry, though, and the bare windows allow the entire cabin plenty of hard, bright sunlight.

"Just a minute," Tom says, kneeling on one knee beside the bed, dragging out a battered wooden gun box from underneath. Tom hasn't offered me a chair, so I stay standing. Besides, whatever it is he wants to show me, it isn't going to take long.

Even though Tom arrived in Buxton when I was a boy, I didn't meet him until I was much older, until I'd opened Sophia's. Once I got to know him, though, I remembered hearing about him—the ex-slave up from Mississippi via the Underground Railroad who lived on the edge of the Settlement in an Elgin Association–approved house, right down to the regulation picket fence and mandatory flower garden out front, but who refused to farm like everyone else, earning his living instead on the railroad whenever there was work, hunting and fishing and somehow getting by otherwise whenever there wasn't. The Reverend King strongly encouraged every new settler to initially work on the railroad, but only long enough to earn the first instalment toward his own plot of land so as to begin raising a money crop as soon as possible, a man's legally owned land something that no other man, white or otherwise, could ever take away from him. Tom came up with the minimum down payment followed by the slowest repayment schedule allowable, taking the full twenty years permissible under the terms of his loan to finally pay it off.

Tom even went about the business of education his own way, was front and centre at the evening adult reading classes that the Reverend King and the other teachers held for the new arrivals, but refused to learn to write, politely insisting he only wanted to know how to read, and then only enough to know how to read the Bible. Fittingly, a worn copy of it along with an old pipe, sharing space on top of a small, mirrorless dresser of drawers, looked to be his only luxury items.

"I want you to have this," he says, standing up from his crouch.

I go over to get a better look at what he's holding in both hands. Once I do, even though I've never seen one before, not in person, I immediately know what it is. "Whose is it?" I say. It's not exactly what I meant, but it's probably as close as I'm going to get.

"Somebody's. Back in Mississippi. Somebody's from there."

Tom's still holding it, and I'm still staring at it. "Is it—I mean, *was* it—yours?" I say.

"Just somebody's back in Mississippi." He holds it out for me to take it from him, like a valet offering a king his crown.

I take it and hold it like he did, cradled across both hands. Each shackle has its own keyhole, and there's a chain about six inches long and three inches thick joining them together.

Tom can tell what I'm thinking. "So he don't run away," he says, "but so he can still work."

I nod, keep looking. I don't know what else to do. I don't know what else to say.

"Put it on," Tom says.

"What do you mean?"

"I mean put it on. Like you was having to wear it."

I don't move, so Tom takes the thing back and sinks to one knee and pulls up my pant leg and clasps one of the shackles around my left ankle. "Ordinarily, that'd be tighter some, on account of it being locked."

I feel enraged. I feel unworthy. I feel honoured. I feel sick to my stomach.

"See now how it feels like to wear both," he says, but before he can attach the other shackle, I bend over and unclasp the first. We both stand up.

"It's okay," I say, handing it back.

Tom picks up his pipe from the dresser and carefully lights it with a match from the box he pulls out of his shirt pocket. He slowly shakes his head. "It belongs to you now," he says.

"Why do you want me to have it?"

Patiently sucking at his pipe until it begins to burn to life, "A man don't live forever." Him, he means. He won't live forever.

"Fine, but why not . . . ?" Exactly. Why not what?

Tom points at me with his pipe. "I want *you* to have it."

"But—"

"Boss, there ain't nothing more to say."

"Tom, look—"

"And you keepin' on talkin', you just sayin' more of it."

*

On our morning walk, on our way to Tecumseh Park, Henry and I detour along King Street in order to stop in at the post office. Schopenhauer and Goethe and Heine may all sound wonderfully beguilingly the same to me, but since Loretta actually understands every word she reads aloud, I need to periodically replenish my Germanic reading list. Obviously, Hegel is out—no musty metaphysics for either of us, no matter how dialectically dressed up to sound like science—and Loretta's sole reading rule is nothing even remotely theological, so Feuerbach and Schleiermacher aren't options either. I've ordered as many volumes as are available of a young philosopher whose name I've become familiar with through the pages of the *Fortnightly*, a Friedrich Nietzsche. The little I've read about his work is intriguing, but it's the other names that his name is often linked with—Socrates, Heraclitus, Schopenhauer—that are most compelling. You know a person by the company he keeps. And it's an astute autodidact who pays attention to who's friends with whom.

It's election time in Chatham and most of the storefronts we pass have signs hanging in their windows urging the populace's support for either the incumbent, Mayor Henry Smyth, or his challenger, Manson Campbell. Campbell is playing the radical this time out, advocating not only that Chatham officially change its status from town to city but that four hundred cords of cobblestone be purchased with taxpayer money with which to pave Queen Street. I'm all for progress and clean boots, so if I manage to remember where and when to vote, Campbell is my man. And if I don't, Chatham will still be Chatham and Queen Street won't be any muddier than it was before.

I leave Henry outside the post office and let the bell over the door bring Larwill to the front counter. There's no smug smile for me today, only the most nominal, barely detectable nod, as if a single genuine greeting costs two hundred dollars and Larwill has only a nickel to his name, and he retrieves my package and produces the piece of paper I need to initial so promptly that I'm almost back out on the street when I'm left wondering if I imagined the entire exchange. But when a woman and her young daughter enter through the door I hold open for them and I hear, "Good morning, Mrs. Carpenter, good morning, Elizabeth, and what can I do for you ladies today?" I'm reassured that my hold on reality is still secure, at least for now. The woman thanks me before replying to Larwill's query, I tell her she's welcome, and Henry and I are on our way again.

There was one election I didn't cast a vote in but would have if I'd had the opportunity—would have had to have been imprisoned or dead to have missed. Or been only nine years old at the time, which I was.

Although Larwill's father's attempt to stop the settling of Buxton had been ultimately unsuccessful, Larwill Senior continued to be a dedicated adversary of both the Elgin Settlement and Archie McKellar. When, in 1856, Mr. McKellar decided to run against Larwill for his seat in Parliament, the Reverend King went right to work, helping to get the 321 Negroes who owned property in Buxton and who had been residents for the necessary three years naturalized and eligible to vote. But, being the Reverend King, voting wasn't enough for him, it was just as important *how* the Negroes of Buxton voted.

When the day of the election arrived, the Reverend King gathered all 321 men in front of St. Andrew's Church and marched with them through Duck Pond Swamp all the way into Chatham. Once there, they entered the courthouse together and each man signed his name in the register, not one having to make his mark, unlike nearly half of the whites who voted. Some of the men who cast their vote that day had been slaves little more than three years before. The Reverend King and the 321 men of Buxton marched home the same way they came, and Larwill lost his seat to Mr. McKellar by the largest count in the history of Kent County.

I let Henry go from my side as soon as we get inside the park, let him chase after a squirrel he thinks he can catch but that I know will make it up a tall maple tree before he can reach him. I put my hands inside my coat pockets and watch

Henry jump up against the tree, his front two feet as high as he's going to get. I let him bark a couple more times before I start walking again.

Henry barks one last time, just to let the squirrel know that he knows he's there, and then he's beside me.

15

The trickle of *hope-you're-well*s and *I'm-just-fine*s that consti-
tuted the first ten years or so of George's and my post-Buxton
relationship eventually dribbled to the desert of good intentions and fond recollections that all unirrigated friendships
must become. A yearly Christmas card is not a nourishing
springtime thunderstorm. By the time I received George's
postcard informing me that Mrs. King was dying, I hadn't
heard a word from him, nor he from me, in over a decade.

A practised grave robber by now, I knew that the dead
neither want nor need our respect; but the dying are a different matter. I didn't know what I wanted to tell Mrs. King before she passed away, but I decided at once that I was going to
tell her anyway. Burwell had an order for two more bodies he
wanted me to fill, but I told him I was busy, they'd have to wait.

"It's not like you to postpone a payday, lad," Burwell said,
amused, if inconvenienced, by my independence.

"I need to visit a sick friend."

"Nothing too serious, I hope."

"She's dying. She might be dead already." Burwell only
understood absolutes: money, death, money.

"Perhaps you can mix a little business with pleasure, then."

Knowing he was only trying to upset me made it possible
not to appear angry but didn't do anything to counteract what

I was feeling. Or thinking. What was the point of being cruel if nothing practical could be gained by it? Burwell, I decided, was wicked for the sake of being wicked. I rode off to Buxton for the first time since my mother's death twenty years before, unable to help being awed by the purity of Burwell's malice.

On the way out of town, I passed by the biscuit factory. It was lunch break, and a string of stoop-shouldered, sun-stunned employees were wordlessly filing outside, a dozen worker moles struggling to adjust to the twin shocks of fresh air and hard winter sunlight. There but for the grace of Burwell once-upon-a-time hiring me to exhume dead bodies for a very lucrative fee go I, I thought.

I'd taken along a half-pint of whiskey for companionship and nipped at it while I rode, puzzling over how someone so obviously bad could have done me—however inadvertently—so much good. By the time I reached the Settlement, I was drunk, but only enough to make me slightly numb to the prospect of meeting the Reverend King again, someone, it occurred to me, so obviously good who had done me—however inadvertently—so much bad.

I tied up my horse at the post office and walked to Clayton House unrecognized. Most of those I'd known there as a boy were either dead or gone. Because of the exodus south after the war, Buxton had shrunk, was a village that used to be a town. Everything was the same, but nothing was as it used to be.

Unlike during my mother's last days, Clayton House was empty but for a single nurse sitting beside Mrs. King's bed. It was obvious from the uniform the woman wore that she was an actual nurse and not a caring neighbour. I was relieved that the Reverend King wasn't there.

It was the middle of the afternoon, but the blinds were drawn and the room was dim. I pushed the already halfway-open door another few inches, hoping to get the woman's attention but not wanting to wake Mrs. King. I used to do the exact same thing with the same door when wanting to visit her as a boy. When the woman didn't respond, I cleared my throat and took a couple of steps farther inside, only to realize she was asleep. I cleared my throat again, louder. The woman snorted herself awake.

"I'm a friend of Mrs. King's," I whispered.

The woman stared up at me from her chair, taking a moment to adjust to the all-of-a-suddenness of the waking world.

"I don't want to wake her, but I'd like to pay my respects," I whispered again.

The woman stood up and stretched her arms over her head, emitted a yawn louder than anything I'd said. "You're welcome to stay and visit as long as you want," she said. "And don't worry yourself with being quiet—poor old thing couldn't hear you if you yelled." The woman, a plump white woman dressed all in white, looked down at the prostrate figure and slowly shook her head and tsked several times like a disapproving but understanding teacher. "Poor old thing."

I only really looked at Mrs. King once I was alone, sitting in the abandoned chair beside the bed. First, though, I'd removed the pint from my shoulder satchel and taken a long pull, strained my eyes in the dark attempting to locate the piano. But there wasn't any piano. I screwed the top back on the bottle and turned my attention to Mrs. King, and braced myself.

But it was just an old, shrivelled woman I hardly recognized. I forced myself to focus, but Mrs. King wasn't there. I was heartbroken I wasn't heartbroken. I didn't know what I'd expected, but it wasn't this, wasn't nothing. There was foamy white spittle at the corners of her mouth and she began to rasp, like she was trying to catch her breath after a long run she shouldn't have undertaken in the first place. I went and got the nurse, making herself a cup of tea in the kitchen.

"Something's wrong," I said.

My surprise at how the woman immediately dropped her spoon rattling to the countertop and passed me on the stairs on her race back into the bedroom was short-lived. After taking Mrs. King's pulse at her wrist and tucking a strand of long silver hair behind her ear, the woman stood up straight and surveyed her patient again, shook her head again.

"It won't be long now," she said. "I've seen a thousand cases like this before if I've seen one."

"Isn't there anything you can do? Or a doctor can do?"

"Just try and reassure her we're here and we care."

"But you said she can't hear anything."

The woman looked at me, blinked twice. "That's true," she said, and returned to the kitchen.

There wasn't any point in my staying. There wasn't any reason for me to stay.

I sat back down beside the bed and took the copy of Montaigne's essays out of my satchel, started reading where the book fell open. When the nurse returned with her tea, she'd just have to get another chair from the kitchen.

*

Even the good ones aren't very good. Even the best of us aren't blameless. I rub both of my eyes, hard, until they crunch in their sockets like fresh gravel underfoot, but I still see what I saw, what I wish I hadn't seen. I stuff Meyers' copy of the *Planet* into the garbage pail behind the bar. Serves me right. You read the newspaper, you deserve what you get.

A couple of years back, England invaded the small country of Matabeleland because, it claimed, English trade emissaries on an innocent mission were attacked and killed there and no satisfactory justice was subsequently dispensed. The warriors' spears were little match for the British army's guns, and the Matabele people were stripped of most of their land and the majority conscripted to work in the British gold mines. Many shiny pocket watches and gold candlestick holders were purchased by many respectable, patriotic British citizens in the years that followed.

And in today's newspaper, signs of a freshly brewing imperialist tea storm, this time originating on this continent, the United States making loud war noises over Cuba. Not, of course, because of a need to safeguard substantial American investments in Cuban sugar plantations, processing plants, and railways, but simply because the magnanimous American people feel a growing desire to liberate the unfortunate Cubans from the tyranny of the horribly repressive Spanish government they've been reading so much about in their newspapers of late. Woe unto them about to be liberated.

But, today, a singular voice of sanity in Meyers' copy of the *Planet*, a concerned congressman from the state of Massachusetts despairing of the United States' most un-Christian embracing of social Darwinism, this never-satisfied lust for yet more and more territories and power. Invoking the recent memory of Britain's latest foray into imperialist action, the congressman from Massachusetts lamented the five hundred casualties the British forces reportedly suffered there, "each one," he emphasized, "a tragically, pointlessly sacrificed Christian soul."

Apparently, the ten thousand Matabelian soldiers who died defending their homeland didn't have souls to lose.

And tomorrow morning, as I breakfast with Loretta—no lying newspaper sliming *my* kitchen table, no gilded stuff-lust sullying *my* untainted soul, thank you very much—she'll ask me to please pass her the sugar for her coffee and I'll answer, "Of course," and hand her the bowl, and the proud American flag of imperialism will flap in the wind just a little bit louder, world domination one sugar spoon at a time.

"I say, David," Meyers says, back from the washroom, "have you seen my newspaper? I left it right here when I stepped away to use the loo."

I look where Meyers can't, at the garbage pail with his copy of the *Planet* and an already-browning apple core resting beside it. I shake my head. "Someone must have taken it," I say.

Meyers peers down the length of the bar in each direction, half turns around with one hand still on the bar to survey the room for the thief. "Honestly, what kind of rounder . . ." Meyers rests both flabby forearms on the bar, stares down at the wood grain like a pouty child whose toy has been taken away. I place a fresh drink in front of him. Meyers looks up. "What's this?"

"Drink up," I say. "You're not missing anything."

*

When Mrs. King's eyes were open, which wasn't often, it was the same as when they were closed: long periods of empty silence interspersed with sudden bursts of gasping, rasping, wheezing, and desperate panting for air. She didn't know who I was even when looking directly at me and when I reminded her of my name, but then, the last years of my time in Buxton hadn't been much different. I didn't stop reading to her, though.

Actually, I did, once—when reading aloud one of Emerson's essays and pausing to puzzle out a sentence—and Mrs. King didn't gasp, rasp, wheeze, or pant, but whimpered, like an animal not so much in pain as abandoned. It was probably only happenstance, but as soon as I resumed reading, the whimpering ceased. It was all the coincidence I needed to keep going.

I visited regularly enough that the nurse would leave Mrs. King and me alone whenever I arrived. Occasionally I'd hear voices in the house—the cook's, a member of the cleaning staff's—but never the Reverend King's. Two decades later and the old man still knew what I was up to.

Sitting there day after day in the silence of Clayton House, it wasn't surprising that I began to hear other voices, dead voices, my mother's louder than any other. I remembered how, once, my mother had been preparing the Reverend King's supper and I was helping, the first damning dusting of arthritic rust on her fingers only slowing her down, not nearly stopping her yet. It was July and hot and humid and the Reverend King was eating light—cold salmon, summer-gushing sliced tomatoes, crunchy fresh radishes, strong iced tea. My job was to arrange the food on the plate and deliver it on a tray to the Reverend King's office. "Food that looks nice tastes nicer," my mother always said. I was pleased with my work: I'd bookended the vegetables, which I'd arranged in rows top to bottom in decreasing size, with two equally long slices of fish. I filled up a tall glass with iced tea from the pitcher and picked up the tray.

"Hold on, now," my mother said. "You isn't done one job yet and you already on to another."

Frowning down at the tray, not wanting to upset the symmetry of my careful design, "What did I forget?" I said.

"You put together Mrs. King's plate first, then you go and give the Reverend King his supper. I want to put all this away so I can make sure tomorrow's breakfast's all set before we leave."

"Okay," I said, and set down the tray. And stared at it.

"C'mon, now, hurry up, that plate not gonna make itself up."

I hadn't visited Mrs. King for over a year, maybe longer, ever since she went silent and stopped playing the piano and didn't recognize me anymore. But now I'd forgotten about her. Not overlooked her, not slightly slighted her, but fully forgotten her. To compensate, I placed bigger tomato slices and extra radishes and a whole other piece of fish across the top of her plate, but my mother shook her head, said, "No use wasting good food, she never eat all that," and cleared it to almost half of what lay on the Reverend King's plate.

The Reverend King thanked me for his meal and asked me to please thank my mother for preparing it. Mrs. King didn't so much as look up from her lap when I set hers on her chair-side table. Once we were home and eating our own supper, "Does the Reverend King . . . I mean, does Mrs. King ever recognize him when he talks to her?" I said.

"You know she don't. Poor woman don't know nobody from nobody." My mother forked another piece of salmon onto my plate. My mother was the one in charge of deciding when I'd had enough to eat, which was rarely ever.

"Do you think she's lonely?" I said.

"Who?"

"Mrs. King."

"Don't talk such nonsense," my mother said, helping me to some more warm green beans. The pad of butter she smoothed across them with her fork melted almost instantly. "You eat your supper, now. I seen those books you brought home from your meeting with the Reverend King the other night. You finish your supper and I clear the table so you can get down to work."

I sliced through the soft pink flesh of the salmon although there wasn't any need to use a knife. My mother's salmon steaks were just as moist and tender as her pork roasts and her beef steaks.

"What about when she was all right, though?" I said. "Even when Mrs. King was all right—I mean, when she still talked and still played the piano, I mean—I can count on one hand the number of times I can remember her and the Reverend King speaking to one another." Now that I thought of it, I couldn't remember them *ever* speaking to one another.

My mother stood up from the table and took away my plate even though it was still half full, even though I was still eating. With her back to me at the kitchen counter: "No man ever suffered so much for his wife as the Reverend King done. Such a good man, such a good, hard-working man— good to so many people in so many ways, and always working so hard, *so* hard—and no wife to come home to and no children to find his joy in." My mother emptied my plate clean into the refuse can with two sharp scrapes of her fork. "Mrs. King, she blessed to have such a man as the Reverend King as her husband. *Blessed*."

I hadn't finished eating, and I knew I was going to be hungry later, but I didn't say anything.

*

I decided when Mrs. King wouldn't suffer anymore. When the gasping and rasping and wheezing and panting began to occur more often than the quiet unresponsiveness, I returned to Buxton with more than a book and a bottle of whiskey in my satchel. There weren't any final words and she didn't recognize me at the last moment and I didn't feel anything but satisfaction that I'd done for her what I'd want someone to do for me. What I'd want a friend to do for me.

16

And then Chatham voted itself dry. It wasn't my first lesson in how what seems so wrong today can become so right tomorrow, but it was the most profitable. When Chatham's most stolid citizens conspired to take advantage of the newly passed Canada Temperance Act and hold a referendum on the ban of the consumption and sale of alcohol, all I'd initially felt was rage and contempt. Rage, that technically I was now a teetotaller; contempt, that someone other than myself had made that decision for me. I'd orphaned my past and murdered my future for the right to obey or break my very own tallied-up Ten Commandments, and the idea that the decision had been made by a roomful of pasty-faced do-gooders who'd never even heard of Mr. William Blake or knew that he'd ordained that "the road of excess leads to the palace of wisdom" would have driven me to drink if I hadn't already been so inclined.

Ordinarily, I stayed out of the bars in the daytime, but I'd just returned from delivering not one, not two, but three perfectly preserved bodies to London, and after spending all night on the road, a sleep-inducing drink or two didn't seem uncalled for. Besides, it was the day that the result of the plebiscite was to be announced in the afternoon *Planet*, and the saloons were a shoulder-to-shoulder sight to see. Not

that there was much suspense about which way the vote was
going to go.

At the time, Chatham counted eighteen saloons, where
good whiskey cost a dime a shot, and the sight of a man stag-
gering down King Street was not in the least uncommon. Yet
the *Planet*, "The Voice of the People," weighed in on the
Yea side of the question in editorial after editorial, local
merchants proudly hung signs in their storefront windows
illustrating their clear support for all things temperate and
decent, and even the already-abstaining inhabitants of Buxton got in on the act, the Reverend King himself leading a
procession of every voting-eligible Elgin Negro into town to
cast their votes in favour of sobriety, civic responsibility, and
clear-minded rationality.

"Scott."

"Hey?"

"I said, says here, 'Officially known as the Canada Temperance Act, this measure, put through the Dominion Parliament by the Honourable R.W. Scott.' That's the fellow
whose idea it was, it seems. Scott."

At the table next to me, a man hunched over a greasy copy
of yesterday's newspaper was talking to another man twirling
one of the ends of his moustache like he was attempting to
roll a cigarette out of it.

"I suppose," the man with the moustache said.

"Not that much can be done about it now."

"Of course not. It's going to be the law."

"It's not as if you could open up your own saloon."

"Of course not. That would be against the law."

I swallowed the last of my drink, laid another quarter on
the table for the bartender to see.

"Says here there's going to be a celebration next week to
commemorate the Queen's golden jubilee," the man with the
newspaper said.

"Is that so?"

"That's what it says."

"I suppose I'll attend, then. If there's going to be a celebration."

"That's what it says."

"I suppose I'll attend, then. I suppose I'll bring Candice and the children along. I wouldn't be surprised if we made an afternoon of it."

Four weeks later, Chatham's first renegade saloon was open for business. Coming up with a name had been the easiest part. *Sophia* means "wisdom" in Greek. It was the very first word that the Reverend King had taught me.

*

The revivalists have taken over Tecumseh Park, so Henry and I detour all the way around and end up on Prince Street, over by the new school. The new school that's now ten years old, the new school no more. Another decade dead just like *that*. Used to be it was enough simply to stay out of churches; now you've got to be careful where you're walking as well.

Even a quarter of a mile away you can hear them. Not the preachers exhorting their tent-cramped parishioners to feel the saving grace of Jesus, to receive the loving embrace of Jesus, to accept Jesus Christ as their personal saviour, but the equally frenzied effect of their soapbox frothing, the thundering *Amen*s and *Hallelujah*s and *Help me Jesus*es of the assembled. To each his own delusion, I suppose, but we're most loyal to our first fairy tales. My Jesus was better. He just was.

Jesus is a prism: hold the Son up to the sun a little to the right and He's Anglican clean and haughty High Tory; slide Him a little to the left and He's a dirty but dignified Everyman, bleeding hands and feet callused and sore just like anyone's who dies a little bit more after a particularly bad day at work. The shriekers and the screamers back in Tecumseh Park know that all they have to do to be saved is say the right words and have faith in the right things, but I wasn't raised that way, I wasn't taught to believe that salvation was quite that easy.

The Reverend King never spoke the word "Jesus" without somehow at least implying the word "work." Work that made you a better person. You making the world a better place. A better you and a better world how we go about the busy business of glorifying God.

Once, when George and I hadn't done our Latin translation assignments because we'd been fishing at Deer Pond so late the night before we'd fallen asleep as soon as we'd gotten home, Mr. Rapier informed the Reverend King, who asked to see us after school the next day. Neither of us had ever been in trouble with the Reverend King before, so we didn't know how frightened to feel on the walk over.

After giving us an opportunity to explain our excuse and then helping us understand why it wasn't an acceptable excuse and then extracting from us a promise to always take care of work before we allowed ourselves pleasure, "Jesus loves us all just the way we are," he said. "But he loves us far, far too much to let us stay that way."

Time helps a mind forget what it doesn't want to know.

Even so faith, if it hath not works, is dead, being alone.

I haven't forgotten.

*

If I was going to set myself up selling illegal liquor, the first thing I needed to do was secure someplace that seemed relatively innocuous yet was still accessible enough that the average caterwauler could locate it even if he was already halfway in the bag. I found it the first day I went looking, a small house near King Street that was buried behind an all-enclosing fence of four tall rows of cedars and which rested upon a mildewy basement big enough to hold, by my own estimation, thirty men and enough liquor to keep them there. The house was empty, had been for months, and the absentee owner's representative said that his client was motivated to sell because of the extensive water damage recently done to the basement.

"A dirty business down there, I'm afraid," the man said after we'd climbed back upstairs. Scarecrow thin, and with a warm Scottish burr stuck to his tongue, the man had shown me around the property with a polite forthrightness that I didn't imagine extended to every agent whose potential client was an anonymous Negro.

"There are dirtier ones," I said.

"A dirty business to make it clean again, I mean. Like a tomb down there now, it is, I'm afraid."

I held off telling him that, if it came to it, I had some experience in that field as well.

He balked when I offered to pay him in cash—"This isn't how transactions of this sort are ordinarily undertaken, Mr. King"—but whether because I'd accepted his price without bothering to make a counter-offer or because the property had already been up for sale for so long, he eventually took my money, almost every dollar I'd saved from a decade's worth of dutiful digging and robbing. It had taken me forty years, but I was now the legal owner of my very own home and place of business both.

After dumping my books upstairs along with what little I'd accumulated in my most recent rooming house, I got down to the real task at hand, transforming the damp, fetid basement into a habitable, illegal saloon. First I cleaned—

there was no question of hiring any help, even if I'd had the money—which foremost meant scrubbing the mouldy walls and floor with bucket after bucket of chlorine and hot water. That there were no windows would, I knew, be an advantage eventually, but at the moment it only meant that an already long and tedious job was made even more so for having to frequently dash upstairs in order to gulp down reviving drafts of fresh air like a suffocating, half-expired miner.

Creating an inviting atmosphere wasn't a priority, at least not in the beginning—the booze would do all the inducing I needed—so I bought cheap straight-backed chairs anywhere I could find them, scoured the dump for broken ones of any kind and repaired them, and built several serviceable tables out of empty pickle barrels I purchased for practically nothing from Miller's Dry Goods. And when I wasn't cleaning up the basement, I was still digging up bodies for Burwell, whom I'd worked out a new arrangement with: in lieu of cash, one fresh corpse in return for ten bottles of bootlegged liquor. Eventually, I knew, I had to get my own underground connection, which wouldn't just be easier and cheaper but would allow me finally to be finished with Burwell. But for now the only thing that mattered was stockpiling as much rotgut as possible.

Burwell's initial amusement at my request for a change in the usual method of compensation ended as soon as he determined that the whiskey wasn't for me. As long as he believed I was pouring his illegal booze down my own throat, he was happy, just one more rusty nail in the coffin of my grave-digging dependence. When he had trouble keeping up with my demand for more and more whiskey, though, and failed to see any obvious signs I was drinking myself into sodden submission, he started asking questions.

"Just out of curiosity, lad, how much are you making?"

"On what?"

"Markup. I assume your thirsty new friends are paying a wee bit more per bottle than what I'm letting you have them for."

I'd known that this moment was going to come sooner or later, and since I hadn't settled on the lie I was going to use to keep him off my entrepreneurial trail as long as possible, Burwell's misunderstanding of what I wanted his whiskey for worked as well as anything I could come up with.

"You agreed to sell the whiskey to me," I said. "You even set the terms yourself. Whatever I do with it after it's mine is my own business."

Burwell held up his hands as if intent upon proving he had ten fingers just like everybody else. "Easy, lad. Of course it's your business. I was merely inquiring as to your profit margin. As one businessman to another."

There wasn't any *merely* about it. Whatever I was up to, and no matter how little extra income he figured I was bringing in, Burwell wanted in on it. To own a piece of the burgeoning illicit-booze business, of course, but even more so, to continue owning me. The tongue that wasn't in Ferguson's mouth anymore told me that Burwell's employees weren't the ones who decided they didn't work for him anymore.

In the meantime, until he could determine the seriousness of my moonshine moonlighting, he could at least make it as difficult as possible for me to do it. Even after I'd delivered him two bodies just the week before, when I showed up with a third a week later he tried to convince me that I was mistaken, that our arrangement had been for only eight bottles per corpse.

"Fuck you, Burwell," I said.

Ferguson and I had already unloaded the body from my wagon and into the boat that they sometimes used, but I grabbed it by its ankles through the thin sheet it was wrapped in and started yanking it out by myself, in the process setting the boat, and Burwell and Ferguson, gently rocking from side to side. The moon was the only light we allowed ourselves, but I heard Ferguson slowly unsheathe his knife. Burwell just laughed. Only when I'd dragged the corpse nearly free of the craft did he bother to speak.

"Now, David. What are you going to do with a dead body?"

"That's my fucking business," I said. "I fucking dug it up out of the fucking ground myself, so I'll do with it whatever the fuck I want."

Over the course of the previous twenty-four hours, I'd spent approximately eleven of them on my hands and knees scouring the basement with enough chlorine that I'd literally burnt away most of my nose hairs—only to discover that, underneath the glaze of mould, there was a seemingly imperishable bloodstain the size of a large living room carpet—four of them at the dump scavenging for broken furniture and fixtures, and four more pilfering and delivering a recently deceased human being. It felt refreshing, invigorating even, to do something so irrationally self-destructive, a little insane something just for me.

Only when the corpse's neck was resting on the edge of the boat—rigor mortis keeping the head from falling backward—did Burwell finally relent. "You know, now that I think about it, lad, I believe you're right." He reached underneath the stern of the boat and held out the two missing bottles.

I was too tired to feel victorious, simply took them. Ferguson slid his knife back into its sheath and untied the line from the dock.

"Why lie?" I said, too exhausted to say more. "Why lie when you don't need to?"

Ferguson dipped the oars into the water. Over the soft splash of their first immersion, "That saddens me, lad, it really does," Burwell said. "That tells me you haven't learned as much as I thought you had from working for me for all these years."

Ferguson had found his rowing rhythm by now, the boat was disappearing down the Thames into the dark.

"If you're not cheating, lad," I heard Burwell say, "you're not really trying."

I put the bottles in the back of the wagon and started home. Thankfully, I was too tired to stay angry. I had more important things to expend my time on. I had blood to scrub out of my floor.

*

Busy getting Sophia's ready for business, I hardly had time to eat or sleep, never mind notice a stray dog. When I did finally spot him, though, it was just a furry flash. As soon as he saw me see him, he rabbited out of sight through the line of trees at the back of the lot. I emptied my bucket of dirty water and chlorine and stood up straight, stretched. There weren't any nearby neighbours, the closest thing being the brick rear wall of the bank several hundred feet from the front door of the house, so whomever he belonged to, or had belonged to, they weren't likely anyone who lived close by.

Then the dog and I began our cat-and-mouse game. Every time I would re-emerge outside with a fresh dirty bucket, there he'd be, waiting for me at the back edge of the property, lingering amidst the trees, but only long enough to see me see him before darting off until the next time, when we'd start all over again. I wanted to get a better look at him, but knew that if I made a move in his direction or even attempted to lure him closer, not only would he probably run away, he might run away for good.

All that was left to do before I could transfer downstairs the tables, chairs, and bottles of booze I'd stockpiled was to rid the basement floor of the bloodstains I'd discovered hiding underneath the layers of mould I'd worked so hard to remove. Compared to the blood, eliminating the mould had been easy, like trying to erase the green of a leaf after first wiping away the morning dew. I told myself I'd give the floor one final scrub and that was it; if it wasn't blood-free by then, I'd admit defeat and start looking for a rug. And this time, whatever the washing result, when I emptied out the bucket, I wouldn't look at the dog. Not directly, anyway.

It was the middle of the afternoon, but, lacking windows, I'd hung up oil lamps in every corner of the basement to go along with the one I kept beside me wherever I was working. The stain looked to be the end result of several different stains, like a number of slim rivers of blood had congregated to create a large lake of blood. The floor tilted slightly toward the middle of the room, so it made sense as far as that went, but where the blood had come from stumped me. I soaked the brush in the bucket and scrubbed the floor so hard I only stopped when it felt as if my wrist was going to snap. Duller, slightly diluted maybe, but still there. "Fuck it," I said, standing up, bucket in hand. I was running an illegal tavern, after all, not a luxury hotel.

From the moment I stepped outside, I made a point of not looking anywhere but at the ground or the bucket, kept at my task without even once so much as glancing at the dog. When the bucket was emptied and it and the brush were set out in the sun to dry, I occupied myself with whatever chore was at hand—pulling weeds, picking up rocks, gathering up debris. Even when I ended up as far as the middle of the lot, dragging a charred log back toward the house, as long as I didn't look directly at the dog, he stayed where he was. From the corner of my eye I could see he'd even sat down now, like he was amused to watch me go about my business. I could also see, aside from the patches of fur missing from his black coat, that a good chunk of his right ear was gone, looked as if it had been bitten right in half, and that one of his eyes was permanently shut tight. Given the condition of the rest of him, I didn't doubt that the socket underneath the closed lid was empty.

I stopped myself from doing what I wanted to do—turn to him, talk to him, tell him not to be afraid, that I wasn't a threat, that I wanted to help—and walked as nonchalantly as possible back inside the house, but not down to the basement this time. Except for my books and the furnishings and supplies I'd been steadily assembling for Sophia's and the few things I needed to cowboy it out on the parlour floor—a mattress, a suitcase of clothes, a bar of soap—the house itself was still as empty as the day I took possession. The kitchen was even barer: a bottle of whiskey, a water pitcher and a glass, a loaf of bread, and a couple of tomatoes. I didn't have anything else to give him, so I tore off a chunk of bread. In spite of his wounds, it was obvious he was still alert and energetic, so he must have been drinking from the Thames, didn't need any water.

I shut the screen door behind me, careful not to let it slam, and walked in a straight line to the middle of the yard with my eyes focused on my feet. I got down on my knees and held out the bread in the palm of my right hand, stared at the earth directly beneath my chin. I could feel the dog creeping toward me a foot or two at a time, always stopping to reassess the situation, to be careful, to be sure. About twelve feet from where I was kneeling he stopped for good, sat down like he had when he was watching me working in the yard. I knew he wasn't coming any closer, at least not for now, so I placed the piece of bread on the ground and walked back to the house.

From the kitchen window, I watched him wait to make sure I'd gone inside before grabbing the bread in his mouth and running off through the trees at the back of the lot. I wasn't disappointed he hadn't let me feed him; if it had been me, I would have done the same thing. A stray has to be vigilant. A stray has to be self-reliant. If he decided to come back tomorrow, I'd make sure to have some meat for him. And a name, too. I decided I'd call him Waldo.

*

I knew Thompson was doomed the day he was moved to testify about Walt Whitman. I remember the precise date—July 11, 1887—because it was the first time he came into Sophia's, only the second night I was open for business.

It wasn't difficult to acquire an instant clientele. It might have been hard to find anyone—especially anyone who considered himself a respected member of Chatham's business community—who didn't publicly support the Scott Act, but if you paid attention to the eyes of the strangers you passed on the sidewalk or the faces you encountered while looking for roofing nails or a new sledgehammer at the hardware store, it was obvious that something was wrong, some stubborn collective itch wasn't being scratched, some essential numinous nutrient was lacking in the local diet. The *Planet* cheerfully reported that church attendance had increased by more than fifteen percent since the implementation of prohibition, but it wasn't God that packed the pews and heavied the collection plate, it was the need to get drunk. Which is just a different way of pronouncing *God* anyway.

The whiskey was barely drinkable and the basement smelt and was still damp and what we were all doing down there wasn't legal, but within forty-eight hours of opening for business I'd already recouped my start-up costs. I was still finding my pouring/charging/refilling rhythm when I had my first security scare. Standing directly behind two bearded men pressing up against the bar with their outstretched empty glasses was another man I recognized but couldn't quite place—rarely a promising combination. I served the two bearded men their drinks and took their coins and prepared myself to do whatever had to be done. One way or another, I wasn't going back to the graveyard by choice.

"Well, well, hello again," the man said.

As soon as the first Scot-splattered words flew from the man's mouth, I remembered who he was: Thompson, the lawyer who'd sold me the house whose basement we were both standing in. Which still didn't explain why he was here. Most of my customers were workingmen, drinking and smoking and doing what workingmen do and will always do, trying their best to forget the workday done and the too-soon one to come.

Thompson removed a five-dollar bill from his leather billfold and placed it on the bar. "Whiskey, please, Mr. King," he said.

I looked at the bill then back at him. "Whiskey is twenty-five cents a shot," I said.

"And given the present circumstances, quite reasonably priced at that," Thompson answered, pushing the five dollars my way. "I was wondering, however, if I might pay in advance for tonight's libations. I'm afraid that occasionally, when I'm enjoying myself as I expect to do this evening, I have a tendency to forget to settle my tab. Not for reasons nefarious, of course, but simply out of innocent absent-mindedness."

"You want to pay in advance for twenty shots of whiskey?" I said, still not picking up the bill. Anyone who planned to drink that much alcohol in one sitting likely wasn't anyone I had to worry about. Not to notify the police, anyway.

"Oh, no, of course not," Thompson said. "That includes a dollar tip for what, I'm sure, will be your more than able service as well."

I poured him his drink and took the money.

By the end of the night, three things had become clear. First, if I continued to provide alcohol and a safe place to consume it, it wasn't unrealistic to imagine myself a very wealthy man someday. Second, that providing alcohol and a safe place to consume it weren't my only job requirements; at the conclusion of every night's labour I could expect to be as filthy and exhausted as I had ever been as a grave robber, with the added insult of smelling as if every cigarette and cigar smoked that night had used me as its ashtray. And third, working among the drunken living as opposed to the recently deceased wasn't necessarily an improvement in working conditions. Over the course of that night's twelve hours alone, I'd had to stop two arguments before they turned into fights, confiscate two blackjacks and one fishing knife, mop up a belch of vomit and a sleeping drunk's pool of urine, and listen to enough lies, self-pity, and out-and-out twaddle to keep any confession-hearing priest busy until the arrival of the twentieth century.

Thompson won the job of being my sole work-shift voluntary acquaintance by default: didn't get cantankerous, no matter how much he drank; didn't carry any weapons; didn't lose control of his bodily functions; and didn't talk about himself unless directly asked, and even then remained elusive to the point of outright evasion. He liked to talk, but only about things that excited him. His own life, apparently, wasn't one of those things. Walt Whitman was.

Wiping down a nearby empty table and noticing him desultorily pecking away at a small notepad, I'd asked, jokingly, if he was writing a poem. What I really wanted to know was if he had any idea where the bloodstains I'd discovered on the basement floor of his former client's house came from, but I thought it best for now to separate work from pleasure, at least until I got a better fix on him. Thompson shut his notepad and deposited it in the inside pocket of his suit jacket and leaned forward with both elbows on the table and didn't stop talking until he'd said what he had to say.

"There is only one poet alive today, and that man's name is Walt Whitman. Walt Whitman the joyful liberator. Walt Whitman the unrepentant fornicator. Walt Whitman the secular man's saviour. Walt Whitman the proud apostle of democracy, science, and steam. And yet, and yet—" Thompson gulped what was left in his glass, like he was afraid of something getting stuck in his throat. "And yet Walt Whitman remains a neglected martyr, continues to live in despair and loneliness and want, and whose immortal poems in their public reception have fallen stillborn in this country as well as in that of his native United States, immortal poems that have been met with denial and disgust and scorn and even charges of outright obscenity, and, in a very real pecuniary and worldly sense, have most certainly destroyed the life of their author."

I'd finished cleaning the table just in time for three men just off their jobs on the railroad to sit down. Before I could get them their whiskey, Thompson continued. A little of the pleasant affability of before returned to his voice.

"Don't misunderstand me, though. All of these admittedly unfortunate circumstances are no more than he himself expected. He had his choice when he commenced upon his task. But Walt Whitman bid neither for soft eulogies, big money returns, nor the approbation of existing schools and conventions. He has had his say and has put it unerringly on record that Walt Whitman's value thereof will be vindicated by Time and Time alone." Thompson noticed the empty glass in his hand. "I'm afraid I'm going to have to trouble you to replenish my drink, Mr. King."

All three men from the railroad were now staring at Thompson. It was difficult to determine what they wanted more: their whiskey or Thompson's neck.

I turned to the biggest, dirtiest one. "A bottle and three glasses, coming right up," I said. And to Thompson, "Why don't you sit closer to the bar, nearer to me?"

Thompson smiled. "So we can talk some more," he said.

"Exactly," I replied.

*

It's time for Loretta to leave for Montreal again. Twice a year, every spring and fall, six nights and seven days of preening, pampering, and all-around polishing. She always stays at the same luxury hotel, the Rasco, supplements every breakfast, lunch, and dinner with plenty of beluga caviar and very cold Mumm champagne, and for several years has employed the same elderly female German masseuse, who arrives at her hotel room every morning at ten to give her her hour-long wake-up working-over. None of it is an indulgence, however, she never fails to point out, particularly when attempting to convince me to join her. Inevitably, it always comes back to my clock.

"No matter how well made a clock is, it still needs to be rewound, does it not?"

We're both looking at the long-case clock standing in the corner of the library, watching it patiently counting the seconds and minutes, mindful of minding its own ticking business.

"Just like people," I say, knowing my part.

"Yes, just like people. And remove that foolish grin from your face. This mocking of yours of things you do not understand, this is as good a reason you need to go away from time to time as any other."

"Just because I don't feel the need to take a holiday like other people doesn't mean I'm mocking something I don't understand."

"I am sorry, but yes, it does. You are like the person who says, 'I know what I like,' but what they are really saying is, 'I like what I know.'"

Loretta directs her attention back to the small box of photographs resting on her lap, but I'm still looking at the clock. I knew that one day I wanted to have my own long-case clock the very first time I saw the one in the Reverend King's sitting room. Aside from the Reverend King himself, I'd never been in the presence of anyone or anything so quietly, unfailingly dignified. The first thing I purchased when this house was built and finally ready to be moved into was an eighteenth-century Scottish mahogany long-case clock made by James Howden of Edinburgh. After what I had to pay to have it shipped over, it ended up costing only slightly less than what I'd originally paid for the half-acre of land that the house is built upon.

"I know enough to know that I do—that I *buy*—plenty of things that aren't just meat and potatoes."

"You do not eat meat."

"It's an expression. It means things that are only essential."

Loretta considers this. "This is not an effective expression. Particularly for one such as yourself who does not eat meat."

"Anyway, the point I was making is that I buy things— rare books, for instance—that—"

"You buy things, you buy things—what you need is not to buy things, what you need is to look at the things you already have with new eyes. This is what every person needs."

All the while she's talking, Loretta is sifting through her most recent collection of photographs. If anything, it seems only to sharpen her focus on what she's saying.

"And I suppose I'll get these new eyes if I travel three hundred miles to eat expensive dead fish eggs and have my back rubbed by a stranger?"

Loretta looks up, sighs for effect. "Please do not try to be foolish. This is not something you need to try to do."

Just for that, I decide to punish her by denying her the pleasure of my continued conversation on the slim chance that she'll actually even notice, pick up where I left off in my book. Actually, it doesn't matter where I last was, as I'm skipping and skimming anyway, one illusion-loosening page of Winwood Reade's *The Martyrdom of Man* as good as any other to revisit and delight in all over again. Whether because my eyes, like the rest of me, are older—itch and burn if I read too long—or because I'm just getting lazy, I prefer to reread beloved books now rather than search out new favourites. In point of fact, it's much simpler than that: I like to hear familiar voices. *The Martyrdom of Man* was, yes, one of *those* books— portrayed Jesus, for instance, as neither the son of God nor even a great moral teacher, but simply as a fallible, if admittedly alluring, human being, and only one of a number of very similar contemporary Jewish fanatics. But just as much as his liberating message, it was Winwood Reade, the thoroughly sensible but always sprightly messenger, who compelled me to listen and learn. As I do now, this time as to why Rome really declined and fell:

> *Industry is the only true source of wealth, and there was no industry in Rome. By day the Ostia road was crowded with carts and muleteers, carrying to the great city the silks and spices of the East, the marble of Asia Minor, the timber of Atlas, the grain of Africa and Egypt; and the carts brought out nothing but loads of dung.*

History made human, all too delightfully human. Just as feisty and refreshing as the very first time I read it.

Probably because she's detected yet another foolish grin on my face, "You are a confused man," Loretta says.

Still smiling, "I was just amused by something I read," I say. "Listen to this. Reade—that's the author, Winwood Reade—he—"

Loretta waves away my kind offer of a complimentary lecture. "I am speaking of you—you, David—as confused."

Well, I'm confused about one thing, anyway. "What am I supposed to be confused about?"

Now that she has my attention, Loretta resumes sorting through her box of photographs. "On this hand, you are a very brave man. You choose a life for yourself—a good life—and you live it as you wish. This is not common, I do not have to tell you this."

I easily avoid any danger of sinning from an excess of pride because I know there's another hand coming. Whenever there's occasion to feel good, you can usually count on the other hand.

"But on the other hand . . ." I say.

"But on this other hand, you are very much afraid."

I lower my eyes to my book without bothering to read what's there. "Ah, I see. And what exactly is it I'm afraid of?"

"How would I know such a thing? But always the way you are unwilling to go anywhere or do anything you have not already been or done before, this is how you are confused, yes? You are a brave man and you are an afraid man."

"That's not what 'confused' means. What you mean is—" What does she mean? "What you mean is, I'm a contradiction."

"Is a contradiction not confusing?"

"I suppose so, but—"

"Then they are the same, yes? And you are surely one who is confused."

Even if I did know what she's talking about, I know it's better to nod instead of argue. I pick up my book again. Almost immediately I put it back down.

"When did you say you leave for Montreal?"

17

I'd quit plenty of other jobs before, and this, I told myself, was just one more, albeit one I'd held longer than any other. I'd finally found someone who would supply Sophia's with the ever-increasing amount of whiskey I needed and who didn't demand dead bodies as currency, and at a much better rate, too. I knew Burwell wouldn't be pleased to lose a veteran grave robber, but he was a businessman, he'd understand. He'd have to.

"So that's it, then," I said.

I'd informed Burwell that this was the last human being I'd ever disturb from his supposedly eternal resting place, and Burwell had motioned for Ferguson to give me the last ten bottles of whiskey I was ever going to purchase from him. I'd decided I would tell him about Sophia's if he asked me again what I needed all the whiskey for, but he didn't. Burwell was sitting in the passenger seat of his wagon, I in the driver's seat of mine. It was our usual sort of meeting place, an empty road beside a fallow field just before sundown.

Ferguson handed me the box of whiskey and I placed it in the back of the wagon without getting out of my seat. Part of me said to climb down and go and shake Burwell's hand; another part of me said to stay where I was, don't get out of the wagon no matter what. I stayed in the wagon.

"I'm sure I'll be seeing you around," I said, neither sure nor desirous of any such thing.

"Of course you will, lad. Why wouldn't you?"

Ferguson had climbed back in the wagon and grabbed the reins.

"So, that's it, then," I said.

"So you've said. Twice."

I rustled the reins; there wasn't anything left to do but leave.

As I pulled away, "I'll be seeing you soon, lad," I heard Burwell call out.

I wondered whether or not I should turn right around and tell Burwell no, he wouldn't, not if I had anything to do with it. But before I could make up my mind, it was too late, I could hear Burwell's wagon going the other way.

*

For some, it's love gone wrong. For others, money gone missing. For still others, good health going going gone and not coming back. To each prospective suicide his own unique inspiration. For Thompson, it was Walt Whitman's garbage.

It was December 24 the entire month of July in the summer of 1887, Sophia's first summer of business, Thompson for weeks before he was supposed to travel to London to hear speak and quite possibly even meet Walt Whitman suffering one long, continuous, nervous night before Christmas. Thompson had learned that not only did Whitman have a younger brother living under the care of the insane asylum in London, Ontario, whom he periodically visited, but its superintendent, Richard Maurice Bucke, was both a disciple and an intimate of the aged poet, and that Bucke had persuaded Whitman to read from his work for the local literary society the next time he was in town. Only by nightly numb-

ing himself with my whiskey and just as unfailingly mono-
loguing my ear raw with what he expected the great man to
look and talk and act like and how he honestly didn't know
what to expect of himself if he was permitted, however briefly,
actually to occupy the same physical space as his long-time
hero, was he able to avoid boiling over before the big day even
arrived and to limit himself to a low but steady daily simmer.

One night—after closing time, no one left but Thompson and me—he talked and talked until I think he said something true. Because, whether or not you want it, run a hot
water tap long enough and you're eventually going to get
scalding water. It began with a poem. No matter how much
whiskey he'd had, Thompson saved his recitation of Whitman's verse for when Sophia's was empty except for us. You
don't survive as an outcast by being stupid.

> "'Of two simple men I saw today, on the pier, in the
> midst of the crowd, parting the parting of dear friends,
> "'The one to remain hung on the other's neck, and
> passionately kissed him,
> "'While the one to depart, tightly pressed the one
> to remain in his arms.'"

I looked up from my mop. Thompson was so rarely quiet
these days, the sudden silence sounded loud. He picked up
his glass and swallowed without appearing to notice it was
empty. He shut his eyes and kept them that way once he
began talking again.

"Please understand, in Whitman's conception of comradeship—and here's the thing one needs to understand,
here's the thing that desperately needs to be understood—in
Whitman's conception of comradeship as best exemplified, of
course, in the poem 'Calamus,' he allows for the possibility—
and that's all I'm saying—all he's saying, rather, all *Whitman*

is saying—he allows for the possibility of the possible intrusion—the wrong word, I'm afraid, but it's all that comes to
mind at the moment—allows for the possible intrusion of
those possibly amorous emotions and actions that no doubt—
because there is no doubt, there really is no doubt—do occur,
occasionally, between men. According to Whitman, you see,
such emotions and actions are to be left entirely to the incli-
nations and conscience of the *individuals* involved. The individuals who are comrades. True comrades. True individuals
who are true comrades."

Thompson opened his eyes to me looking at him. He
looked back at me like he was waiting for me to say something
he'd been slowly dying his entire life for someone to finally,
mercifully, say. And because I wasn't the one to say it—could
only nod into my bucket and nervously re-soak my mop and
sincerely hope that one day he'd hear it—Thompson stood
up from his table and wordlessly exited upstairs to merge
with the night slowly dissolving into morning. It wouldn't be
the last time he quoted from Walt Whitman while I cleaned
up, but he never recited another line quite so explicitly . . .
comradely ever again.

The day he returned from London, I found him sitting
on the ground with his back flat against the locked door of
Sophia's when I arrived to open up for the night. Thompson's
wrinkled, whiskey-stained suit showed he'd been sleeping
in it, probably since the day he'd left Chatham. There was
another, more recent stain spread across his crotch that I was
fairly certain wasn't whiskey but that had certainly started out
that way.

There are two kinds of regulars: those who drink so as not
to have to speak and those whose sole purpose in public drinking is to speak and be heard. Everybody gets served the same
whiskey, but a successful publican knows whom to politely

ignore and whom to patiently endure. Thompson waited until I'd lit the lamps and poured him his first drink before starting to talk. It takes a few minutes for one's eyes to entirely adjust to the lamps' soft defeat of the basement's darkness. Thompson's voice mingled with light and dark like a smoke ring on a damp fall night.

"Yes, he spoke, I heard Walt Whitman speak," he said, answering the question I hadn't asked. "He spoke on the subject of Thomas Paine. Of how Thomas Paine wasn't the notorious infidel that the Christian clergymen have made him out to be, but, instead, was a man who had done more to secure the independence of the United States than any other. He didn't read from his poetry. He never mentioned his poems."

I kept busy readying Sophia's for the evening's second customer, but kept an eye on Thompson's glass as well.

"The assembly hall was ill lit and dank. There were only thirty odd of us, although ten times that, at least, could easily have been accommodated. But I took a chair in the middle of the first row and it wasn't long before the dimness and the mustiness and the scraping of empty chairs didn't matter. I—" Thompson finally took a sip of his whiskey. "*We* waited for Whitman to appear."

The lamps had done their job by now, tricked night into day one more time.

"A few minutes later, Whitman appeared on the platform. He walked slowly—he used a stick—and his carriage was stiff, as if another, concealed stick was keeping his spine in place and his body upright. He must have had a stroke—he *must* have—because he talked even slower than he walked, he talked like every word he spoke cost him physical effort. His beard was long and white. What has been said about his long white beard is accurate."

I topped off Thompson's glass. He didn't thank me, didn't even acknowledge me.

"And his jacket was buttoned wrong."

Thompson drained his drink, set it back down on the table with a smack that could only have meant either he was done for the night or he wanted another without delay. I didn't have to ask to know which one it was.

"The last button on his jacket was buttoned where the second button should have been. He looked like a confused old man. He looked like a damn fool." Thompson downed the refill like he was attempting to kill the disgust that the words he'd just spoken had left behind in his mouth.

"So he looked unkempt," I said from behind the bar. Bartenders get paid to listen, not lecture, but this seemed as good an exception to the rule as any. "Dottiness is an old man's privilege."

Thompson didn't appear to hear what I said, let alone consider it. "Then it was over. People clapped their hands and some people pressed around him to talk to him, but I had to get outside. I walked and walked without knowing where I was going. The fresh air helped. I sat down in a park when it seemed safe to stop moving."

A man, a workingman, with a newspaper underneath his arm and dead eyes where his life should have been, found a table far enough away from us that, after I served him his whiskey, Thompson continued where he'd left off.

"I don't know how long I sat there—half an hour, an hour maybe—but when I got up, I knew what I had to do, there was only one thing I *could* do. My ex-colleague at the practice, the one who knew Bucke, the one who had told me about Whitman coming to town, had also told me that Whitman was staying at the Noyes Hotel. I needed to speak to him. Privately. I needed to speak to him immediately. I hired a carriage and was there in ten minutes."

I poured Thompson another drink, but he ignored it, went to the cold fireplace and put his hands in the pockets of his jacket and stared at the empty grate.

"I told the concierge I had a message for Mr. Whitman from Dr. Bucke, and he gave me the room number without asking any questions. His room was on the third floor. I didn't know if I possessed the courage to knock until the instant I felt my knuckles against the grain of the wood on the door, but once I did, I knew everything was going to be all right. When there was no answer, I knocked again, twice this time, and knew that, even though I didn't know what I was going to say, once I saw him, I would."

Thompson squatted on his heels in front of the fireplace, took the poker from its stand, and pushed around the coal-black dead embers inside. "But no one answered. I knocked again, and again, but no one answered. I still don't know how I managed it, but I tried the door handle, and it turned, and I found myself inside the room. But the room was empty of anything that had been Walt Whitman. He'd obviously left. Whitman was gone."

Thompson scraped the same six-inch expanse of the fireplace's hearth with the poker, back and forth, back and forth, a filthy windowpane that won't come clean. "And then I saw it. In the corner, beside the bed. A tin canister. Walt Whitman's garbage. I grabbed it—I hid it underneath my coat as best I could—and went out the hotel's back door."

I knew I was hearing a confession, not having a conversation, but, "You took his garbage?" I said.

Thompson stood up and put the poker back in its stand but didn't turn around from the fireplace. "I locked myself in my hotel room and didn't rush myself—I *made* myself be thorough, I *forced* myself not to miss anything—and I went through every item in that canister as meticulously as anyone possibly could."

"The canister filled with Walt Whitman's garbage."

"I don't think I've ever been more careful with anything in my life."

I don't think I've ever believed anything anyone's ever told me more.

"And do you know what, David?"

"What?"

"It was just fucking garbage."

I didn't know what to say, so Thompson said it for me.

"It was just fucking garbage."

*

Who knew? Apparently there really does exist too much of a good thing.

"A pair of pants—that I can believe, I said. Come spring-time, what man hasn't had occasion to pull on a pair of pants only to find that they're a little snug. That's what winter is for, isn't it? Plumping up? To help keep warm? That's what all of God's creatures do, don't they?"

Even if our bimonthly Saturday night bottle of whiskey wasn't half empty, I'd still know George is drunk. I would never take his Saviour's name in vain in George's presence, and he'd never invoke his Lord's limitless love, might, or forgiveness in mine.

"But a jacket?" he says. He swallows the last of his drink, sets the empty glass back down on the kitchen table. "I told Mary it must have shrunk—over the winter—we must have put it away in the fall when it was wet, it must have shrunk."

I'm watching George tell his story while I pour two more drinks. When the bottle hits the halfway mark, I always mix the whiskey with two fingers of water. Diluting liquor this good is a bartending crime, I know, but the whiskey has done its part—elevated each of us to a place where only mystics and poets and other lucky madmen are intended to linger—and now it's up to us to stay afloat here just as long as we can, to not cross over and up to that next level of intoxication that turns bards into babblers and seers into sentimental bores. Nirvana isn't easy work.

"Because this is a jacket, understand. Not a shirt or a vest—a spring jacket. And it won't . . ." George begins to laugh: I set down our drinks and myself at the table, feel my own smiling face bubbling beginning to join him. ". . . it won't button up. 'Maybe I *have* put on a few pounds this winter,' I tell Mary." George sips his fresh drink, places it carefully back down like he knows, if he's holding it while he finishes his story, he's bound to spill it. "And Mary says . . ." George laughs again, shuts his eyes, and nods his head in time with every fresh exhalation. ". . . Mary says, 'Either that, or all your clothes are getting smaller.'"

The two of us fall about ourselves so loudly, Henry just has to come into the kitchen to see what all the fuss is about. He sniffs at the air with a raised snout; he looks at me and then George and then back at me; finally decides that, whatever it is we're up to, it's not nearly interesting enough to stay awake for, trots back into the library to lie back down on the rug in front of the unlit fire, tail wagging contentedly the entire time.

Since Loretta is in Montreal, not only is the house unheated, every window is pried wide open to the crisp early April air. As a boy, my favourite season was winter, every overnight snowfall another frozen morning miracle, months and months of a cold confetti sky and the entire world just as fresh and clean as the inside of a brand new prayer book. Now I prefer the spring. But that's no surprise. Once one's own endless winter starts to creep into sight, beginnings, not endings, are much more pleasant to contemplate.

George looks around the kitchen like he expects to see something that isn't there. "And how long is your friend away?" he says.

My *friend* is Loretta. Loretta the unmarried white woman I occasionally cohabit with. Which isn't how I'd prefer my oldest friend to think about the woman I love, but which is in keeping with the accepted Buxton line, namely, that only married people live together, and only people who have the same skin colour get married. And George is a Buxton man, so that's all right. And I'm not a Buxton man, and that's all right too.

"Monday," I say. "She'll be back on Monday."

George shakes his head. "Don't you get lonely?"

"It's only a week."

"I couldn't do it. If I'm away from my Mary for even just an evening—like tonight, for instance—I can't wait to get back home."

"And your company is just as enjoyable to me."

"Ah, you know what I mean."

I smile, nod, because I do. But it feels good sometimes to feel sad missing someone. Missing them reminds you why you want them around. Which isn't the same as being lonely.

"I never feel lonely," I say.

"Come on. Everybody gets lonely."

"I don't."

"Ah . . ."

"I don't. But when it's time for her to come back, I do start to get lonely for *her*. For Loretta."

Now it's George's turn to nod and smile.

"But maybe you're right," I say. "The longest she's ever been away are the trips she takes to Montreal. Lately she's been talking about going overseas. Back to Germany. Maybe a month straight of myself *will* make me lonely."

"Or crazy."

"Or crazy."

A brisk breeze flutters the Meyers' Drugstore calendar on the wall by the window. Each month features a different poorly sketched British landmark—Big Ben, London Bridge, Westminster Abbey—and on the once-a-year occasion Meyers hands them around Sophia's, he's like a brand new father passing around celebratory cigars.

"Why don't you go too?" George says.

"We've talked about it. But someone would have to run things for me. For a month, maybe more. And then there's the cost."

"Ah, go and see the world. None of us is getting any younger."

"You don't need to tell me that," I say, massaging my sore right elbow, my pouring elbow. "But like I said, there's the matter of—"

George waves away the rest of my sentence. "Shut that place of yours down for a month. Or two. Or however long you need. You can afford it. I may not know much, but I know when a man has set himself up right, and you've set yourself up real, real nice."

"I don't know," I say.

George raises his glass; holds it there until I see he wants to offer a toast. I lift mine too. "You're a good man, David," he says. I wait for more—a punchline, a jokey disclaimer—but all there is is George still holding his glass aloft. "You deserve good things."

"Everybody does," I say.

"Yes. And that includes you too."

We finally clink and drink, set down our glasses.

George is tasting his lips like he's trying to determine the precise flavour of something.

"What?" I say.

Now he licks his lips, pushes his drink toward me. "Try this," he says.

"I mixed it the same as mine."

"I didn't say you didn't. Just try it."

I don't tell George how to run his factory, so he should let me handle how the drinks get made, but I lift his glass anyway.

When he sees me lick my own lips, he picks up my glass, samples what's in it.

We both start laughing at the same time. And laugh, and laugh, and laugh. Long enough that Henry gets up from the rug and goes upstairs.

Once we've settled down:

"Here, give me that," I say, taking back what had been my drink, four generous shots of one hundred percent water.

"You think I'm going to trust a man who served himself a glass of four parts water and no parts whiskey?"

I pour some of George's drink into my glass, I pour some of my drink into George's. His elbow on the table, George leans his big head on his big fist and watches me attempt to undo my mixing mistake. "Very professional," he says.

I pour some more of my drink into George's glass, then some of George's drink into mine. I give each glass a final clockwise swirl and hand him back his drink. "Judge them by the fruits of their labour," I say.

George sips, shuts his eyes, leans his head back on the back of his chair. "Mmm," he says.

"You approve?"

"Mmm hmm."

"I'll take that as a yes."

Head still tilted backward, eyes still closed, "I never doubted you for a minute," George says.

*

The woods make more sense after you've moved to the city. The annoying nothing of before, miraculously transformed into the wonderful absence of after. Conversations you don't want to have with people you wish you didn't know rarely transpire while out walking with your dog in an early morning mist with only the squirrels and the birds and the occasional brave or foolish hare witnesses to a forty-eight-year-old man surprising himself as much as his delighted, barking dog by suddenly running figure eights between and around a long row of just-budding elms for no other reason than his body tells him to.

When I reach the finish line at the last tree, I can feel my lungs inhaling and exhaling my heart rate back to normal without my having asked them to. I'm wet and cold from the mist, but my hands in their gloves and my feet in their boots and my head underneath its hat are dry and warm and content. I shut my eyes and stand in place and am certain that anyone who has ever claimed to have been any happier than I am right now is a liar.

"Thank you," I say.

The warming sun and the cool wind take turns showing my exposed face what they can do. The wind and the leafless branches of the still spring-naked trees work together to say what they have to say.

"Thank you," I shout.

It's been thirty years since the last time I prayed.

My voice—my thanks—echoes back to me.

18

A man has to work, but a man who works for himself is happier. *I* was happier. Not just because I was making and not spending and so saving plenty of money, but because the only person who told me what to do and when to do it was me. Even if I did have to tell myself to do everything and to do it all of the time.

Then some fool had to go and dynamite the house of Hugh F. Cumming.

Ordinarily, the well-being of someone like Cumming—banker, insurance agent, failed West Kent Liberal nominee—wouldn't have concerned me in the least, except that this someone also happened to be the president of the County of Kent Temperance Association. Dynamitings weren't an everyday occurrence in Chatham (the front page of the *Planet* screamed DYNAMITE FIEND! STARTLING OUTRAGE! *Peaceful Town Startled from Its Slumbers by Human Thunder. Providential Escape of H.F. Cumming and Wife from a Horrible Death*), and if public opinion was correct, the explosion that took place at Cumming's home on Victoria Avenue the night of August 7 was somehow instigated by those whose business interests were suffering as a result of prohibition. And since my business interests were, in fact, flourishing for precisely the same reason, I had a keen interest in the perpetrators being caught and law and order being promptly restored. Odd how all that needs to happen for you to become respectable is have somebody threaten to take away your money.

I had no way of knowing if either of the provincial inspectors in charge of keeping Chatham dry were aware of what was going on at Sophia's, and I didn't wait to find out. The meek might inherit the earth, but it's the pushy who own it until then. The *Planet* regularly listed the names of individuals and businesses found guilty of Scott Act prosecutions, but mine and that of Sophia's were never among them. The Reverend King always emphasized to new settlers the need to set aside a portion of their weekly earnings from working on the railroad or wherever else they were making their initial living for the purchase of land and equipment and seed, would ceaselessly counsel them to be wary of the danger of not seeing the forest for the trees. "A penny wise, a pound foolish," he'd say. The weekly bribes I paid out to the police were less money in my pocket in the short term, but I was never fined and Sophia's was never shut down.

"Well, there's little doubt about it now," Meyers said, rattling his copy of the *Planet*.

Because God is a merciful God, He gave the world newspapers so dull people would have something to say. Meyers waited, as usual, for someone else standing at the bar to ask him to elaborate; and because, as usual, no one did, he went ahead and explained himself anyway.

"It says here that last night in Wallaceburg, McDougall's stables were set on fire." McDougall was the police magistrate and another leading local prohibitionist. For a change, what was coming out of Meyers's mouth mattered.

"Fires happen all the time," I said from behind the bar.

"Indeed, yes," Meyers said, pushing his spectacles up his nose, "but it appears that this particular fire was not the result of simple carelessness. It says here—" Meyers lost his place, traced the page with a fat finger for where he'd left off reading. I took the paper from him.

What must have been the world's stupidest arsonist-for-hire, a man by the unlikely name of Martin Martin, had been arrested before the fire had even been extinguished. Martin, it turned out, was married to the daughter of Will Aber, a Wallaceburg hotel-keeper, whom McDougall had fined for a Scott Act violation, and who had publicly threatened the magistrate that he was going to "burn out one of these days." Martin had been spotted walking away from the McDougall farm carrying a half-empty can of kerosene. The article also reported that no arrests had yet been made in the case of the Cumming dynamiting. I handed Meyers his newspaper back.

"The people, it appears, have spoken," Meyers said. "At this rate, this damnable prohibition will be repealed before the year is over." Nodding assent to his own declaration, "And not a bloody moment too soon, if you ask me." When neither voices nor glasses were raised in immediate agreement, "Of course," Meyers added, "one does have to take a dim view of the rounders who committed these heinous deeds. You do have to wonder, I mean, at the moral fibre of those behind all of this senseless violence." Getting the same silent response, Meyers crawled back inside his glass.

I went in the back to check on Waldo. I followed my usual routine when approaching him now that I'd finally coaxed him inside: slowly opened the door; used his name several times as I inched toward him; gingerly unfolded the butcher-paper-wrapped hunk of ham hock in my right hand. A single tail thump admitted me closer. Carefully bending down to offer him the hunk of meat, I could see that he was finally lying on the blanket I'd laid out for him. Dogs don't lie. They might bark at you, they might chase you, they might even bite you, but a dog won't lie to you. In dogs I trust.

I was watching Waldo eat when the door opened—not slowly—and Burwell blocked most of what little light from the bar illuminated the backroom.

"First an entrepreneur, now an animal enthusiast. I am impressed, David. You've come a long, long way, lad, from the stealing of dead bodies."

Waldo dropped the meat from his mouth mid-chew, snarled. When he let me hold him back by the loose skin around his neck, I knew he trusted me. "What do you want, Burwell? I told you, we've got nothing left to talk about." I used my other hand to stroke Waldo's head. I could feel vibrations of rage through his skull.

"Perhaps I'm here for pleasure. Word *has* got around that yours is a very convivial spot to sample those refreshments which are temporarily illegal in our fair burg."

Whatever he wanted, he wasn't going to get it that way. I was surprised: Burwell hadn't done his homework. If he had, he would have known that my dutiful bribing had made me immune to that particular strain of blackmail. I felt the way I did the first time I beat Mr. Rapier, my teacher at Buxton, at chess.

"Say whatever's on your mind, Burwell. I'm getting tired of holding this dog back." With every sentence Burwell spoke, I could feel Waldo pull a little bit harder; it was as if Burwell's voice had a uniquely enraging effect on him. I let Waldo pull an inch—no more—closer, and it did the job, made Burwell take a step back. I patted Waldo's pulsing head.

Seeing me see him recoil, however slightly, Burwell gave up whatever idea he'd had of intimidating me and said what he'd come to say. "I think we should be in business together, David. Not as employer and employee this time. As partners."

"I don't need a partner. I'm managing just fine on my own."

"You don't need a partner now, perhaps, but in the event of unforeseen difficulties it's very advantageous, believe me, to have someone one can count on to help lighten the load of increased responsibilities and new, less than pleasant obligations."

I felt relieved, emboldened even. If that was Burwell's best shot, it wasn't enough even to nick me, let alone leave me wounded as intended and begging for his help. In spite of my hand pinching his flesh, Waldo strained a little farther Burwell's way. It was like he wanted to kill Burwell's voice.

"You know that I know that Ferguson is standing outside that door somewhere," I said. "Now I want you to know something. If you don't turn around and leave the same way you two came in as soon as I stop talking, I'm going to let this animal do what he's wanted to do ever since you walked in this room."

Burwell lingered only long enough to look at my eyes, to see if I was telling the truth. He turned around and walked behind the bar and then toward the exit. He didn't need to tell Ferguson to follow. I told Waldo he was a good boy and closed the door behind me.

Before Burwell got to the stairs, "Next time I'll make sure he gets what he wants," I said.

Burwell stopped briefly and smirked like he was amused at how things had played out, but he smiled too wide, looked precisely like what he was, a man not so much frightened as embarrassed he didn't get what he'd thought was already his.

"They seemed like nice-enough chaps," Meyers said. "Although the big fellow, he's not much for conversation, is he? Friends of yours, I take it?"

"I've never seen them before," I said. "And they won't be coming back."

Thompson came up to the bar with his empty glass, a rarity for him. Thompson enjoyed being waited on. That and being listened to when he couldn't stop talking were his only real patronly needs.

"I'm afraid I have a confession to make," he said.

Not today, Thompson, please not today; and not with Meyers, Meyers of all people, standing right beside you.

"When I sold you Sophia's," he said, "I'm afraid I didn't disclose everything I should have."

I refilled his glass, waited. It wasn't until I picked up the bottle that I realized my hand was slightly shaking.

"The reason this place was for sale for so long and why the owner was so eager to sell was because it had—it had an unsavoury past."

"Please don't speak in riddles, Thompson, I'm in no mood."

Thompson nodded into his glass; lifted it, emptied it. "There used to be dogfights held here, in the basement, where we're standing right now, in fact. Absolutely beastly spectacles from what I understand. Not that I ever attended such a revolting event, of course. But the point is that I knew about them when I was showing you the house. And I'm afraid I let my desire for the commission from the sale compromise my professional candour. You see, I was having some financial difficulties at the time, and, well . . ." Thompson drifted off with his sentence.

"Bloody hell," Meyers said, for once absolutely right.

Now I knew where the bloodstains on the floor I couldn't remove came from. And why Waldo had been lingering around the rear lot of the house. He'd lost an ear, an eye, and hunks of his own flesh, but it was where he used to be fed, probably the only place he ever knew to call home.

I poured myself a shot; shot it. I refilled Meyers' glass and carried the bottle to Thompson's table and did the same with his.

"It's all right," I said.

"David, let me just say—"

"It's all right, Thompson."

And it was. Because Waldo and I were both home now. Home for real. You can only build the house you live in, not the earth it rests upon.

"I shouldn't have said anything, I suppose, I shouldn't even have opened my big mouth. If it hadn't been for that Boswell person, I wouldn't even—"

"Thompson, it's all right." I doubled up his drink. Thompson thanked me by not saying anything else.

Halfway back to the bar, I stopped. "What Boswell person?" I said.

Thompson set down his drink. "That man who just left. The one with the rather large companion."

Burwell, he meant. "What about him?"

Thompson motioned me over. Voice lowered, leaning across his table, "Rumour has it that Boswell was the organizer of the dogfights. Quite a lot of money to be made, apparently, by that sort of thing. Barbaric as it is. It's none of my business, you know, but I'm not sure that Boswell and his kind are the sort you want hanging about Sophia's. I say, David, are you all right?"

"I'm fine," I said, and took my place back behind the bar. After making sure everyone who needed a drink had one, I looked in on Waldo, lying on his new blanket in the backroom. He was fine too.

*

Bartenders don't make house calls, but here I am.

It's been a couple of weeks since Thompson completed his perfect suicide note, and because he wasn't at his usual table at Sophia's tonight, I let Tom close up while Henry and I go looking for 164 Scoyne Street, the room and board where

Thompson's been staying ever since the bank took away his house. I know the address because it's only a few doors down from the building that Loretta wants me to buy as an investment property. Loretta is always on the lookout for a fresh foreclosure, someone else's misery someone else's potential good fortune.

The mud tracks that Henry and I shed behind us lie undisturbed, will stay that way until the pounding rain fills them in and smooths them over and no one will even know we were here. At three o'clock in the morning, it's possible to pretend that your dog and you are the world's only living animals. Tonight's not the kind of night I want to pretend. The bottle under my arm is for Thompson if he's still alive, for me if he's not. I could have come right over when it became clear he wasn't going to show up tonight, but I'm here now—here, instead of at home in bed next to Loretta. And here's 164 Scoyne Street.

I'm in luck. The entire house is dark except for a single window on the second storey on the east side. The weak yellow glow has to belong to Thompson. Whether he's up there in spirit as well as in the flesh isn't so certain. I let Henry nose around for someplace new and compelling to pee while I look for a rock not too big but not too small. I find one and aim and smack the windowpane almost precisely in the middle. Henry looks up at the click of rock meeting glass while lifting his leg. We both wait.

A silhouette looking at us looking at it; then the reluctant tug of damp wood against damp wood and the window groans open. Thompson sticks his head out, looks down. "You shouldn't be here, David."

Believe me, I want to say, the thought has crossed my mind too. Instead, "We missed you tonight," I say.

"No one missed me tonight."

Limp literalism: the surest symptom of the long-gone melancholic. I try to think of something sufficiently straight-forward to say, but Thompson beats me to it.

"You thought I did it, didn't you?"

"Can I come in?" I say, holding up the bottle.

"There's no point. Go home, David."

In lieu of a sound counter-argument, I watch Henry finish the dump he's decided to add to his various urinal markings. A dog with a full bowel and bladder is a dog never lacking in purpose and direction. Lucky dogs.

"Let's have a drink," I say.

"I'm not thirsty."

"Since when has that had anything to do with it?"

I think I can see Thompson smile. Hope yet.

"Just one quick one," I say. "I promise. I don't want to leave Henry out here too long."

The window goes empty and I know that Thompson is coming down to let me in. I leave Henry sitting beside a thin sapling bending in the wet wind like a furious driver's lash. I scratch him between the ears. "I'll be right back, pal, we're going home soon." I avoid his eyes as I walk around to the front of the house. No matter how many times you've left a dog, no matter how many times you've always returned, always the same look of bewildered abandonment seared into its eyes. And knowing that you know you'll be right back never helps. Every goodbye a fresh test of faith.

Thompson says nothing as he unlocks the door, just leaves it open for me and trudges back up the stairs through the darkness. I close the door behind me and follow him. It's the same thing once we get to the second floor. Thompson stands in the middle of his small room with crossed arms and a lank of greasy hair stuck to his forehead. That he hasn't bathed or slept or probably even eaten recently is obvious.

"Have you got two glasses?" I don't bother asking for a towel to dry off.

"No," he says.

A quick examination of the room tells me he's not just trying to get rid of me sooner rather than later. Aside from the neatly made bed, a mirrored bureau, and a single wooden chair, there's little to suggest that the room has recently been occupied. There are not even any pictures or keepsakes or books. I suppose I'd imagined drunken disarray. There's no sign of the perfect suicide note either.

"Where are all your books?" I say. Get him talking about his books. Thompson can't not talk about books.

"You have them. I sold them all to you."

Thompson just stands there, waits for me to contradict him. I pull the cork out of the bottle of Wild Turkey I lifted from my own private stock instead. "You don't need glasses when the liquor is this good," I say, lifting the whiskey to my lips. I offer the bottle to Thompson. He looks at it, then at me, like the sourest prohibitionist. Accordingly, I take another, longer swig. Incredible: angry insolence even while on a suicide watch. The thought of which makes me even angrier, this time at myself, so I swallow a third time.

"Now you've had your drink," Thompson says, uncrossing his arms and going to the door.

I stay where I am. "Yours and mine both."

"Yours and mine both." He's got his hand on the glass knob now.

"So. This not-drinking business. Is it temporary or permanent?" It's not what I'd planned to say, but, considering I had nothing else planned, it seems as sound a strategy as any.

"Both," Thompson says, looking pleased with his answer. Private jokes irritate me, even those coming from a man who has absolutely nothing to joke about.

"Impressive," I say. "You've managed to transcend time. Just like your dear old Uncle Walt."

Thompson takes his hand off the doorknob. "Don't," he says.

"Don't what?"

"Don't talk about things you don't understand."

I sit down on the edge of the bed. It's hard—hard as a newly cut piece of plywood. "Well, you're right about that, anyway. I've never understood how a grown man could swallow any of that 'What I shall assume, you shall assume' nonsense. But I suppose the human mind will believe whatever it wants to believe. *Needs* to believe." I raise the bottle and drink, wipe my whiskey-wet lips on the arm of my coat.

Thompson's face turns a decent approximation of a healthy shade of red, rage and indignation managing to accomplish what health and happiness haven't. He opens his mouth to speak but stops himself before anything comes out. In a determinedly calm voice: "It won't work," he says.

I shake my head, offer over two upturned hands.

Thompson sighs like he's weary of talking to a particularly slow child. "Making me angry enough that I'll forget myself. Forget myself and what it is you came here to find out if I'd done. Which I should have done if I'd had the courage to do it."

"Don't call it courage."

"Integrity."

"That either."

"What would you call it, then?"

"I'd call it a mistake."

"That's because you're not in possession of all of the facts."

"Which facts?"

"The facts that are my life."

"I'm acquainted with those facts," I say. "I've seen far worse facts."

"That's because you're not in possession of all of them."

I stand up from the bed and go to the window to check on Henry, take the bottle with me. He's still there, sitting in the darkness and the rain, waiting for me to come back. I take a long drink before I speak.

"Fact: you're a white man in a white man's world. Fact: you're an educated man in an ignorant world. Fact: you're free to be as happy or as miserable as you choose to be." I take another drink.

"You don't believe that," Thompson says.

"Of course I do. How could I not?" Too much whiskey too soon gangs up on me, makes me feel nauseous and dizzy at the same time. I sit back down on the edge of the bed carefully, like it's my idea.

"You know life isn't that simple."

"Not for everyone, no," I say. "But for any man born free it is."

Thompson runs his hand through his hair, adds an extra lank of greasy bang to the palate of his forehead for his effort. "Let me understand you," he says. "Because I wasn't born a slave, I'm not allowed to be unhappy."

"Oh, you're allowed. You just shouldn't be."

Thompson picks up the bottle from where I left it on the floor, looks at it only for a moment before putting it to his mouth. "And just why the hell not?" he says.

I hold out my hand. Thompson takes another drink then passes me the bottle. "Because it's a sin," I say.

Thompson looks as if he's actually considering what I've said. "What about you, then?" he finally says.

"What about me?"

"Are you a sinner too?"

I push the cork back inside the bottle. "I need to take my dog home," I say.

Thompson nods like I've finally said something he can agree with. "Leave the bottle," he says.

I do what he asks—set the whiskey on the bureau—and let myself out. Thompson will make it through the night.

*

I was still young enough that physical exhaustion wasn't anything a decent night's sleep and a mug of strong black tea in the morning couldn't correct. But it was the other kind of fatigue—the sort that came from having to listen to a bar-hugging bore like Meyers jabber on and on all night about his holiday to Northumberland as a small boy with his father ("the wild icy seas, the great cliffs, the willowy storm clouds racing across the winter sky")—that wilted the will, no matter how willing. But I was learning. Learning, for instance, how to hear without listening. And learning precisely how much patience a paying customer is owed with his change. And one day I was going to have my own house to come home to—a real home—where there'd be hot water to wash away the workday with and a comfortable chair to commence the rest of the night in and wall-to-wall bookshelves spilling over their wise wares like an overripe fruit tree just drooping to be plucked. Happiness, I knew, had to be bought, just like everything else, and I was willing to pay the price.

Thompson, my last lingering patron, had finally departed, and all I had left to do was bury out back the contents of the evening's accumulated dirty ashtrays and lock up. It was a short walk home to the mattress I'd placed on the floor of one of the empty rooms upstairs. Even though it meant having to go downstairs to Sophia's again, I left Waldo in the backroom until I was done outside. The week before, he'd almost caught a raccoon before eventually settling on loudly treeing him, and a barking dog wasn't the kind of word of mouth Sophia's was looking for. I'd dug the hole and was on one knee with the bucket of ashes and dead butts when I heard, but didn't see, Burwell.

"You need an errand boy, lad. On your knees is no place for a businessman, respectable or not."

I finished what I was doing—tapped the bottom of the bucket to empty out the last of the debris—before standing up. It was September blustery, and a patch of tall maple trees near the rear of the property bowed in the wind, the light of the exposed moon revealing Burwell and his three-hundred-pound shadow walking toward me. The wind died down and the trees stood back up and I couldn't see either of them again until they were standing only a few feet away. I didn't say anything. They were the ones who were where they weren't supposed to be; let them do the talking.

"What do you say we go inside and have a drink, lad?"

"I'm closed."

"I thought illegal saloons never closed."

"This one does."

Burwell grinned as if genuinely pleased, shook his head. "All business, just like me." He reached into the pocket of his jacket and pulled out something that looked like a brick. "It's customary to seal a deal with a toast, but to be honest, I've never had much use for customs. Here you are."

It was a fat stack of bills, twenties by the look of it.

"Go on, take them," Burwell said. "They're yours."

"Burwell, I don't know what—and I don't want to know what—this money is supposed to mean, but—"

"You think too much, lad," Burwell said, pushing the stack of bills closer, nearly jabbing me in the stomach. "That's a sign you've got too much on your mind, too many irons in the fire. But that's going to change now that you've got a partner to halve your worries." He poked me, gently, in the midsection with the money. "Come on, take it, it's your fee for cutting me in. I recognize you were the one who put up the initial capital and took the risk. You have to be compensated for that, it's only what's fair. And I think we both can agree that five hundred dollars is fair. *More* than fair."

I looked at the money, then at Burwell and Ferguson, and instead of being frightened, felt only tired. Tired and bored.

"All right, Burwell, let's settle this once and for all, all right?"

"My thoughts exactly, lad."

"All right, here's how it's going to be. No, I'm not going to take your money, so you can put that back where it came from. And no, you're not weaseling in on my business, it's mine and it's going to stay mine, and you can either start up your own place or drop the whole idea altogether, but you can put it out of your mind that I'll allow anyone—you or anyone else—to take a piece of what's mine. It's never going to happen."

Burwell was smiling again, but this time he wasn't amused. I could tell by the way his eyes narrowed behind his spectacles through the smoke of his cigarette. "Is that the truth?"

"That's the truth. And one more thing: if you think you can intimidate me with threats of violence against either me or Sophia's, you're wrong. I swear on my mother's grave, you're wrong. Because you know why, Burwell?" Burwell answered with a cloud of smoke. It wasn't answer enough. "I said, do you know why, Burwell?" My slightly raised voice appeared to wake up Ferguson; I saw him slowly withdraw each of his mallet hands from the pockets of his long coat.

"Why, lad? Why is that?"

"Because now I know what freedom tastes like. And once a slave gets a taste of freedom, he never goes back. Ever."

Burwell took a slow drag on his cigarette, exhaled a mouthful of smoke just as slowly. "I'm surprised at you, lad, truly surprised. You would think by now you would know my methods. Why would I resort to crude acts of physical aggression when all I need to do is ask you for what I want?"

"Because I already said no. And now you're just talking in circles. And do you know what else? I'm tired, and I've said all I have to say. So unless you or—" After all these years, I still wasn't comfortable talking about Ferguson like he wasn't standing right there. "—you or your help plan on killing me right here and now, I'm going to bed." I didn't really think either of them would do anything, at least not right now, but I picked up the empty ash bucket anyway.

"Answer me just one question before you retire, lad."

I switched the bucket from my left hand to my right, from holding it by its handle to gripping it tightly underneath its inside lip. "What?"

"Where were you on the date of August 7?"

"Who cares?"

"So you can't account for your activities on the date in question?"

"What the fuck are you talking about, Burwell?"

"It's a simple question, lad, the kind that gets asked in a court of law every day. Where were you on the date of August 7?"

"I don't know, Burwell. And what's more, I don't care."

"That is not an attitude I would recommend you adopt when you're standing before judge and jury, lad. It's damning enough that three respected members of Chatham saw you— you, David King—at the scene of the recent act of dynamiting that has shook up our formerly sleepy little town, but without being even able to remember where you were on the nights in question, well . . ."

The maple trees bowed again, like they were praying to the wind, while I took in what Burwell said. "Bullshit," I said. "There aren't three people who saw me there, because I wasn't there, and you know it."

"Naturally *I* believe you, lad. But unfortunately, three separate individuals all claim to have witnessed a Negro—that Negro being you—at the scene of the heinous act in quite compromising circumstances. And not only are all three men willing to swear under oath they saw you, but all three are also quite prominent members of our community. From what I understand, one of them is even a member of city council."

The moon went away with the wind, but my eyes were used to Burwell and Ferguson by now, I could see both of them just fine. "And how is it that you have access to this information?" I said.

"Coincidentally enough, all three gentlemen have taken advantage of my lending services in the recent past. Quite heavy borrowers, all three of them, in fact. But I'm pleased to say that their debts might soon be wiped from the ledgers in their entirety."

"If they lie for you."

"If they provide a service for me, yes."

I thought for a moment. I took another moment.

"Oh, and I would forgo any idea of claiming you were here, serving illegal drinks to a bunch of law-breaking degenerates who are your witnesses. Not unless, of course, you want your establishment to be closed down for good, not to mention raising the no doubt substantial ire of these same law-breaking degenerates. No one likes a tattletale, you know."

I took a deep breath. I relaxed my grip on the bucket. There wasn't any other way out, I didn't have any choice. "Let's go inside," I said. "Let's straighten this out over a drink."

"Exactly what I had in mind," Burwell said. "After you."

"Always the gentleman," I said.

I took the lantern from where I'd left it hanging on the wall just inside the upstairs door. Because I'd been almost ready to go home, I hadn't left any lights burning in Sophia's. Before taking the first step downstairs, I locked the door behind us from the inside. Ferguson pointed at the lock and shook his head rapidly.

Addressing Burwell, "We don't want any unexpected visitors," I said.

Burwell considered this.

"I'm leaving the key in the lock," I said.

Burwell nodded at Ferguson, and I led the way downstairs.

"Tell me how you see the profits being split," I said.

"Why, fifty-fifty, of course, lad."

"But if I'm working here every night, I should get a wage too, shouldn't I?" I picked a number I knew Burwell wouldn't agree to. "How about fifty dollars a week, plus my fifty percent take?" We'd reached the bottom of the stairs.

"Light a lamp or two, lad, it's as dark as a dungeon down here. And of course you're entitled to a wage, but how about something that won't insult your partner's intelligence? Let's say ten dollars to start, and we'll go from there."

"Let me put the lantern down and I'll get our drinks." I was the lead elephant, with Burwell and then Ferguson following close behind. I led us to the bar, where I set down the lantern and palmed three shot glasses from underneath. "Come in the back, I'll show you where I keep the good whiskey. And forty dollars would be a little fairer. Remember, I won't just be swinging drinks here, I'll be keeping an eye on our investment. That's not something you can expect from a ten-dollar-a-week hired hand."

"By all means let's have the best you've got, lad—*we've* got, I mean—but bring the bottle out here. You can serve

Ferguson and me as a proper bartender should. And I see your point about you being our eyes and ears. Let's say twenty dollars a week."

Hand on the door handle to the backroom, "Whatever you say," I said, "but I thought I'd show you where the safe is while we were at it. Another time, I guess. And I think thirty dollars would make me happy."

Burwell followed the light, came around the front of the bar after all, Ferguson, of course, trailing right behind. "Oh, well," he said. "Procrastination *is* the thief of time."

"Someone I used to know always used to say that," I said, turning the handle.

"He was a wise man," Burwell said. "And let's say twenty dollars. I wouldn't want to—"

As soon as the door was open far enough for him to squeeze through, Waldo leapt at Burwell and I jumped aside and knocked the lantern off the top of the bar; Waldo didn't need to see what he wanted. I knew Ferguson was somewhere in the screaming, roaring dark behind me and that he'd be going for his knife, so I put my head down and charged as hard as I could, hoping to hit anything but blade. Burwell's screams became cries, like the sound of a woman wailing over the body of her dead child.

Given its size, Ferguson's stomach was surprisingly hard and unyielding, and he managed to wrap me in a headlock, but I got the bearing I needed and smashed the three shot glasses into his genitals. Ferguson's hands fell away from my head and I dived past and behind him across the floor. I looked for something to use on him while he was bent over with his hands covering his balls, but without the lantern I could only see the ghostliest of outlines of tables and chairs. Before I could grab a chair to bring down on his head, Ferguson straightened up and whipped his knife out of its sheath.

I ran.

I ran for the stairs and found them and tore to the top, figuring my speed advantage would give me time to unlock the door before Ferguson stumbled to the top after me. Which I did, but only barely, Ferguson's fleetness of foot as unexpected as his firm fat. By the time our feet touched the back lot, it was a race too close to call.

I ran in a straight line, in the direction of the rear of the lot, and didn't look back, somehow remembering what the Reverend King always told the children on race day, on the last day of school. Of course, there'd been a life lesson to learn too: "Pick a goal in life, children, and do not deviate from it and do not look back. Never look backward."

I only looked back once, when I couldn't hear Ferguson's feet pounding behind me anymore. Then I looked again, and again, until I stopped running. I walked back to the middle of the lot and Ferguson's face-down, beached body.

The black man pushed Ferguson over onto his side as far as he could in order to retrieve his knife; slid it out and let the great dead weight fall back to earth.

"Why?" I said, catching my breath.

The black man stayed squatting, dragged his knife back and forth across a clump of dewy weeds. "Saw a white man with a knife chasing a Negro."

"How did you know it was the Negro who needed help?"

"Didn't," he said. "Suppose I just never seen it the other way around before."

Satisfied his blade was clean, the man stood up. He was old, maybe as old as sixty.

"My name is David," I said.

"Tom," the old Negro said, putting out his hand for me to shake.

19

Clichés when you're ten tend to become eternal verities once you're approaching forty. Particularly when you have two dead bodies to dispose of, preferably before sunrise. Out of the frying pan and into the fire, for instance, suddenly made a whole hell of a lot of sense.

Tom helped me haul Ferguson's body into the back of my wagon, but I left him outside to keep an eye on things so I could assemble what was left of Burwell. Waldo was lying on the floor only a few feet away from the body, panting, watching over his kill. He looked like he could have just come inside from a particularly spirited game of fetch. When he saw me at the bottom of the stairs, he wagged his tail.

"Good boy," I said, carefully making my way toward the bar. But I didn't have to worry; what had to be done was done. I led Waldo into the backroom and patted his rug and he immediately lay down, head resting between his paws as he watched me close the door on him. Waldo had done his job. Now it was time for me to do mine.

Burwell's throat was torn out and a chunk was missing from his right cheek and both sleeves of his coat were tattered from wrist to elbow, but otherwise he was intact, if bloodied. Actually, most of the blood, the source of which was where Burwell's neck used to be, was pooled around the outline of the body, but it was now slowly flooding across the floor. I'd worry about that later. I placed a burlap potato sack over Burwell's head and tied it in place with a long piece of string, Tom not needing to know anything more than here was another white man who had to vanish. I tossed Burwell over my shoulder like a bag of flour. I'd never noticed before how small he was.

Tom was silent until I'd laid out Burwell on the ground beside the wagon. "I'll take the feet," he said. And so I took the head and we placed him in the wagon beside Ferguson.

"I'll ride in the back, if you don't mind," he said.

"You don't have to come. I'll take care of it." Even if I didn't have any idea how.

"If it's all the same, I'd like to see this through."

To see with his own eyes that it got done. "I understand."

Tom looked up at the beginning-to-bruise sky. "Best we get a move on, then. Sun-up not long now."

As if on cue, a bird twittered awake in one of the trees, and we climbed in the wagon and were off.

*

Knowing we had to leave town was the easy part; deciding where to go after that was the problem. I didn't have any clearer idea who Burwell was today than I'd had the day twelve years before when he'd hired me, but even if no one was going to miss him, he and Ferguson had to disappear for good. No one was going to miss Ferguson.

I kept driving deeper and deeper into the country, the only thing I could think to do being to bury them both in the woods. It wasn't the bodies being discovered that concerned me; rather, now that it was becoming light, someone seeing us digging the graves. After a decade without incident removing countless corpses from the ground, I wasn't about to go to jail or worse for planting two last ones.

BUXTON TWO MILES, the sign said.

It wasn't Damascus, but it would do.

*

"Wait here, please."

I heard voices inside from where I stood on the porch, my cap in my hand. I'd wondered what George's wife was like. Pretty and pleasant, I discovered. Imagine, I thought, what she'd be like if it wasn't six-thirty in the morning and there wasn't a stranger knocking on her front door. It was the same house George had grown up in, but with a large addition built onto the back and with a whole other floor added on top.

George came to the door and shook my hand, but without inviting me inside. No one shows up at your doorstep at six-thirty in the morning with good news, particularly after not having seen you in twenty years. George closed the front door.

"What's wrong?" he said.

"I need your help."

"I assumed that. What do you need my help with?"

It was like two decades had been two days. There was more of him—a lot more of him—but other than that, he was still George and I was still David. I told him enough of what had happened and what needed to happen for him to understand.

"I swear to you, it was them or me," I said. "I didn't have any other choice."

George nodded at Tom, who was standing beside the wagon I'd parked alongside George's house. "I know you didn't," George said. "I wouldn't help you if I thought you did."

I kept my eyes on the porch floor.

"Drive around to the back of the factory," he said. "I've got an idea."

*

On our return to Chatham, I offered Tom half of all that was left of Burwell, the five-hundred-dollar billfold. Which, it turned out, was nothing more than a Missouri bankroll, an impressive stack of counterfeit money stuck between five real twenty-dollar bills on top and another five real twenties on the bottom. You had to give the man credit: even dead, Burwell was still cheating his way to a better deal.

"Wouldn't feel right taking money for what I done," Tom said, riding up front with me this time. "I did what I did because it needed doing."

"I understand that. I'd feel better, though, if I could do something for you."

It turned out Tom had come upon Ferguson and me while cutting across Sophia's back lot on his way to an all-night shift at the sugar plant, a job he despised. "Man can't hear himself think in a place like that," he'd said. And now, after not showing up for work, he didn't even have that.

"It seems to me," he said, "the business you in, you might be able to use a man at the door to make sure the wrong sorts of people don't bother you or your customers."

"Sort of like a watchdog," I said.

"Seems to me you don't have no worries in that particular area."

I smiled; Tom, too. Double homicide tends to bring people together.

"Are you sure you'd want to stand around all night just waiting for trouble?"

"I expect I'd be sitting," Tom said. "Nothing fancy, a stool maybe, if you could manage it. And I expect the idea is to make sure trouble don't happen before it does."

"That's exactly the idea."

It was a lovely fall morning, sunny and cool all at once. The wind was mild, southwesterly, and you could smell the smoke coming from the potash factory.

Every time I learned that George had moved up another rung in the company, I'd wonder what they actually did there—what, for example, they were always burning in their big furnace. And that morning, after finally meeting George's wife, I'd gotten my answer, had found out first-hand not only what they burned all day but how, if you wanted to burn up something else, there'd be nothing left of it once you had, nothing at all except maybe a few grey clouds of smoke.

*

One more fatality-free dynamiting a couple of months later—this time to the home of Israel Evans, another Scott Act inspector—finally led to the arrest of one Mr. Jason Macy of Port Huron, Michigan, a convicted American felon whose room at the Royal Tavern was discovered to contain a Ranger No. 2 revolver and three fulminating caps and a fuse. Although the county Crown attorney failed to gain an admission from the accused of his part in a conspiracy by local hotel-keepers to blow the Scott Act off the face of Kent County, Macy was found guilty and sentenced to fourteen years in Kingston Penitentiary, the judge declaring at the sentencing that "You came to this country to commit one of the most diabolical crimes known in this land. It is proper and right to make an example of you. The laws of the land must be maintained and justice vindicated. Such as you must learn that law is supreme."

Until I learned of Macy's conviction, I was never sure that one of Burwell's supposed secret witnesses wouldn't come forth and claim that it was the Negro named David King who was responsible for the dynamitings, the one who ran the illegal saloon people called Sophia's. But I should have known better. Even if Burwell hadn't been bluffing and did have three bought-off accusers lined up and ready to lie, his sudden and permanent disappearance rendered more than just myself free. Dead men can't collect on promissory notes.

Once I read news of the conviction in the *Planet*, I wrote George a letter asking him if he would care to visit me in Chatham sometime. When he wrote back suggesting the following Saturday, I answered that that would be fine and closed Sophia's for the first time since I'd opened for business.

I hadn't known Loretta for very long, but when I told her not only how I hadn't seen my oldest friend except for once in over twenty years but how I owed him a debt so large it was impossible ever to repay, she prepared us enough strudel, coffee cake, and marzipan to make George fat if he hadn't been already.

After he'd obliged me by eating a little bit of everything, I asked him if he'd like a cup of coffee or tea.

"You don't have any whiskey?" he said.

"You don't drink," I said.

"Oh, so you mean there might be things about me you don't know. I can't imagine the same thing about you."

George laughed and rubbed his belly and I took a bottle and two glasses down from the cupboard.

We haven't missed a first Saturday of every other month for the last eight years.

20

Loretta's excited: there's a blind man on the undertaker's table.

"What's the difference?" I say. "The dead can't see."

Loretta is applying the finishing fidgeting to her camera set-up. "This is something you believe you need to tell me?"

Artists. I cross my legs and keep my mouth shut and am thankful for a chair in which to pass the time. Ordinarily, Loretta likes an empty room when she works, but today she said she'd like some company. How often does someone have a chance to watch a beautiful woman take a picture of a blind dead man?

"Are you sure I'm all right here?" I say. The chair Loretta has pushed against the wall is directly behind the table covered with her subject.

"You are where you should be."

"Are you sure? I don't want to interfere with your picture. I can easily move."

"You are where you should be. Now please do not be restless. It distracts me, yes?"

The blind man looks blind, even with eyes that wouldn't be seeing anything anyway. It's the pupils, the way they look used up, callused, like he'd been straining unsuccessfully to see his entire life, long after he knew he couldn't.

"So," Loretta says. "I have given you sufficient time to consider our journey to Germany, yes?"

"*Our* journey? It sounds like you've already decided for me."

"Of course not. This is a journey no other can decide to take for you. But I have decided I am to go at the end of this June. I have begun to make the necessary inquiries."

Loretta is behind her camera now, clicking and adjusting things I don't even know the names of. That I'm surprised she's settled on going, with or without me, surprises me. I've known she was planning on returning to Germany for months now. I stare at the body on the table.

Sometimes, as children, George and I would take turns pretending that one of us was blind while the other was his guide. Being the blind man was by far the better role. There was always the worry you'd trip in a pothole or bang your head on a tree branch if your seeing guide got lazy or distracted, but that was what made it so much fun—not knowing what was going to happen next. You weren't going to fall down or hurt your head being the guide, but the entire time you couldn't wait until it was your turn to be the blind man again.

"How long do you think you'll be gone?" I say.

"This depends. If you accompany me, not so long—perhaps one month—but if you do not, perhaps longer. Perhaps then I will visit France as well."

France. Montaigne, Voltaire, Rousseau. France sounds like a place in a book, even more than Germany. Not having been there, I suppose that's what it is. Unless I went.

"Understand, I recognize the appeal," I say.

Loretta is focusing on the dead man through her camera.

"Like I said before, though, there are a lot of loose ends I'd need to tie up first."

"Yes, you have said."

"I'd have to free up some money as well. I don't even know how much money."

"Yes."

"And don't travellers . . . don't they need something to show someone when they go somewhere?"

"A passport."

"A passport, right. I don't have a passport."

And then Loretta is done, is taking apart her equipment. "Yes, you would need to get a passport."

I feel embarrassed. I feel eight, not forty-eight. I wish Loretta's face was still busy behind her camera so she couldn't see mine. "Passports need pictures, don't they? I don't even have a picture of myself."

Laying away her camera in its black, felt-lined storage case, "You do now," she says.

It takes me a moment to realize that I was the blind dead man whose photo she was taking. "You fooled me," I say.

"Of course," Loretta says.

*

"I'm the man you want to talk to. I can get you anything you need—peaches, pears, beets, corn, yams—and every can just as fresh as a daisy."

"I do appreciate the generosity of your offer, but Mrs. Meyers does all of our fruit and vegetable shopping at the farmers' market."

"You see," Franklin says, setting down his glass on the bar, "right there, that's where you're going wrong. A pear in a can is a *clean* pear, one hundred percent guaranteed, no questions asked. You can't get that kind of freshness from a pear off a tree, you just can't. My God, you're a man of science, Meyers, you of all people should understand that."

Meyers pushes his glasses up his nose. "You might have a point there," he says, taking out his snuff box.

"You're darn right I do."

I wouldn't miss this. Listening to Franklin lecture Meyers on modern science is like horseradish on an empty stomach.

"I'm thinking of the children," Meyers says. "Mrs. Meyers and I want only what's best for them." Meyers takes a snort of snuff up each nostril.

"That's what I'm saying. You want to put your children's health and happiness first. Which is why you want to eat clean food. Canned food."

"I say, I do see your point."

"You're a man of science, I knew you would."

I would *not* miss this.

*

"Good evening, David."

"Thompson."

Thompson sits and settles at his usual table while I pour him out his usual drink, both of us committed to pretending that the other night didn't happen, that Thompson hadn't come about as close as anyone can to killing himself while still being around to feel ashamed about it the next morning. It's difficult to make friends—real friends—after adolescence; having things in common to lie about helps.

"Well, it's finally starting to feel like spring," Thompson says as I set down his glass.

"It's about time."

"Feels as if it's going to rain again, though."

"That's spring."

"That it is."

I take care of a couple of other customers at the bar, Meyers included, before stepping into the back. Henry, lying on his side, wags his tail without opening his eyes, an aging dog's entitlement. I get the package I brought with me to work and bring it out front to the bar. Henry wags goodbye as I close the door.

I unwrap the book from the cloth bag I carried it in and take it with me to Thompson's table. "I believe this is yours," I say, but Thompson looks at it like he's never seen it before, only heard about such an antiquarian wonder in bibliographic lore.

"It *was* mine," he finally says, taking it from me without opening it, holding it open-palmed in both hands.

"Do you want it back?"

Still admiring the book, the dark green cover with the words *Leaves of Grass* splashed in gilt across the front, "I believe my days of owning first editions are over," he says. "But I'm sure you won't have any trouble finding an interested buyer. Copies of Whitman's own self-published first pressing are very, very rare." Thompson is still holding the book like it's a cushion with the rarest of emeralds resting on top.

"How about a trade?" I say.

Thompson searches my face—hard—for even the most nominal hint of pity. Not finding any, "What do I have that you could possibly want?"

"I'm going away for a while. I'm not sure for how long— a month, at least—and I need someone to look after Henry for me."

"Your dog?"

"It's the only Henry I know."

Seeing I'm serious, Thompson carefully rests the book on his knee, holding on to it with one hand, taking a sustained drink of whiskey with the other. To himself as much as to me, "I'm afraid I don't know much about the care of animals," he says. "I'm afraid I wouldn't know the first thing about looking after a dog."

"There's not much to know. You feed them and walk them and make sure they've got water. Believe me, Henry's easy to get along with. If you can't get along with Henry, you can't get along with anyone."

"I'm sure, I'm sure, it's just . . ."

"Just what?"

"Just that this is a very valuable book."

"And Henry is a very valuable dog. So much so, if when I come back he's just the same as when I left him, you can have the rest of your library back. I haven't got room for all my books anyway, let alone yours." I pick up Thompson's empty glass. "You think about it. And if you decide to do it, I left you some advice inside the book."

I leave Thompson alone with *Leaves of Grass* and the page I bookmarked, the one with the poem "Animals."

> *I think I could turn and live with animals, they are so placid*
>   *and self-contained*
> *I stand and look at them long and long.*
> *They do not sweat and whine about their condition;*
> *They do not lie awake in the dark and weep for their sins;*
> *They do not make me sick discussing their duty to God;*
> *Not one is dissatisfied—not one is demented with the mania*
>   *of owning things;*
> *Not one kneels to another, nor to his kind that lived*
>   *thousands of years ago;*
> *Not one is respectable or industrious over the whole earth.*

A few minutes later, I return to Thompson's table with a fresh drink.

"You've got a deal," he says.

*

Tomorrow is set: Chatham, to New York, to Liverpool, to somewhere else over there—over the ocean—until, somehow, to Germany. I don't know the details, but I don't have to, Loretta does. For the next six weeks I plan to depend on Loretta's dependability.

Tomorrow isn't the problem, though; it's tonight I'm having trouble with. Sleeping, specifically. Not that there's anything to worry about. But then, that rarely has anything to do with it.

Sophia's is shut tight and locked up until I return, and Tom is going to look in on things anyway just to make sure, as well as keep an eye on Franklin. It's time Tom had a holiday too. I gave him fifty dollars when I handed over the keys and told him to buy himself something he didn't need. Tom gave it some thought. "I don't suppose I'm in the market for any of that," he said. I know Sophia's will be here when I get back.

Thompson has his instructions as well: what and how much to feed Henry; where and how long to walk him; where and whom to seek help from if he takes sick or is injured. But I know Henry will be fine, if a little confused and lonely at first. Henry was a stray, just like Waldo, but he's been with me long enough that there'll have to be a period of adjustment. But he'll adjust. That's one of the things that us strays do best.

And since Thompson will be staying at my home while I'm gone, looking after the house as well as Henry, he has another responsibility to attend to. Thompson has to take care of my rose bush. I seem to have become a gardener by accident.

One of the Reverend King's conditions of residence on the Settlement was a picket fence with a garden out front that had to include flowers. By the time I was living in Chatham, I swore that the first home I owned—the first home I could legitimately call my own—was going to be wilfully barren. Besides, although my body had never had to rise before sunrise with the master's bell to begin a long day's enforced labour in the fields, my brain had heard enough stories about what it was like to suffer thirteen hours under the unyielding Southern sun picking, ginning, and pressing cotton to feel an uncomfortable ache of empathy whenever I passed a farmer's field, or even a large vegetable garden. This was one Negro whose hands were never going to get dirty—at least not with dirt.

True to my word, even the half-acre upon which my house was built is untilled and unembellished, a stone fence enclosing the entire property the only improvement I can be held responsible for. But somehow a rose has appeared. A pink rose. I didn't put it there, but there it is anyway.

Stacking a delivery of firewood behind the house—it's never too early to ready fall's first cords—I noticed what I assumed to be a larger than normal weed that needed pluck-ing. Except for a single large maple tree, the backyard is bereft of anything alive, simple soil the majority of the time, mud whenever it rains. What I'd thought was just a weed, though, wasn't. A small rose bush had taken root; how, I don't know. My instinct was to yank it out of the ground—it was young and delicate enough, it wouldn't have been difficult—but I left it where it was, decided to let nature takes its course and do the job for me.

A week or so later, I checked back, ready to remove the uncared-for corpse. But between the steady April rain and spring's increasingly sunshiny days, the thing had managed not only to survive but actually to grow, three tiny buds sprouting at the ends of three separate spindly branches. I couldn't help but be impressed.

I got into the habit of following its progress every couple of days, after a while Henry picking up on the new routine and accompanying me on my inspection. It was like a much slower version of when Loretta had shown me how she developed her photographs before she began sending them away to be done, the thing you were waiting to see slowly becoming itself, taking all the time it needed to be exactly what it was.

After work one night, I told Loretta about the rose bush, about how it reminded me of her developing her photographs.

"You are talking about a living bush?" she said.

"What other kind would I be talking about?"

"I do not know. But you caring for a rose bush, I cannot see this in my mind."

"I'm not caring for it. I'm just . . . watching it."

"I see."

And then it didn't rain, and it didn't rain, and then it didn't rain again. I asked Franklin when he came downstairs to Sophia's for a whiskey break, "Is it raining?" and he immediately set down his whiskey on the bar, whispered, "What's wrong?"

"Who said anything's wrong? I just asked you if it was raining outside."

Franklin looked at me like he was trying to remember an agreed-upon code word, silently mouthed the word *rain*.

"Oh, for—" I went upstairs and outside to check for myself. It still wasn't raining.

The next day, I filled an empty whiskey bottle with water and poured it over the bush. After the bottle was empty, I poked my finger into the ground and it was only wet a quarter of an inch down. Henry followed me back inside the house while I refilled the bottle and then back to the bush while I watered it again, and then one more time after that. This time the earth was soaked deep, to the bush's roots. *To create a little flower is the labour of ages*, Mr. Blake wrote. He must have been a gardener too.

The day after that, one of the buds was open when we arrived with two whiskey bottles of water. A pink rose. I let

Henry go first, then I knelt down on one knee and smelt it too. Honest perfume. I smelt it again.

I've left Thompson the two whiskey bottles with detailed, written watering instructions. It would probably be easier if I had an actual watering can, though. Maybe when we come home next month I'll stop in at McKeough's Hardware and buy one. It's not as if I can't afford it.